CENT
LIBRA

3 0

1

D0345957

COMPLICE

XB00 000006 9028

From the Chicken House

I'd do anything for my friends – really, I mean it. But what if by doing it you hurt other people, or even yourself? What would real friends do then? The friends in this novel find out. Boy, do they find out. I hope I never have to.

This is a pulsating debut from a brilliant young writer.

Barry Cunningham
Publisher

ACCOMPLICE

Eireann Corrigan

Chicken House

2 Palmer Street, Frome, Somerset BA11 1DS

Text © Eireann Corrigan 2009
Published by arrangement with Scholastic Inc.,
557 Broadway, New York 10012, USA

First published in Great Britain in 2010
The Chicken House
2 Palmer Street
Frome, Somerset BA11 1DS
United Kingdom
www.doublecluck.com

Eireann Corrigan has asserted her rights under the Copyright, Designs and
Patents Act, 1988, to be identified as the author of this work.

All rights reserved.
No part of this publication may be reproduced or transmitted or utilised in any
form or by any means, electronic, mechanical, photocopying or otherwise,
without the prior permission of the publisher.

Jacket design by Steve Wells
Interior design by Steve Wells
Typeset by Dorchester Typesetting Group Ltd
Printed and bound in Great Britain by CPI Bookmarque, Croydon, CR0 4TD

The paper used in this Chicken House book is made from wood
grown in sustainable forests.

1 3 5 7 9 10 8 6 4 2

British Library Cataloguing in Publication data available.

ISBN 978-1-906427-56-6

for Nina Stotler –
my co-conspirator and collaborator,
my partner-in-crime

WOLVERHAMPTON PUBLIC LIBRARIES	
XB000000069028	
Bertrams	18/08/2010
YA	£6.99
ALL	01114985

ONE

The picture they usually use is one from the Activities spread of the yearbook. Chloe's got denim overalls buckled over a white T-shirt and her hair's wound into these two loose braids. Like an even blonder version of the girl on the hot chocolate box. She's gleaming. Beaming. And then, of course, there's the sheep.

It's a picture we took at the county fair, so Chloe has a lamb cradled under one arm. The networks loved that – Chloe and her little lamb. In the original snapshot, Chloe's other arm is linked through mine and we're leaning toward each other. But when the story first hit the papers, someone picked out that photo and cut me out of it, so it looks like Chloe has her head tipped toward nothing. The way dumber girls do, like something's just so hilarious they can't even hold their heads up right. Laughing Chloe and her Lamb. Lost, little Chloe.

It's not like I took it personally. It was exactly the kind of picture that we figured networks would use.

It was all part of our plan.

TWO

In the few days after Chloe disappeared, I paid more attention to my own face than I ever had before. I needed to look confused and stunned and afraid. And the more I had to arrange my face to look that way, the more I felt that way. After the first little while, I realized it helped to picture what Chloe would look like, feeling those things.

I bit my lip a lot. I took noticeably deep breaths. Shook my head as if I was trying to clear my thoughts. The hardest face to put on was the puzzled one. Like when Chloe's dad rapped on our screen door, asking if she was upstairs with me. And when my mom grilled me on whether or not Chloe talked to any strangers online. Or later, when we all had to sit down with the police officer. I chewed on the inside of my cheek the way Chloe did when she was trying to remember something. I said, with what I hoped was a helpless look in my eyes, 'I'm sorry . . . I just don't remember Chloe saying anything about going for a ride after school.' And then I cried for real, mostly because I was so scared, and that way I could cover my face with my hands and not have to look the cop in the eyes.

I had sort of figured that my mom would keep me home from school. I mean, that seemed like the reasonable thing, especially since we'd been up almost the whole weekend, either with the Caffreys or making sandwiches for the mobs of people gathered with flashlights on our property. But that Monday morning, she called up to my room like it was any other day. At first, it felt like any other day. I almost forgot what we'd done, that my mom wouldn't be honking the horn on the way down the hill until Chloe came running out of the barn. Chloe wasn't going to comb her hair in the car.

Realizing it made me gasp. It felt like when you eat too much ice cream and your head hurts, except it felt like that in my chest. I went downstairs clutching my stomach, like I was faking a stomachache. My parents were already in Phase United Front, though. Mom used her gentle voice, but she said, 'Your dad and I have discussed this and we think this is the best plan.'

'Plan? How is it a plan?' In my head, I was thinking, *You don't even know what a plan is. Because we have a plan. We have a much better, more detailed plan.*

'Finn, honey, this isn't a debate. Your father and I have considered this very carefully. You need to be around your friends right now. And we don't know how long this is going to go on . . .' My mom trailed off and looked stricken. And then I made myself look stricken to cover for the fact that I knew exactly how long it would go on, and honestly I wouldn't have minded an eleven-day vacation from school.

'Well, what if she comes home and I'm not here?' I said.

Because that's what a normal kid would wonder, right? That's what you'd ask if your best friend had just vanished.

'Then we'll come straightaway and pick you up. Really, honey, your dad's going to stay right by. I'll be at the Caffreys' most of the morning and then I'm putting in a few hours at Dr. Winter's house.'

Then, when I started to slink back up the steps, my mom said something weird. She said, 'Finn, honey, there's nothing to be afraid of.'

I was afraid. I was scared to look people in the eye at school. Every time the school secretary came over the intercom, I expected she'd call my name down to the front office. They'd tell me that they'd found Chloe. The same cop who had coaxed me to try to remember whether anyone had been looking at Chloe strangely lately would show up, ready to cuff my wrists behind my back and duck my head into the squad car.

But that first day back, everybody straightened up when the intercom interrupted class. Even Señora Dutta put her hand to her chest when the secretary called down to remind her about the register. She clutched at the collar of her shirt as if she was trying to slow her heart down or something. Chloe – or the lack of Chloe – had us all on edge. They brought in a counselor that day. The principal was really proud of that move – in the months afterwards he brought it up a lot like it was some radically kind motion on his part and not a completely reasonable choice. It was just this young guy who looked like Harry Potter who they probably sent over from some college or something. The only person more tentative than a student teacher has to be a student guidance counselor. They sent me down to talk to him. Of course they sent me down.

It didn't feel kind, being sent down to the makeshift mental ward. I felt sent away, probably because I felt like I should be sent away. And when I got to the library-slash-counseling-center, there were a bunch of PTA moms setting out a spread of cookies and donuts. We're never allowed to eat in the library, but I guess when someone as popular, pretty and smart as Chloe goes missing, it counts as a special occasion.

'Oh, Finley.' Kara Mae Clairemont's mom is one of the only people in the world who has ever called me Finley. The other is my grandmother, which is just weird. Finley was my mom's maiden name. So essentially, my grandma insists on calling me by her own last name. And Kara Mae Clairemont's mom went to high school with mine, so it's odd that she insists on using it too.

Mrs. Clairemont draped her arms around me and squeezed me like a grandmother would. She kept her hand on my shoulder and steered me into the doorway of the conference room. 'Doctor?' The guy she was calling Doctor looked like he was maybe twenty years old.

But Mrs. Clairemont didn't seem to notice that the doctor didn't appear old enough to rent a car on his own. 'Doctor – this is Finley Jacobs. She was Chloe's best friend. She IS Chloe's best friend.' Her hand rubbed circles into my back. 'It's so important to support each other during a time like this. To trust each other with our feelings.' I wanted to tell Mrs. Clairemont that her daughter once spread a rumor that

Chloe's brother Cam had fetal alcohol syndrome, but I just nodded and let her close the door after her.

The kid sitting across from me looked like he had a paper round. 'I'm not actually a doctor.' Shocking. 'I never know what to say when people call me that.' In Psychology we'd call this *building rapport*. I tried to look like the young undoctor's canned conversation was putting me at ease. I didn't want rapport. Chloe and I had covered this. We had figured it would be Mrs. Holmes, the same old guidance counselor we had always refused to confide in. But still, I reminded myself of the plan: Get in. Act appropriately shocked, sad. Shut down. Get out. I almost felt sorry for the undoctor. Here he was, trying to get his grief counseling merit badge, and I was too busy getting my black belt in fake kidnappings to care.

'So your name is Finley?' He wrote it at the top of a yellow legal pad and underlined it.

'Finn.'

'Oh, Finn. Like Huck?'

I hate when people say that. Hated it when I was a little kid. Hated it last year when we read the book in class. Sure, just like a ten-year-old boy. Thanks.

'No, it's just Finn.' That's all I'd give him. Let him think I was illiterate.

'Well, you can call me Ace.'

'What?'

'I mean, if you're more comfortable with that.'

'I'm not comfortable with that.'

'Why?'

'Because it's a drug dealer name.'

'Oh? You know many drug dealers?'

'This is Colt River.'

'Yes?'

'We don't have drug dealers in Colt River.'

'Did Chloe know any drug dealers?'

'Are you a cop?'

'No.' But even as he said it, Dr. Ace wrote something down below my name on his yellow legal pad. My palms were wet again. I could probably leave handprints on the table. I tugged my sleeves down and kept my hands in my lap. This was exactly the kind of conversation Chloe and I said I shouldn't get myself trapped into.

Maybe Dr. Ace saw my face tense up, because he exhaled and pushed the chair away from the conference table. I heard the wheels squeak. He said, 'I'm sorry. *I'm* nervous.' He splayed out his fingers like, *Hey – what can you do?* And smiled. He had a nice smile.

I don't really fall for that kind of thing. 'You're nervous because you're just starting out?'

'I'm a student.'

'I figured,' I told him. 'I didn't want to insult you.'

'I wouldn't have been insulted. We're all students. We're all learning.'

That made me laugh. A little. 'That's the kind of thing Chloe would say.' And it was. She would've probably ended up Googling Dr. Ace or trying to bump into him after school. She would've even liked that his name was Ace.

'So you guys are good friends.'

'Yes.'

'Grew up together?'

'Almost.'

It was fourth grade. My mother made me carry over the welcome-to-the-neighborhood pie while it was still warm. The Caffreys didn't even have a real house yet. They lived out of a trailer while a bunch of men in coveralls and work boots turned our old barn into a house. My parents had sold off all the cows the month before the new family moved in. So that summer, our fence moved about twenty acres closer to our house. And then the Caffreys moved in and installed solar panels above the old hayloft. They built a pen for llamas, talked about raising ostrich for meat.

When Chloe first got here in fourth grade she was just some weirdo city kid. She wore Halloween costume dresses all the time with knee socks and sat alone on the bus. I was the only person who knew who she was and I only talked to her out of fear and pity.

'It must be tough to be here without her,' Dr. Ace said. I just looked at him. 'Something like this must be a hard thing to go through without her.'

I put the look on my face that Chloe got when she was considering something. She looked to the side, like she was trying to read a list written over in the corner. 'The whole thing is scary.' That's what I let myself say. The truth.

'Are you scared?'

'This is Colt River.'

'You've said that. But what does that mean to you?'

'Nothing ever really happens in Colt River.'

'Except . . .'

'Except my best friend's gone.' I did him the favor of finishing the sentence. And then I added, 'That's pretty much the only thing that's ever happened. And she's missing it.'

Only she wasn't. Chloe was holed up in my grandmother's basement, probably watching the local news with headphones on.

'What would you say to Chloe if she were here right now?' Dr. Ace might as well have jolted me with electroshock.

'What?'

'Sometimes it helps to envision the person for whom we're grieving, to take the opportunity to say what we need to hear ourselves say.' He sounded like one of the cards my mom bought my aunt during her divorce.

'I'm not grieving for Chloe. She's not dead.'

'I didn't mean to imply—'

'Everyone's acting like that – like she's dead.' They were, and I hadn't counted on that either. For the first two nights, it was like the whole town was coasting on adrenaline. No one slept, people stomped in and out of our house all hours of the night. You could see traffic winding down our road at two in the morning. I'd never seen actual traffic in Colt River.

By the time I got to school on Monday morning, though, things had calmed down into an eerie hush. Everyone spoke in funeral voices. There were a lot of hugs in homeroom and in the halls beforehand. I think people were starting to imagine the worst that could have happened to Chloe. Chloe had predicted that would be the hardest part. She had said,

'You're going to want to tell people I'm okay because you're a good person. You're going to want to make everyone feel better. But remember most of them will be caught up in the moment. They won't know they're doing it, but they'll be faking it.'

Chloe had said, 'You have to remember what will happen if we get caught.' There were things I couldn't think about because they were so terrible. Like Chloe's mom. Even Dean West, who'd been in love with Chloe since the seventh grade. I knew he was probably going nuts and he wasn't going to be in there talking to Dr. Ace. Dean didn't talk much in front of anyone.

At the same time, Chloe was right – there were plenty of people who were just playing the part they'd been cast in the new soap opera of Colt River. Like Mrs. Clairemont and her cookies and the girls who had come up, one by one, to squeeze me at my locker before school. Maddie Dunleavy and Lizbette Markell had set up a table in the hallway and sold Bring Chloe Home ribbons for three bucks a pop. I don't know who chose green, but it looked like half the school had spinach leaves pinned to their chests. Those people sitting in homeroom with swollen eyes and solemn faces – most of them weren't our friends. They didn't really know Chloe.

Even Dr. Ace was just playing a part. I felt like telling him he should write Chloe and me a cheque. By the time we were through, Colt River would be big news and he'd be able to put this stint on his CV. Instead I asked him, 'How long will you be here?'

'Hmmm.' He sounded like it was the first time he'd considered it. He said, 'I don't know.' He meant that it depended on whether or not they found Chloe. And how they found her.

I took the card that Dr. Ace offered after he ran out of questions. It didn't even have his name on it. It said: *Rutgers University Student Counseling Services.* I snickered a little – all that work and we didn't even get a student social worker from Princeton. He said, 'You can come talk whenever you need to.'

I tried to look grateful. And then I said something weird. Something stupid. I said, 'When Chloe comes home, I bet she'd like to meet you.' And then I felt my throat close up, like my body was cringing on the inside. I pictured the little Chloe in my head, slamming her head on the old metal desk in a miniature version of my grandmother's basement. But when Dr. Ace looked up, he blinked, and the only thing that flickered in his eyes was pity. I could see it written across his face – *You poor girl. You think she's coming home.*

If we had planned for Chloe to stay missing for longer, I might have risen to the top of our class. For once in school, we weren't leaning over each other's desks and writing in each other's notebooks. I didn't want to look at everyone looking at me anymore, so I kept my eyes on the board. Listened to my teachers rather than the whispering behind me. And most of our teachers spoke more slowly. It was like the whole school was moving through syrup. It's weird to think that might have helped my college applications just as much as anything else.

After I left Ace to doodle in his yellow legal pad, I slipped into English class. Or tried to. Dr. Glenn stopped talking when I slid into the room. 'I'm s-ss-sorry.' I sounded like Dean. 'I was in the counseling center—'

'Of course, Miss Jacobs. Take a seat.' Dr. Glenn isn't a sentimental guy. He's kind of a hardass. But he didn't ask me for a written pass. And that's how I knew his pacemaker was functioning in full heart capacity. After about four notebook pages of notes, I heard snuffling from the corner behind. Looked back to see one of Lauren Szabo's hands wiggling in the air. The other was covering her face. You know during the Oscars, when they replay the most emotional parts of the nominees' performances? So you can see just how amazingly talented they are? That's what Lauren looked like signaling her tragedy in the back row.

She kept pinching the bridge of her nose. Apparently that's the face Lauren puts on when she's pretending to be trying not to cry. Dr. Glenn looked over his tiny glasses at her. 'Yes, Miss Szabo?'

'May I please be excused to the counseling center?' It became a refrain that echoed through most of my classes, especially after Lauren returned to report on the new counselor: 'He has such *understanding eyes*.'

Lunch was kind of an ordeal, mostly because I couldn't figure out if I was supposed to have an appetite. Usually upperclassmen get to sign out at the front office and we go to Subway or get pizza at Vito's. That was all that got me through Monday morning . . . counting down the minutes until I could shake loose of everyone and escape every single set of eyes in the building. But when I got to the office, the clipboard with our names was gone. 'Sign-out is suspended until further notice,' the secretary chirped. Until she saw it was me reaching for the pen. 'Oh, Finn. How are you *doing*?' She leapt out from her desk and started patting my hand before I could move it away. 'Sweetheart, Mr. Gardner cancelled sign-outs. Under the circumstances, we think it's best for everyone to stick to campus.'

'Does he think someone kidnapped Chloe?'

She stopped patting my hand then and started straightening out the piles of forms. It was a weird kind of relief to make someone else feel uncomfortable for a change.

'There's a lot of reason for all of us to stick close together right now.' Behind me, a line started forming, kids jostling and wondering what the hold-up was. 'No signing out today!' Mrs. Axelbank called out in the bright voice.

'Are you kidding me?'

'It's because of Chloe.'

'What? Why?'

'What does that have to do with lunch?'

'This is bullshit.'

That was Teddy Selander, and it was actually good to hear someone say it, to hear that not everyone's world had shut down because Chloe slid off the face of the planet. 'Why can't we sign out?' But when I turned, Teddy clamped his mouth shut, stepped back like I might hit him.

'Sorry, Finn.'

'Why are you sorry?' But Teddy had already spun around, headed toward the cafeteria.

We'd said we couldn't call each other or even text each other. Cops can trace that kind of stuff. Part of Chloe's checklist had been to toss her cell phone in the old well back behind my house. It was about the thousandth time I'd wanted to call her. There were things we hadn't known. And the biggest one was the kind of power we had all of a sudden. I felt like a superhero, like I had some kind of invincible cloak of grief around me.

Teddy Selander was an asshole. He'd been an asshole since the sixth grade when he'd moved to New Jersey from wherever they breed his particular kind of asshole. But all of a sudden, we'd made him act like a decent human being. It was the kind of thing I wished we could put on our college applications.

THREE

It started as a joke. A sick joke really, the kind that Chloe and I could only tell each other because anyone else would think we were terrible people.

In the first week of our junior year, after the seminars about getting into college started, we had to eat lunch in the auditorium two days a week. Soggy sandwiches while the college guidance team lectured us about the admissions process. Not just the grades we'd need, but the personal essay we had to write, the letter of recommendation that went with the submission, the list of extracurricular activities. That was the same month they found Margaret Cook – the girl who was kidnapped from the campsite in Yosemite. In the middle of the night, surrounded by her family. The guy had taken her last year, back when we were still sophomores, and all summer long, she was all over the news. She became a ghost story, a warning label: *You're never really safe.* And being pretty with cheerful red curls haloing your head didn't change anything. *People* magazine put Margaret Cook on their cover and published the postcards she'd written out to her friends and never got to mail. A TV camera crew followed some psychic around who believed that she could sense her around the park ranger's cabin and they actually dug around there, with bloodhounds. Initially, Chloe and I and pretty much every other kid in Colt River ate it all up.

By August, Margaret Cook was old news. We figured she was dead. Pretty much everyone besides her family seemed to figure she was dead. Her parents still went on talk shows, but eventually the networks stopped showing trailers of them. And then junior year started and it felt like every other year of school hadn't counted – they'd just been practice for three advanced courses and SATs study in the evening and Higher Math and the 140 sheep that Chloe and I cared for to show off our sense of responsibility.

But even the sheep weren't enough. We signed up for a Labor Day beach clean-up, because, you know, colleges needed to know there would be no untidy beaches with us around. When we got home, my dad was standing in the middle of the kitchen with a jar of pickles, eating kosher dill after kosher dill, with brine all over his chin. On the TV on the counter there was some lady standing in front of a big red house, announcing that Margaret Cook had knocked on her parents' door that morning. Her hair had been cut off. She seemed to be in relatively good health, showing symptoms of shock and malnourishment.

My dad's kind of sensitive in this really weird way and he was all choked up about it. 'That little girl came home.' And then he got even louder. 'That little girl CAME HOME.'

'Holy crap!' Chloe dropped her backpack at the door and

bounded over to the TV to turn up the volume. 'It's Margaret Cook. It's Margaret Cook, right? Why is she wearing a head-scarf?'

My father choked back another pickle. 'They cut off her hair. They cut off that poor little angel's hair.'

'She's our age. She's a year older than us.' Chloe knew all the stats. And even as we got used to the news of Margaret Cook's resurrection, Chloe couldn't let it go. The rest of the night, she kept flipping back to CNN.

'Nothing's ever going to be the same for her. She's just walked back into her life and nothing's ever going to be the same.' Chloe sounded stoned. She sounded like kids did that time they had a hypnotist get people to cluck like a chicken and stuff at our eighth grade formal.

'Yeah, that's awful,' I said.

'Maybe it's awful.'

'What do you mean, *maybe*? She got kidnapped. It's been months . . . who knows what some pervert did to her—'

'Yeah, but she's home now and everyone knows who she is.'

'Exactly. That's horrible, Chloe . . .'

'Yeah, yeah I know.' But she didn't seem convinced. Even when late-night reruns came on and she got up to leave, Chloe was still a little out of it, like Margaret Cook was this loop she couldn't get free from.

Which was how Margaret Cook followed us into our college seminar. Chloe came straggling into the auditorium, still in the process of snapping shut and pocketing her cell phone. She was a good ten minutes late and no one said a word, which is what happens when you're the kind of pretty that when you go to the movies people watch you and not the screen. And it helped that she smiled at everyone. That sounds like nothing, but I mean *everyone*.

Chloe smiled at the crusty-haired gamer guys who took over the computer lab during study halls. The bitchy future manicurists of America. The cranky maintenance workers. She moved through everyone seamlessly, cheerfully. And it never felt like she took anyone's adoration for granted. Chloe worked at it – just like how she printed out banners with witty slogans every school council election. It's not like anyone would consider running against her anyway. But she still campaigned.

Except for being the charm queen, Chloe was just kind of normal. And maybe that was her charm – she worked hard but didn't test spectacularly well. She didn't cut herself or take two trains into New York City to buy her clothes in SoHo.

That day I was glad to see how normal she was . . . relieved. She wasn't carrying a single magazine with the face of Margaret Cook on the cover. She was just the same old frantic, breathless Chloe sinking down with all her stuff into the seat beside me.

The seminar was the third of about fifty we'd have on how to get into college. Colt River is farm town, but it's not the same kind of farm town that my parents grew up in. Back then, you went to college if you were hoping to get out. Now you need college, even if you're going to come back and work on your dad's place. Mostly because you have to know when to sell your dad's place. You have to crunch numbers and keep up with new-fangled crops and herds. You know, like ostrich.

The college talk pretty much went like this: It's not a buyer's market anymore. It's true there are thousands of universities and colleges in the United States but more teens than ever are applying for slots in those esteemed establishments. And for the next few years, until something extraordinary happens to level off the playing field, those elite schools – the ones we'd already picked out based on the stickers our parents wanted on the family SUV – they got to pick and choose.

You could tell the guidance lady had practiced this speech in front of a mirror a few times. For one thing, she paced around like our football coach on the sidelines. She waved her arms and pointed. And she kept singling out kids for eye contact. She yelled a lot. I really sort of half expected her to whip out one of those whiteboards and draw 'x's and arrows with a marker, as if she was diagramming plays. We had some options! We were not powerless! We had to look closely at the possibilities!

One of the possibilities was to apply to the West Coast, the Midwest, the South. Any place but the Northeast with its glut of college applicants. 'There are airlines, people.' You could tell she'd practiced bellowing that line out loud. 'We have this thing called the railroad. You don't have to limit your choices to the narrow scope of a two-hour drive from your parents' houses.'

Clearly College Guidance Lady didn't grow up here. My parents considered Delaware pretty far away. That part of the pep talk was valuable to the two or three asshats who thought that three summers at the Jersey shore made them surfers. They were going to apply to the University of Hawaii, aloha very much, and the rest of us could drown in the foam crush they'd be spraying out from beneath their bitchass boards. Everyone else sat there and assumed that College Guidance Lady wasn't talking about us, because we'd worked really hard and had planned to go to a top college like Amherst since the sixth grade. We'd been carrying tupperwares of piss all around Saint Barnabas Hospital for years just to prove that someday we were going to make topnotch med students. We were the Class Council secretary, treasurer, archivist. We were envied in the tiny Colt River High School Orchestra for our ability to pluck pizzicato solos on the viola. We were special.

Only not. What College Guidance Lady seemed to be saying was that we weren't as extraordinary as we all thought we were. 'Where do you see yourself in three years, Mr. Ryden?' It was like College Guidance Lady had rehearsed that one too – ask the kid who's most obsessed with the whole application process, the one who dreams in HB application forms. The one who's dressed as a Princeton tiger every year for Halloween since we were six. Because he's not wound tight enough or anything.

'I'm hoping to attend Princeton University, ma'am.' And that was why Kenneth was Kenneth. Because did he really have to clarify? Did he think College Guidance Lady would think he meant Princeton Air Conditioning Repair School? She was clearly screwing with him, setting him up for God knows what kind of spirit-deflating exercise, and he still called her *ma'am*. Next to me, Chloe covered her eyes with her hands. *God*, I thought, *sign us all up for the Army. Anything to make this stop.*

'And so are *two hundred thousand* other high school students. What makes you so special?' And poor Kenneth actually went to list things. 'WHAT MAKES YOU SO SPECIAL?' College Guidance Lady boomed. 'Ladies and gentlemen, it's not enough anymore to be the captain of the cross-country team, the vice-president of debate club, or even the president of our local chapter of Future Farmers of America. Lots of young people have resumes peppered with fancy-sounding titles. Lots of young people get straight As. You need to think about what makes you stand out. Every year, hundreds of thousands of American students apply to colleges and think that because they are well-rounded, they are going to roll right on to campus.' When she said that last bit, College Guidance Lady actually did a rolling hand motion. She looked like she was on her way out of the auditorium in a conga line.

No such luck. She straightened up a little. 'Ladies and gentlemen, if you think being well-rounded is enough these days, you've been misinformed.' And that's when the murmur started. It sort of rolled over the rows of seated kids. Because we had been misinformed. And had spent hours, hundreds of hours, listening ardently to that misinformation. Girl Scouts, marching band – I cannot tell you how many hours I'd spent in some dorktastic costume. Because we were supposed to have some longass list of activities to convince college admissions committees how well-rounded we were.

It was nuts actually to see our whole class kind of flipped on its ass a little. In the back rows, the same kids who are usually slumped over during assemblies were still slumped over. But they were grinning a little, laughing at the kids who'd bought into the bullshit. Kids like me and Chloe.

But Chloe didn't even look that upset. She was dead calm compared to half the kids who were sitting around us twitching tearfully. That's when she made the joke. It was just an offhand comment, hushed in the rest of the well-behaved riot brewing around us.

'Now, do you see why Margaret Cook's so lucky?' Chloe poked me. 'She's got a ticket anywhere.'

I said, 'You're sick.' And she tossed her head back and cackled.

College Guidance Lady just kept going. 'Admissions committees want students who understand the world around them, who have unique perspectives.' And I raised my eyebrows, heard Chloe suck in her breath, trying not to laugh. 'They want people who matter. Individuals who have overcome adversity.' By then we were rocking in our chairs. *Margaret Cook is going to Harvard* . . . I remember whispering that to Chloe, just to see her squirm harder in her seat, just to get her laughing even harder.

That's how the whole thing started. That's when it got on its way to becoming real.

FOUR

Lunch was miserable that first day back.

Most of the girls Chloe and I usually ate with were ensconced at the front table – the resident queens of tragedy. Easy to spot, so I dropped my bag off on the floor beside the table. Said 'hey' in what I hoped was a suitably stricken tone and then left to push my tray along the line in the cafeteria. Picked up chips and salsa and a bag of cookies. Got to the table to see Priyanka and Elena patting the seat between them.

'Finn, it's so smart of you to try and eat. We've got to keep our strength up.' That came from Priyanka, who was sitting at the table with three cans of Diet Coke lined up in front of her.

Chloe and I had slumber parties with these girls. We'd played truth or dare and told secrets and none of them could even imagine the secret we kept between us. None of them had any idea how daring we actually were.

'Have you heard anything?' Elena had her chin on her hand.

This startled me so much I almost dunked a cookie in the salsa. 'From who?'

'I don't know . . . from the Caffreys? How are they?' One of the things I noticed about our friends was that they sounded a lot like their moms when they were trying to sound concerned. I mean, I knew everyone was concerned. But none of it sounded real. At all. And I didn't want to talk like this. I wanted to tell Priyanka that cutting bangs into her hair was a mistake. Or to ask Kate Herndon if I could copy her Math notes. Those weren't the kind of conversations we were having now, though. It was going to be a long time before we could talk like that.

But I wasn't about ready to talk about the Caffreys. Or think about them, really. Elena at least had some useful information. 'They're not letting us out for lunch because of all the reporters outside,' she said.

'Really? There's reporters?' I said it before I could practice it in my head, and then hoped I didn't sound too excited.

But Elena was right there with me. 'News trucks. All the big networks too.'

'Guys . . .' Priyanka sounded scandalized, but started fussing with her bangs immediately.

'What? It's important. And maybe it'll help Chloe.'

'We're not supposed to talk to them.' I said it automatically. I was so tired. I couldn't remember if Chloe and I made that rule or if it was someone else.

It didn't matter. By the time the dismissal bell rang, there were cops all over the school.

They weren't there to arrest me. I knew it because they

weren't facing the doors of the school. It took a while to convince myself of that, to talk my heart back into the right part of my chest. They were there in simple protect-and-serve capacity. Squad cars blocked off either side of the driveway that circled the school and cops stood along the sidewalks. The only vans there were the usual minivans. Whatever media had descended was lurking somewhere else.

It felt as good to step into the open air as I thought it would. For one thing, I was never out of school that early. Usually we'd have yearbook or sax ensemble or community service board. Sometimes when Chloe had school council, I would sit in as an honorary rep or wait around in the library until she got done. It felt luxurious to walk out of the building when the bell rang at three. I just let the stream of kids around me carry me up the sidewalk. We were all going home. Most meetings had been canceled by school officials. Sports teams had practice but that was about it.

It felt weird to spend so much time by myself. It wasn't just Chloe I couldn't talk to. There were clusters of kids around me, kids we'd grown up with. And I had nothing to say to them.

Losing Chloe had united us. Or them at least. All over the quad, people were clutching at each other, hugging like they might never see each other again. Sometime over the weekend, the Parents' Association had posted signs all over school instructing us to use the buddy system. No one should walk home alone; we should get home before dark. It felt like the freshman camping trip when Craig Nordgren spotted a bear in the woods.

Chloe was going to get a kick out of it. All the planning she'd done last year, putting together school pride week – or freshman year when school council assigned her with organizing the buses to Basking Ridge when our swim team made the state finals. Chloe preached school spirit like it was religion, and then all it took to unite the many fractions of Colt River High was her disappearance. I wanted to take out my phone and take pictures for her.

I knew I was supposed to stand around for a while, talking about how we couldn't believe we hadn't heard anything about Chloe yet. But the iPod in my backpack won out. I walked down the sidewalk with my head down, until it felt safe enough to smile up at the trees.

I walked home thinking about the Caffreys, and the world I walked into the night before fourth grade started, carrying my mom's peach pie over to the trailer where they were temporarily settled. I heard Cam first – you always heard Cam first when you got close to the Caffreys. I guess they knew he was autistic even way back then – that was part of the reason for moving out of the city. Not much reached Cam, but he'd spend two hours brushing a horse. He was really into systems – he liked maps and schedules and lately he'd been sort of obsessed with the skeletal structures of the animals on the farm. So Colt River was a good town for him. He never went to school with us – he got bussed over to some research facility in Princeton – but by the time of the disappearance, everyone in town knew Cam and knew to let him take his own time with things.

That night, Cam was building something with dominoes. It covered the whole table that I could see from the trailer's screen door. Later Chloe would say I banged on the door, but I don't remember it that way. My hands were cooking against the pie plate and Cam was looking right at me. I just hadn't learned yet that didn't mean he saw me. So I yelled. And when I yelled, Cam yelled and then he jerked his hands and then the clatter of all those dominoes falling filled the steel cylinder of the Caffreys' trailer. Chloe rushed over to the door to swing it open and I almost fell backwards. Mr. and Mrs. Caffrey came tearing out from some back room. Their mom went right to Cam and sort of held his arms at his sides. And Mr. Caffrey took the pie without even saying thank you. He barely looked at Chloe and me when he said, 'You girls should stay outside and play.'

'What's wrong with your brother?' I remember asking Chloe. It must have been the first question that a lot of people asked Chloe.

I never heard a different answer than the one she gave me that night, either. She just stared at me and said, 'Nothing.' As if it was that simple and obvious. Back then when people looked twice at Chloe, it wasn't because she was pretty. Her two front teeth stuck out almost horizontally and she was so skinny that her elbows and knees jutted even further. That first night, she was wearing a blue checked dress – like Dorothy in *The Wizard of Oz*. It wasn't a real dress – it was one of those Halloween costumes, the kind made of really thin material so that your mom makes you wear long under-wear underneath. Chloe just wore it on its own, like it was a real dress. She even had on sparkly red shoes. And when I asked her about the costume, she said something like, 'It's not a costume.' In the same flat voice she used to say that nothing was wrong with Cam.

I had waited a long time to have a kid live close by. It didn't even have to be a girl – just someone around my age who didn't suck. Another set of legs climbing on to the school bus from my stop on the corner of the long road alongside our farm. I wanted a neighborhood like the ones on TV where kids ran back and forth between each others' houses and ate at each others' dinner tables all the time. My neighborhood was, well, us. The farm. Back then, I couldn't even ride my bike to the nearest house.

So finally there was the possibility of something else. But one kid was inside crying over dominos. And then there was this girl dressed up like Dorothy, clicking her heels in a lawn chair outside of her trailer. Not what I'd pictured at all.

I helped torment Chloe until February. There's no other way to say it. She dressed like a cartoon and her teeth made me cringe and even though my dad never said it out loud, he seemed sad now when he looked out our kitchen window on to what used to be all of our land and saw another family living there. So I helped pick on her. I laughed when other kids pointed and I could draw an accurate diagram of the strange angles of her skewed smile. She looked like some doll that had been tossed into the dryer for too long.

Right after our Valentine's Day party, when we were supposed to be packing up little envelopes and waxy bags of candy, Chloe was bent over her cubby, wearing her Dorothy dress, and Ryan Neylon started it – darting up and flipping up her skirt. Yelling guesses about the color of her underwear. And maybe because she didn't react – Chloe never yelped or cried or even raised her hands behind her to clutch her skirt down – Ryan did it again. And then he started kicking her. Behind the knee where it makes your whole leg buckle. Other boys got in on it so that when she'd gather her balance someone else would kick her. Even after we could hear her knock hard into the wooden bench in front of the cubby, Chloe kept straightening back up. And the boys kept kicking.

Suddenly, I'd had enough. I stood in front of Chloe and when the next foot shot out, it stopped right before it connected with me. I stared them down with Chloe frozen next to me. No one said anything and there wasn't a brawl or even an argument. This was back when being just as big as the boys was a good thing. I was as strong and as fast. So it's not like I was brave because I might have gotten kicked. It was brave because it meant standing next to the weird girl and claiming her as my friend. And we were friends then – the kind I'd pictured when my parents had explained another family was moving on to our gravel road. The green cereal bowl in our kitchen cupboard became Chloe's and we spent most of that next summer sleeping out in a tent that her dad put up next to the trailer.

We never talked about Ryan and the other boys kicking her. The only reason I knew it mattered was that Chloe never wore the Dorothy dress again. The red shoes winked on her feet until we got to middle school. But those became almost cool, especially when it rained, because then Chloe would leave a trail of red glitter everywhere she stepped.

It's probably hard for a stranger to picture the before and after of Chloe's transformation. How beautiful she became – after the thick metal retainers came off and the sharp angles of her skinny body softened up in junior high. Colt River is a small town, though. We were in classes with the same eighty kids who used to scream names at Chloe on the school bus. And no one brought it up. I didn't even think most of them remembered. And if they did, if some girl like Maddie Dunleavy started slyly mentioning *The Wizard of Oz* and looking over at Chloe, well, there wasn't anything to do about it. Chloe was the kind of pretty you couldn't argue with.

The only reason I knew the way Chloe looked mattered to her was because we never joked about it. It was one of the things Chloe didn't talk about.

In the picture the newspapers used, Chloe's smiling so widely, you'd never think she usually covered up her teeth with her hand. You wouldn't know that Chloe only smiled like that next to someone else, usually me. Her hand would tighten around my waist or my shoulder and I'd know she was fighting the urge to cover her mouth. If you knew Chloe and you saw that picture, you'd know it was doctored. When Chloe stood alone for a picture, she smiled serenely – this weird quiet smile, without teeth. Like she was resigned to being beautiful and would just stand there for the second it took you to record it.

FIVE

At home, both of the Caffreys' cars were in the driveway, but that was all. No news vans, no cops. Cam's horses were grazing behind their fence and my dad's truck wasn't back yet.

'Finn!' My mom was great and all, but she wasn't really the waiting-with-cookies-at-the-door kind of mother. If it was before four, she was usually at some scrapbooking class. If it was after, she had her appointment with Oprah. But that day I could see her from all the way down by the mailboxes. She was standing on the steps, her hands on her hips.

'Yeah?' I started running without thinking. Part of me wanted to run away, but the whole day got to me, and I got scared. I started running to my mom like a little kid.

'Finley Claire Jacobs – what in God's name are you doing?'

Of course I thought she knew. It was like the eightieth time since we did it. Every time anyone spoke to me, I thought they knew.

'I'm sorry—' and holycrapthankyoujesus, my mom held a

hand up to cut me off.

'I don't want to hear it. Frankly, I am trying to be under-standing but you need to be a little more considerate, Finn.'

'What?' Because that seemed sort of mild for helping my best friend fake her own kidnapping.

'I just got off the phone with Caroline Herndon. Kate told her she saw you walking away from school.'

'Yeah?'

'Alone.'

Honestly, aside from taking detailed Math notes, Kate Herndon was pretty useless.

'Yeah.'

'Yeah?'

I wasn't going to say it again. So I stood there and looked at her and waited.

'Do you not see a problem here?'

'They canceled clubs.' For a second, I really thought she was mad that I'd skipped sax ensemble.

'Of course they canceled clubs. Honey, Chloe is *missing*.' My mom tilted her head and examined me. It was like she was trying to make a diagnosis. She rubbed her eyes a little, looked at me again and apparently decided it was time to bust out the deluxe parenting skills.

'Finn, are you okay? Sit down with me here.' She lowered herself on to the top step and I climbed up next to her. 'I can't imagine how this is.' Probably not. 'To some extent it's hard to believe all of this is real.' To some extent, yes. 'And I still don't think you're telling me everything you need to.' Nope, probably not.

I wasn't one of those girls who said, 'My mom's my best friend.' Girls like Kate or Kara Mae Clairemont said that. And they said it because the only other people who put up with all their crap were their own moms. My mom definitely listened and gave good advice – Chloe probably went to my mom more than her own, mostly because Mrs. Caffrey usually had her hands full with Cam. But it wasn't like my mom and I hung out by the lake and talked about what was going on. We didn't trade make-up or predict each other's futures. I didn't tell Mom my secrets.

That was me and Chloe.

Mom went on. 'You probably don't think you know anything. But I'm sure there are things that Chloe might have confided in you . . . like maybe she started talking to someone online. Or maybe she was sick of the situation at home.'

'Chloe didn't run away.' Not a lie. She sort of skulked away.

'Okay.' Mom rubbed her temples again. 'I have to say I hope she did run away, Finn. I hope that we get a call from her soon. No one would be angry at her, you know.'

I thought about how my mom and I had lined the kitchen counter with slices for bread, making sandwiches for all the men who showed up to search for Chloe. I remembered the dull look in Mrs. Caffrey's eyes, how she looked more like Cam as each hour passed. I thought about the cops at school that day, even stupid Teddy Selander, who couldn't go out to get pizza for lunch.

'Why would Chloe run away?' I asked, knowing she wouldn't be able to conjure a reason. That was the point we were banking on, after all. *I* was the moody one. People might be able to convince themselves that some ex-con seduced me over the internet and arranged a meeting at the bus station near the car rental place. Not Chloe, though. What prison poetry could compete with the adoring looks she got every day? It wasn't just Dean who looked at her like she carried the sun around with her in her backpack. Chloe had been to the prom every year, even as a freshman. She got free refills at Slave to the Grind from the college guys who worked the counter. She lived in a house that had its own spread in *Architectural Digest*.

My mom still seemed to be searching for an explanation to offer. 'Well, that was what I was hoping we could figure out together.'

'She would have called me.'

'And she hasn't?'

I put the edge in my voice that was supposed to be there.

'If Chloe calls me, I'll make sure to give someone a heads up.' Narrowed my eyes and set my jaw. 'You want to check my phone? You know, just in case?' I started to unzip the front pocket of my backpack.

But Mom stopped me. She reached for my arm and then kept a hold of it, turned my hand over in hers like she did when I was a little kid. 'Finn, they're going to drag the lake tomorrow.'

The gasp I let out was real – this was something Chloe and I hadn't thought about. 'How do they do that?'

'The police will bring out boats. They'll have nets. There might be people trained to look there. You know . . . divers.'

'Are Chloe's parents paying for it?'

'What? No, sweetheart. That's something that the police do, when they think someone might have had an accident. That's what we all pay taxes for.'

I pictured everyone in Colt River pulling a hundred dollar bill out of his pocket and throwing it into a metal trashcan. So that Chloe and I could set it on fire.

I learned to swim in our lake. It had some Native American name from the Lenni Lenape tribe that once lived in our area, but around here it was just the Lake. Chloe and I were morons for not imagining they'd look there. When they ran the nets through the water, maybe they'd catch the toy boats we'd once painted and sailed in the summer time. Or old eye-droppers from when we took samples of it for the sixth-grade science fair.

I thought about sneaking to my grandmother's house, but what would I do then? Convince Chloe to call it off? Tell everyone we did it so we'd have ourselves some fascinating college application essays? Besides that, the soccer mom phone chain reached my parents when I walked a mile and a half home from school on my own. It's not like it was going to be a simple thing to sneak out the night before they dragged Lake Hopatcong for the body of my best friend.

SIX

It took me longer than usual to dress the next morning. Mostly because I didn't want to force myself down each step and face the third day of Operation Evaporation. I started groaning when I hit the first floor, but my parents weren't in the kitchen waiting for me to fake sick again. Instead I stared down a plate of corn bread and a jar of jelly and a note from my mom. It just said, *Down at the Caffreys.* I felt sick all over again.

By seven forty-five, my parents hadn't come back. When I ran out of reasons to stall, I finally hoisted my bag over one shoulder and let myself out through the side porch. I walked down the hill and tapped on the Caffreys' front door. I couldn't remember the last time I'd knocked on their door, let alone the front door. Usually, Chloe and I would just make sure the screen doors didn't slam shut behind us.

Mr. Caffrey answered the door, pulled me in toward him for a hug, and called out, 'It's just Finn.' And my own mom strode in from the kitchen. She was drying her hands on a dishtowel tucked into the waist of her jeans. 'Hey, you ready to go to school?' It felt strange to follow my mom into the Caffreys' kitchen. To see my dad at their table with a cup of coffee in front of him. There was a plate of my mom's corn bread in the center of the table and baskets of food along the kitchen counter. It looked like my parents were borrowing Chloe's house. Or like we were all celebrating a holiday together.

My mom stood at the bottom of the steps and called up, 'Sheila, I'm just going to buzz Finn to school. Can I pick you up something? A bagel, maybe?'

I looked at my dad. He got it. 'Your mother believes in therapeutic carbs.'

'Nothing wrong with that.' Mr. Caffrey sounded like he was aiming for hearty. It was like the plaid shirts he always wore around town. It didn't really fit him.

'Where's Cam?' I asked.

'We arranged for the bus to pick him up early. There's going to be a lot of vehicles here and if Cam saw those, we'd never get him off to school.' Mr. Caffrey looked over at my dad like he needed to explain something. 'We thought it was important for him to be at school. Cam really needs the structure.'

'It's a great program he's in,' Dad answered, nodding his approval.

'It is. Sheila and I are so lucky.' He stopped then, and we all stared at the grain of the wood table. I found myself nodding. Thought about how it must feel to have built this careful world around all of Cam's needs. And then to have lost Chloe in it.

My mom gathered me up then. 'Speaking of structure – let's go, Finn. You got everything?' She held the door open for me. I kissed my dad on the cheek and then sort of pressed my own face to Mr. Caffrey's. He said, 'You take care, Finn,' and his voice sort of scraped along with his chair across the kitchen floor.

'You okay?' Mom asked when we got into the car.

'Yeah. Are they?'

'I think they're holding up.'

'Where was Mrs. Caffrey?' And then, because I knew she was upstairs, 'I mean, what was she doing?'

'She's having a hard time today.' My mom said it matter-of-factly as she hit her blinker and turned the wheel.

'Is she okay?'

'I think she's very frightened. She hadn't gotten out of bed yet.'

I sucked in my breath at that one. Mrs. Caffrey had always had more energy than anyone I knew. She'd been one of those moms who makes everything from scratch and who irons all the laundry. The Caffreys had one of those gigantic whiteboards on their screened-in porch where she keeps all the family's activities on track – Cam's stuff in blue, Chloe's in red. Mrs. Caffrey was always running through the house with her car keys and a water bottle, like she was running the suburban marathon.

When we pulled up to the school, we saw only one squad car out front. No news vans either, so I let myself relax a little. I started to think, *Maybe it's already blowing over*, but then that would mean that we did all that for nothing. And how would Chloe take finding out that life had moved on so quickly?

At school, it was clear that most people knew they were dragging the lake. A lot of the girls looked like they'd been crying. The usual box of tissues that Mr. Pearl kept on the desk had been replaced with a roll of the scratchy toilet paper they stock our bathroom with. He'd brought boxes of donuts in also, but only the guys were eating them.

'How are we all doing?' Mr. Pearl asked once we were all settled in. I knew from the way his face was tilted that he was trying to make eye contact, but I tried to keep my head down in my notebook.

'Mr. Pearl?' Regina Sklar raised her hand. 'Will they let us know if . . . if someone finds out anything about Chloe?'

Regina was always a pretty decent person. She asked like someone who actually cared, and I made a mental note that after Chloe's comeback, we should ask Regina to go get coffee or something. It was girls like Maddie Dunleavy who I'd rather throw coffee at. She didn't even let Mr. Pearl answer; she practically leaped over her desk to tell us, 'My dad promised he'd call.' Maddie's dad was the mayor. Which sounded all important, but our town was smaller than most small colleges. 'He said if they pulled up a body, he would have to close school.'

I guess if I actually thought there was a chance of Chloe floating up, that would have made me gasp. I mean, other girls did. But instead, I sort of marveled at the wonder that was Maddie Dunleavy. Mr. Pearl looked like he could use a drink. He swallowed a couple of times and then said, 'Okay, Maddie. Let's just let those people in authority do their job. Our job is to concentrate on the work we're doing in school.'

This time the principal announced the suspended lunch period over the intercom. He said that upperclassmen would stay in for lunch until the community felt safe. And that was pretty much all he said. No mention of the activities of the Colt River Police Department. He just wished us a peaceful and productive day.

Mr. Pearl fitted in a reminder about the counseling center before the bell rang and then we were spilling out into the hallway, but even that we all did solemnly, like we were practicing for a procession. I spent most of the morning waiting for my parents to call my cell. I don't know why I needed to hear it from them. Obviously no one was going to find anything. But I still wanted the whole thing to be over.

When no one called by sixth period study hall, I asked to be excused to call home. Everyone in the class looked around at each other as if they knew exactly what I was thinking. Whatever. I didn't know what I was thinking.

Mom picked up on the first ring. 'Finn? You okay?' She sounded really worried, like she was already grabbing her keys and headed toward the door.

'Yeah, yeah, but you said that you'd call . . .'

'Oh, no, honey . . . I meant I'd call if there was a reason.'

'Are they still there? The cops? At the lake?' I didn't know why my voice was rising. It wasn't like Chloe and I were serial killers who'd weighted down bodies and sank them down into Lake Hopatcong after sax ensemble rehearsal.

'No, they're just about done here. Nothing's changed. Is everyone okay there? How are Kate and the rest of the girls?'

'Fine – we're all just waiting to hear something.'

'Well, do me a favor and let someone else call and spread the news. I'm sure the police will issue a statement or something soon, but let's not have it come from us. I'll pick you up at three? Or are you going to get a ride with someone?'

'I actually thought I'd go check on Nana's house.'

'Oh, Finn, I don't think you need to worry about that.'

'No!' And then I thought to myself, *Slow down there, camper.* I sounded a little too desperate to go to my grandmother's house. I tried again, 'I promised her I'd check on things.' And then I trotted out the trump card: 'It might take my mind off all this.'

'Can someone go along with you?'

'I'll bring . . . Regina.'

'Regina Sklar?'

'Yeah, her parents aren't letting her go into the city for dance lessons.' If I didn't feel my own mouth moving, it could have been some other voice inventing all of it on the spot like that.

'Well, okay. That's very sweet of you to be thinking of your grandmother. Please tell Regina to stop by the house sometime soon. I'm glad to hear you two are spending some time together.'

'Yeah, I will. We'll just go over and sort the mail and water the plants.' I sounded breathless. I tried to remind myself to slow down. 'I'll call you when I'm ready.'

'Or if Mrs. Sklar's home – if it's no trouble, see if maybe

Regina's mom could give you a ride home. Tell her I'd really appreciate it.'

'Sure, okay.' It was actually one of my story's more brilliant elements. My mom didn't really know Mrs. Sklar. She was probably one of the few parents who wasn't already programmed into Mom's cell phone. So Mom wasn't going to call her up and hear that she and her daughter were on their way into the city for dance lessons as usual.

It was becoming so easy to lie.

SEVEN

My grandmother is a lovely lady. She makes granola from scratch and gets weirdly obsessed with reality show contestants. She also travels a lot, but the cruise she took that fall was the only time that I hid a missing girl in her basement.

I made sure to get everything packed before eighth period so that when the dismissal bell rang, I didn't even need to stop at my lockers for books. I was out the back exit before Maddie could pronounce the phrase *Daddy's press conference*.

But someone had beaten out my speedy retreat. Dean West was already halfway across the parking lot, wearing the same red-checked jacket he'd had for Saturday's search party at our place. That night, he had helped me pass out sandwiches and fill up water bottles at our kitchen sink. My mom fawned all over him, but he just smiled weakly and nodded – he didn't try to speak in front of so many people.

Dean spotted me when he climbed into his pick-up. He nodded toward me and then reached across the cab and threw open the passenger door. 'Lift?' he asked. Hardly any of us juniors had our licenses then. But they'd held Dean back one year, right before middle school, probably on account of his stutter. Now he seemed even older, parked all the way in the back of the lot, gazing past me at the kids pouring from the school doors.

'I'm supposed to go to my grandmother's. I can walk the few blocks. But thanks, really.' I finally forced myself to stop talking and wondered if all Dean's conversations were like that – all slanted. For every one word he pronounced, the other person said twelve. 'You okay?' I asked. Which was just as moronic, because Dean West was certainly not okay. But he just shrugged and turned the key in the ignition. I slammed the door shut and tried not to imagine how he felt. Once, Colt River's resident source of radiance had unexpectedly beamed her smile Dean's way. And then, just as suddenly, she was gone.

Standing there by the empty space, I watched him peel out of the school lot. I needed to make sure he didn't circle back and follow me to Chloe.

Donahue's Grocery was on my way to Nana's, but I didn't want to have to talk with Mr. or Mrs. Donahue behind the corner, and went on to the drugstore just a little out of the way. I stocked up on as many of Chloe's favorite snacks as I could: Baby Ruths and Ritz crackers and Ring Dings and circus peanuts. Pretty much a celebration of preservatives, but at least none of it would go bad. I bought batteries for the flashlights and hoped no one would notice that part. At the last minute, I remembered to stick in a bunch of magazines,

People and *In Touch*, wondering if Chloe would be on next week's covers.

Buying all that crap helped slow me down too because I couldn't exactly sprint with all that crap in my arms. So I actually walked to my nana's like a normal person, let myself in, and just barely stopped myself from screaming down the basement.

Chloe called for me instead.

'Finn? Finn?' Her voice sounded scratchy, like she had a cold.

'Don't yell. Stay there.' I barked out the orders while I double-checked the deadbolt and made sure the back door was still locked too.

'Finn.'

'Shut up! Seriously.' But I was already tearing down the basement stairs. I almost ran her down completely because I didn't realize she was halfway up the steps. It was so weird to see Chloe, then. It really was like she was a ghost. We must have hugged each other for a full five minutes, swaying back and forth on the steps until we sort of tumbled down the rest of the way and landed in a heap against the wall.

'Can I turn on the light?' She sounded like a little kid. With a sore throat. I realized her voice was hoarse from not talking for days, and felt immediately lousy for all the time I had thought to myself that Chloe had it easy. 'Oh my God, I can't believe you're here. How long can you stay? What's going on?'

She couldn't stop dancing around. My pajamas were too big on her and she looked like a little kid. She must have

French braided her own hair, which was weird to see because we'd always braided each other's hair. She saw me looking and touched the top of it proudly. 'What do you think? I must have practiced for hours, but I can do it myself now. I have to hang upside down to reach. Sit down.' She wheeled over my grandmother's tweed ottoman. 'Sit down. Let me do yours.'

'Chloe, you can't braid my hair. If I leave here with a French braid, what's my mom going to say?'

'Oh, like anyone would even notice.'

I handed over the drugstore bag and all the goodies and she shrieked again. I had to stop myself from clamping my hand over her mouth.

'Shhhhh,' I said. 'Chloe, they *would* notice. You have no idea – everybody notices everything now.'

'That's because you're a celebrity.' She trilled the word, being goofy with it, pulling out the magazine at the same time. 'Oh, awesome.' She breathed out heavily. 'You got Ring Dings. Finn – you are the greatest person who has ever lived.'

It was always hard to stay grim when Chloe was excited about something. Even if I'd felt like the furthest thing from the greatest person in the world. Only Chloe could make a trip to the drugstore seem like a holiday. She made everything momentous, even in the honeycomb of rooms in my grandmother's basement.

We'd worked out a bunch of rules. The lights in Nana's house ran on timers. For the most part, Chloe was supposed to stick to the basement. There were two basement windows and we'd covered both of them with layers of towels.

That way, Chloe could use a flashlight without any of the neighbors noticing lights moving around. The timers went on from 5:30 p.m. to 11 p.m. In that time, Chloe could grab a shower as long as she stuck to the first-floor bathroom. She could watch the portable TV we had moved from the kitchen into the basement. She could use the microwave. She could use the bathroom at any time, as long as she didn't turn on any lights on her own.

It was a lot to remember. But it beat just sitting in an abandoned shed somewhere and worrying if anyone would come across her. This way, Chloe could be relatively comfortable until the last couple of nights, when we'd have to move her to the place where she would say she had been held the whole time.

'I think maybe you're going to have to stop showering,' I said. 'Maybe after tonight?'

'God – this is really hard.' Chloe sobbed a little and I believed her. But then I thought about her dad sitting blankly with the palms of his hands pressed to the kitchen table. She, on the other hand, looked like she always did, like nothing at all had changed. She looked like she'd stayed home from school, or was the only one to show up for a slumber party.

She must have seen me studying her because she squeezed my hand and asked, 'Finn, are you mad at me? I'm doing everything we said.'

She sat down on the ottoman and hugged her knees. I didn't know anyone who could stay mad at Chloe, and at that moment I thought maybe they'd forgive us if we came back now. We'd say she fell and hit her head or something. Or just come clean with the whole thing. People would be so glad to see she was okay, they'd let it go. Or Chloe would just have to cry and plead a little. *Don't be mad at me.*

Only, I didn't have the same superpowers as Chloe. No one would have trouble blaming me. After all, I'd been the one walking through the halls at school, lying. It was me who'd looked straight at her mom and swore I had no idea where she could have gone.

But Chloe didn't know any of that, I made myself remember. And I knew it had to be hard for her to be all by herself in here. Chloe was like her mom – she never slowed down for anything. She must have been climbing the walls.

'I'm not mad,' I said. 'But this whole thing has gotten out of hand.'

'We said it was going to be hard,' Chloe reminded me. 'We said we'd probably want to back out, remember? We said that.'

I did remember. But we'd been talking about her, not me. It was something we said when we pictured Chloe closed up in the cellar, going stir-crazy or getting lonely. It was something I said when I imagined it was Chloe who would want to give up.

'There's just a lot we didn't think about,' I told her now.

Chloe threw back her head and laughed giddily. 'No way. You thought about everything. Every single piece of it. Face it, Finn – you just don't want to admit you're a genius.'

'I'm serious.'

'I know. But it's going to be okay.' She reached out and

squeezed my arm. 'You're freaked out about the lake.'

I'd thought I would have to explain to Chloe about them dragging the lake. I'd imagined her getting a little hysterical and me having to calm her down.

But she kept going and was completely calm about it. 'It was on the news this morning,' she said. 'Not the morning shows, but the New Jersey part of the local stuff. Did you see it?'

Once when we were camping out in the tent in the old pasture, Chloe shook me awake in the middle of the night. She'd seen a black bear through the tent's mesh window. She didn't sound scared at all. It was more like wonder in her voice, and she'd said the same thing: *Did you see it?*

'I was at school,' I said.

'Your mom's making you go to school?'

'It's better than staying at home and talking to cops all day.'

Chloe nodded like she understood. But then she went on to talk like she'd been watching a show on the Discovery Channel. 'You should have stayed home today to see the process, at least. It was actually pretty interesting. I mean, can you picture people scuba-diving in our lake, like it's a tourist attraction or something?'

'They weren't looking for a coral reef, Chloe. They were looking for your body.'

'I know that.' But it didn't seem like she really got it.

'Your mom seems to be having a really rough time,' I said. I wasn't trying to make her feel guilty. I just figured it might snap her out of it a little.

But Chloe just shrugged. 'My mom's fine.'

'Chloe, I don't know—'

'She's fine, Finn.'

The edge on her voice was sharp enough that I didn't want to go near it. We sat silently for a few seconds and then Chloe asked more softly, 'How's Cam?'

'I haven't seen Cam, really. Your dad said he's been going to extra hours at school.'

'Has anyone questioned him?'

When we were putting this whole thing together, filling our notebooks with lists that we thought obsessively covered all our bases, that was the part that had worried Chloe the most. Not everyone understood Cam. He was abrupt and sometimes that made him sound like he was angry. And if you messed with his stuff, he really did get angry. He might have been more into trains and horses than drinking games or porn, but he looked like a man, like a college guy sometimes, until you got him talking. And then once you got him talking . . . well, then he just seemed off. It wasn't like he would talk to the police and fit their idea of a protective big brother.

Chloe had worried that people might assume the worst about Cam, that it would just be the easiest answer. So we were careful to make sure she took off on a Friday, when Mrs. Caffrey usually brought Cam to the transportation museum after school. We made sure people would start looking for her before Cam was anywhere near home.

'I don't know if the officer took his statement, but it shouldn't have been too bad. Your dad found the horse before

Cam and your mom came back from the museum.'

'Okay. So that's good.'

'Yeah, that part's good, Chloe. But the rest of it—'

'The rest of it is already happening. It's not like a ride we can just get off.'

I wanted to tell her it wasn't like a ride at all, that there was nothing fun about it. Not fun like it had been to plot it out together, to figure what would need taking care of, how most of the town would react.

In the local news, they flashed her picture with the grin we usually share together. And the newscaster said something like, 'Teachers and classmates are shocked at the disappearance of this bright, energetic, young beauty.' And here she was bounding around the basement, like the only cheerleader for Team Kidnap.

'So did you see all the newscasts last night?' I asked. This would cheer her up. The anchor lady had called her a *young beauty*.

Chloe flashed a smile. 'I did – I'm sorry about the picture. Did they tell you they were going to cut you out?'

'I didn't know anything until we saw the papers. Your mom must have given them the picture. Anyway, they needed a picture of you, Chloe, not me. Otherwise what would the newsladies say? "No, folks, it's not the pie-face girl missing, it's the cover girl next to her."'

Chloe shrieked at that. '*Pie-face?* What does that even mean? You're so weird about pictures.'

'Everybody's weird about pictures unless they turn out like yours.'

'Whatevs.'

'Listen,' I said. 'I'd better go. My mom thinks I'm with Regina Sklar.'

'Are you serious? Where did you pull that one from?'

'Regina asked about you.'

'Yeah?'

'Really. And she was cool about it. She wasn't all weeping into the shirt of the hot student counselor.'

'What?' Chloe shrieked again and I hushed her, laughing. She grabbed a pillow and hugged it close to her chest and I told her all about Dr. Ace and his new fan club. It felt like any other time we had put off homework by talking. Except that day, it wasn't like my mom would just raise her eyebrows if I showed up late for dinner.

'Okay, okay,' I said. 'I really have to move my ass now. There's candy in the bag too. Are you eating enough?'

Chloe motioned to the pile of cereal bars and cookies in the corner. A jar of peanut butter sat next to one of grape jelly. 'Yeah, it's going to be really suspicious when you find me after nine days and I've put on ten pounds.'

'We'll figure it out,' I said.

'I'm trying to exercise a little down here.' She crouched down and held up one of my grandmother's old Jane Fonda videos. 'There's a VCR built into that TV. It's pretty blurry and I keep the sound off most of the time.'

I snorted. Chloe snapped her head up, a little insulted. 'Oh, don't get mad,' I said. 'It's just that – if you could see how people are zombie stomping around up there . . .' I pointed up to the street. 'And then to picture you down here doing aerobics.' I giggled a little bit. 'My grandmother's aerobics . . .'

'Shut up!' But she was laughing too. 'All right next time, bring some Tai Bo.' Then her face shifted. She looked almost afraid. 'I don't want you to go.'

'I should have been out of here ten minutes ago. It's going to be okay. I'll come back as soon as I can.'

'Finn – you don't know how lonely it is.'

I thought of how I'd been walking around, how hard it had been to talk to anyone because of how impossible it was to look people in the eye.

'I do.'

I left Chloe sitting on the basement carpet. She was trying to open a bag of circus peanuts with her teeth. She called out 'bye' as forlornly as some little kid who'd just been put on time out. I didn't have the heart to remind her to keep her voice down.

EIGHT

Both cars were lined up in the Caffreys' driveway when
I got home. If someone had really taken Chloe, I would
have stopped at her house after school. I would have knocked
on the kitchen door, but I wouldn't have listened for someone to say, 'Come in.' I would've just gone on inside to sit
next to Mrs. Caffrey. In my head, I knew that was what I was
supposed to do.

Instead I walked straight up to our house and let myself
in. Called out for my parents. No one. I went out back and
checked on the sheep. I unrolled hay and checked on a
couple of our ewes. Unwound the hose and dragged it over
to fill the water trough. Sat out there for a while and watched
the sheep surge toward the new green.

The house felt eerie and empty, so I put on the TV. At first
I flipped past the news and then made myself put it back. It
was just a fluff piece about celebrity drink driving. Chloe and
I used to imagine what it would be like to be famous. Some
celebrities didn't even do anything. They went to parties and
they wore dresses. They flashed tabloids. Chloe and I were

working harder than any of them to get this done.

The piece about Chloe made the news wrap-up. That meant people from the whole tri-state area were staring up at the sheep picture. I wondered where we'd be if she came home right then. If we toured New York University that very minute, how many people would recognize her? They closed with the images of the police boat in the middle of the lake. The anchorwoman looked somber, saying, 'This morning's events do not appear to have led authorities any closer to the answer of young Chloe Marie Caffrey's disappearance.'

When the screen door slammed, I hit the remote to turn off the TV. I leaped up from the couch to see my dad standing in the hall.

'Hey.' He looked at me from under the brim of his baseball cap. 'You're not next door?'

'I had to take a look at the sheep.'

'Yeah? Everyone doing okay?'

'Seems like it. What do you think?'

'About the sheep or about next door?'

I shrugged and tried to not look scared. I took a breath and asked, 'How's everyone doing next door?' Next door was beginning to sound like its own country.

Dad went to the fridge and opened it up. He started carrying out sandwich stuff and piling it on the counter. 'I think today was a rough one.'

'But they have to be happy, right? I mean that no one found . . . or that Chloe wasn't . . .' I couldn't finish. I couldn't make my mouth say it all.

'I don't think anyone's happy about anything right now. And now exhaustion's hitting – Mrs. Caffrey can't stand up. Can you believe that? It's like she's just breaking down.'

'What do they think happened?'

'I think we're all just hoping Chloe made a really big mistake. Because otherwise . . .'

It was a little sick to have this conversation while Dad was making sandwiches.

'Otherwise what?'

'Otherwise it doesn't look good, Finn.' Dad pulled out a chair for me and nodded toward it. I sat, obedient as always. 'The Caffreys have money, sweetheart. More than most people. It's pretty well known around here. And even if you weren't from Colt River – well, by now, the house has been on the news, so people know. But no one's said anything about ransom. If someone took her, they don't want money.' Dad watched me as he talked, like he was measuring me for cracks.

'So I'm hoping.' Dad stopped talking and focused on the food in front of him for a minute. He started again. 'I have to say that I'm hoping that Chloe just made the stupidest mistake of her life. Maybe she went to meet some guy. Maybe she felt pressured around here. You know all we've been talking about lately is what a perfect kid Chloe is. We all think of you and Chloe as perfect – you know that. I don't know.' He slathered mustard on one side of a piece of rye, so I knew that one was for me. 'But nobody's perfect, right? It has to get to be a little much, carrying all that around.'

'So what are you saying?'

'Well, maybe Chloe just felt like setting that down for a while.'

'Chloe didn't run away.'

'Because she would have told you first.'

'Yeah.'

'But what would you have said?'

'What?'

'Maybe it seemed like a good idea at the time, right? I mean, you couldn't have known. And then, everything got out of control . . .'

'Dad.' It was weird to feel so hurt, like his theory landed so far off the radar. But my throat ached and tears rushed to my eyes. I couldn't have faked it better. 'What do you think? I'm some monster?' Part of me kind of wanted him to say yes. It would have all been over if he had said yes.

I stood up and Dad reached up for my hand.

'I'm sorry, kiddo,' he said. 'I'm really sorry. It's just wishful thinking, you know?'

I shook him off. 'I'm going up to my room.' Dad didn't even call me back. I wished my door locked from the inside. Just to keep people out for a little while. From my bedroom window you could see the huge arched glass of Chloe's. When we were small, we used to try blinking Morse code messages to each other with flashlights. It was a hard language to learn.

Chloe's light was on, so I rushed to shut my bedside lamp off. I didn't want Mrs. Caffrey to know I was home. Got under the covers without even changing into my pajamas. Chloe and I both used to have glow-in-the-dark stars all over our ceilings. Dad had put them up in my room, and since Chloe loved them too, Mr. Caffrey and Dad then put them up in her room as a surprise for her birthday. The summer before we went into high school, we took them down. They seemed babyish. Or at least Chloe said so. We sneaked ladders up while the dads were playing squash so it wouldn't hurt their feelings. It was stupid, but I hadn't wanted to take mine down. And so I'd left three up, the ones that were supposed to be Orion's belt. Sometimes when I had trouble sleeping, I stared up at them. That's what I did that night.

I wished Chloe and I could have disappeared together. We could have both been watching late night *Law & Order* reruns and eating circus peanuts. We would have been together. And I wouldn't have had to wake up in the morning, slink past the Caffreys' house, and go to school again.

I missed Chloe. I missed who we were before.

I didn't close my eyes until the yellow window of Chloe's bedroom down the hill went dark.

NINE

D ad and I rode quietly in the car the next morning. The day felt dim. I wasn't going over to my grandmother's house. My mom had spent the night at the Caffreys' place. I guess because the cops were through at the lake, the news vans were back parked along the street at school.

'Jesus.' Dad practically whistled the word. 'Everything I pay in taxes, and someone can't clear these shitheads off school property?'

'It's fine, Dad.'

'None of this is fine. We've talked about you and the press.'

'Yes, Dad.' It sounded like we were arguing about curfew or the necessity of clearing my plate at supper.

But he was more intent than that. 'And what did we say?'

'We said *No press*.'

'That's right. I'm not about to watch them turn you into a target.'

I didn't have to turn around to know that he stayed there in the drop-off lane and watched me walk through the gauntlet of reporters to school. No one recognized me anyway. I wondered how long it would take before they all knew me on sight. I saw Kate standing off by the courtyard, bent toward a woman dressed in a tan trench coat. You might have thought the lady was one of the richer moms, except for the camera hovering above them. Kate kept dabbing at her eyes with her sleeve until the trench coat lady pulled a hunk of Kleenex out of her pocket. It was better than Career Day, really. Before I even made it to the building, I'd already learned being a tabloid journalist means carrying tissues for the hysterical sobs of attention-starved failed gymnasts.

In the hallway, people parted in front of me. The reporter lady might not have known who I was, but inside the school doors, I'd achieved some minor celebrity status. Chloe and I had talked about this too. How nothing ever happened in Colt River. So when something did, everyone would latch on to it and try to make it theirs.

When we were in seventh grade, Chloe and I were in a car accident. Mrs. Caffrey was driving and Cam and Chloe were in the backseat, with me riding up front. Mrs. Caffrey ran a stop sign. It was a dump truck that hit us, so it wasn't going fast, but it was big and dirty. I remember that at the same time I realized it wasn't going to stop, I also noticed how dirty it was. Cam and Chloe were wearing seatbelts, but I'd taken mine off so that I could twist around and talk to Chloe behind me. That was a big sticking point in our house, and for a month or two, my dad was considering filing suit. It was really strained whenever either of us was around the other's parents.

My mom's point was that you didn't sue friends. My dad kept saying, 'That's why people have insurance.' In the end, Chloe's parents paid my medical bills, and after a while everything died down.

They paid for plastic surgery. Because I hit the windshield. With my face. The crash left a crescent-shaped scar on my face. It looks like a quarter moon shining on my cheek. Chloe said that you could hardly tell, and if you did notice it, it actually looked kind of cool.

But every night I put this scar cream on it. Chloe said it was pretty much gone, but she wouldn't have said that if it had been her face. Nobody would say it if it was her face that got marked up.

When we started imagining the kidnapping scenario, like really considering what the reality of the situation would be, Chloe brought up the car accident. She talked about how weird everyone acted the next morning, when she went to school and I was still in the hospital. She said that it felt like there was some weird competition between all the girls. That all of a sudden everyone claimed I was their best friend. Everyone was crying in class and by the way the girls in our grade told the story, I'd just barely, miraculously survived.

Chloe kept asking, 'Don't you remember how everyone acted when you first came home after the car accident? What school was like when you first got back?' But when I tried to retrieve those memories, I ended up thinking more about the dump truck. I got stuck remembering how for a while, my mom and I would change the bandages on my face and measure how bad it was together.

Now, when it was my turn to be the center of attention, I let it happen. When the girls flocked to me, when Kate and the rest fell in line behind, I tried to look grateful. Pressed my hand to my chest over my heart. Just like I'd seen them do. Just like how they had seen their mothers do.

The lady in the trench coat showed up during lunch that day, wanting to interview me about Chloe. I'd stopped in at the bathroom near the office, the one that the school thought we wouldn't use because it had *Ladies Room* and not just *Girls* stenciled across the door. I just hadn't felt like dealing with the lunchroom crush of thirty girls crammed in front of the mirrors.

The reporter lady was just standing there at the sink. She looked done. And when I thought about it, it must have really sucked to be chasing weepy teenagers around for a story that wasn't going anywhere. She was pretty in a frozen way – I imagined when she'd been my age she'd pictured herself crossing her legs behind a desk on the evening news or flirting with a morning co-host or something. And instead she was under the fluorescent lights of the Colt River High Ladies' Room. Chloe and I had said that I should dodge the press as much as possible. We figured if it looked like I was seeking out reporters, then it would look really suspicious for me to be the one to find her. But it wasn't like I'd gone into the bathroom looking for the lady.

So when I bent to wash my hands at the sink next to her, I just asked, 'Are you here because of Chloe?'

And she said, 'Yes. I am,' in this really weary voice.

'Chloe's my best friend.' And she didn't even react to that, so I knew that Kate and Maddie and everyone else auditioning for their cameos on *48 Hours Mystery* had fed her the same line. I tried a new one: 'The Caffreys live on my dad's old farm.'

The reporter's eyes snapped up to meet mine in the mirror. 'Jacobs? Finley Jacobs, right? I'm Kirsten Manahan with Channel Eleven. It's good to meet you, Finley – how are you? How is your family doing?' It was like her batteries had been replaced. She took my arm and steered me out into the hallway. I saw her look past me and wave her hand. For a split, scary second, I thought she was signaling a cop. But it was just a camera guy. Kirsten Manahan steered me into a classroom, saying, 'We've been hoping to speak to you – because you must be looking for a way to help Chloe, right? Maybe we can give you a chance to speak out and do that.'

I thought it was weird that someone had given the newspeople a classroom. And I panicked a little because this was it, my self-orchestrated debut. The teacher had hung this enormous periodic table across one of the classroom walls, and I found myself thinking that Kirsten Manahan could be my own experiment. She settled back into one of the classroom chairs and motioned for me to sit back in the teacher's swivel armchair.

Really, she wanted to hear about our idyllic childhood on the farm. And she wanted more about the horse. Everyone wanted to hear about Chloe and her horse. I remember concentrating really hard on each shellacked strand of the reporter's helmet hair and trying to tell the story the way a girl whose best friend had disappeared would tell it. Like I could hardly bear to remember it. As if it hurt that much to tell.

And the more I told, the more it did hurt. Because the things I kept describing – me and Chloe running around catching fireflies in jelly jars, the two of us awake at six, stacking bales of hay, or staying up all night waiting for the new lambs – it sounded so ideal and perfect and innocent. Especially since I knew that we weren't like that anymore. Especially since I knew we'd never be able to describe each other that simply again.

That was the only interview I did before the other ones. Dad flipped out when he saw it on the ten o'clock news, and told me that next time I'd better tell them to go to hell or at least call him or Mom. He was really dialed up to Level Rage, ranting about calling the networks himself or going to court to get a restraining order against the press. And Mom pointed out quietly, 'Really, Bart – whatever coverage we can get, it's probably good for Chloe.'

I wanted to yell out, 'Exactly. That's the whole point.' By that point, I was counting down the hours. Until then it just meant suffering through it – the way my mom said everything quietly these days, the Caffreys' press conferences, the search parties, all the kids at school wearing their dumbass Chloe ribbons. Because the more press, the more exposure, the better it would eventually be for Chloe. And, by extension, for me.

I knew that Chloe would be pissed I did the interview,

too. It broke one of the rules we'd come up with – I had to keep a low profile until Rescue Day. Otherwise it would look too suspicious, too convenient. By then, though, six days into it, I was feeling that Chloe could suck it. She sat on a pile of blankets all day, watching talk shows and eating Pop Tarts and seeing her own picture flash across the news. I was already tired of hearing her memorialized in the hallways at school, sick of seeing her face in makeshift shrines all over town. The afternoon of that first interview, I rode my bike down to the library and then along the towpath by the river. Every time the pedals spun around, I heard them asking, 'What have you done? What have you done?' God. It felt like I was drunk on some kind of liquid guilt. Every time I passed another poster of Chloe with that lamb tucked under her arm, I pedaled harder, but that just made the voice in my head louder. So I ended up just walking the bike home, making myself turn away every time I saw the white flag of a MISSING flyer stapled to a telephone pole or tree.

Now, if I had the chance to do it, if the whole world was still paying attention to me, I would call my own press conference. And even with all the flashbulbs shuttering in my face, I'd tell them: Chloe was never missing. At least she was never missing to me.

TEN

At first it felt like some kind of school assignment – the kind of project teachers usually expected Chloe and me to partner up for. In eighth grade we'd had to care for a robot baby like a real baby. The year before that, we'd balanced household budgets. For this, Chloe and I invented a mystery. What started as a smoldering joke ignited into a game and then into a full-blown sport.

Early into writing the rulebook, we decided it was Chloe who'd have to go missing. She was the Margaret Cook expert, after all. And there was the pretty girl formula. If I'd suddenly vanished, it would be news in Colt River. Hep Carter would run some front-page story and pass around ballpoint pens from the *Raritan Valley Tribune* up at the high school. It's not like I needed a self-esteem transplant, but I was realistic. When it comes down to it, I was a farm kid. I looked like a potato in pictures and usually wore the same jean jacket until the sleeves started to unravel.

Chloe might have lost all her baby teeth here, but she was still city people. And city people cared about other city people. Especially hot city people.

They didn't start the search parties until the second night. That first night, Friday, a phone chain went around town. We were already at the Caffreys' with Cam. Even knowing the formula, we didn't count on how quickly the city tabloids would roll in with their vans. The Holiday Inn on Route 202 was pretty much packed with ladies with Judge Judy hair and sweaty cameramen by Saturday morning.

Chloe had wanted to smear the horse with blood. When we finally figured out how to signal her disappearance to the rest of Colt River, she thought we should step it up, leave a bloody handprint on the saddle or something. That would up the ante. People would be more alarmed so that the news would spread faster. It had taken me days to talk her out of that one. Mostly because it meant we'd have to explain it afterwards. We'd have to cut her.

The riderless horse was spooky enough. I heard Mr. Caffrey find him. He'd been working from home that week and I heard the low whistle under the window. Then I heard him start calling for Chloe. Caught a glimpse of him chasing after Caraway and then leading the horse to the stables. I saw him check the gates. At first, Mr. Caffrey must have thought Chloe was just goofing off. But we're pretty careful about the animals. My cell phone rang next. Then the land line. It had started.

When the first news vans came, someone asked to get some shots of the horse, saddled up just like he was when Mr. Caffrey first found him. I only know because I heard him tell my dad. He was pretty bent out of shape about it. Dad kept trying to talk him down, going on about how people just wanted to help out, so the news people needed details. Mr. Caffrey rarely raised his voice, but he was yelling about that – saying that there was nothing about seeing the horse that was going to help anyone find Chloe.

That night, on the late-night news, they just showed a shot of some other horse – not Caraway – saddled up and trailing reins. It was actually the first time I got that sick feeling in my stomach. These were the people that Chloe and I were chasing. And they were pretty good at playing the game.

I hadn't been near the stables during the daytime since Chloe's disappearance. For once, my dad didn't fuss about it. He must have just taken over cleaning the stall. Besides, you could never keep Cam away from the horses. He'd be looking after them too. A couple of times, I'd snuck out at night with some apples and carrots, trying to make it up.

At night the stables were different. Maybe because of the whole nativity thing, they felt holy. It smelled cleaner, because it was cooler at night. The horses shuffled in the stalls. They snorted and swished their tails back and forth so it sounded like leaves rustling in the wind.

I wondered if Margaret Cook had animals. Because even if I'd looked like Chloe, it couldn't have been me who hid out. I could never have been away from Chauncey that long, or Gabe, or even the sheep. Animals were just easier company for me. They nuzzled at your palm; they asked for what they needed. Gabe studied me with his wet eyes and for once I wasn't worried about what got seen.

Ever since I was five, our dog Chauncey had slept outside, below my bedroom window. If Chloe and I camped out, he slept outside the tent. If I slept at her house, then he slept on the Caffreys' back steps. I knew he'd track me down if I ran off. He was one of the few creatures alive who loved me more than Chloe.

The fourth night after the disappearance, after the ten o'clock news was over, I brought Chauncey with me to the stables. I realized that Chloe hadn't asked about Caraway, which was a little weird. But some things I still passed off as her still being a little bit city. A tried and true farm girl would worry about her horse. Sitting in the stables, I wondered what my life would have been like had the Caffreys never moved out here. Who would I be if I wasn't Chloe's best friend? We told each other we'd be lost without each other, but the truth was we probably would have been just fine. I'd spend more time on my own, but that wouldn't make me any different from any of the other farm kids. The truth was, this was the loneliest I've ever been.

I wondered if Chloe was thinking like that. If sometimes she saw the faint smile-shaped scar on my face and pictured what her life would be like if the accident had been fatal. I knew she would've been fine without me. I thought it and nodded the way I saw my dad nod to himself sometimes. Her status would have just risen faster if she'd tragically lost her best friend.

Maybe Chloe would have written her college essay about me. She could have described how the cracks spread across the windshield before the glass showered on to my hair. She could have said that she promised right then and there that her life would matter for both of us. She could have written an essay that sounded brave and sensitive and noble all at once. And, according to College Guidance Lady, it still wouldn't have gotten her into a top-tier school.

That night, I ended up dozing off on the floor of the stable, with my head on a rolled-up horse blanket and Chauncey curled up in my legs. I woke up to screaming while it was still dark outside. I thought at first that maybe I'd opened my eyes into one of my own nightmares. Looked out at our houses and saw that it was Cam's light that was on. What kind of essay would Cam write about all of this? How much of it was getting through to him?

The thing about Cam was that he liked everything to stay the same. Lunch at 11:30. Same lunch in the same kind of brown bag. Two napkins in the bag and a colored straw. I'd never seen him reach out to Chloe. Sometimes, he'd duck under their mom's arm. That was Cam's way of hugging, but it was reserved for the parental figures. Once Chloe and I were building a fort out of old fence posts and a rusted nail tore through her palm. Cam was sitting right near us with one of his books. His eyes didn't even flicker when she screamed.

But that didn't mean he didn't care. Even if it was just that Chloe was another piece of the routine he lived by, that counted for something. He'd miss that.

That's what I was wondering on my way back up the stairs to my bedroom – what Cam was calling out for.

ELEVEN

Dean West was in love with Chloe, but I was the one who wrote the letters he kept zipped in the front pocket of his backpack.

We weren't trying to be mean. For one thing, Chloe really did think he was hot. That wasn't really his problem. It was the way talking to him stressed people out – everybody got embarrassed when Dean talked. Sometimes he got going and managed three or four sentences just fine. Everyone felt relieved for a second. And then a word got caught somehow – it was like he was choking on it. His whole face contorted and his lips worked around the sound over and over. It looked terrible and sounded painful, so everyone just sort of looked around at each other helplessly, waiting for it to be over. Dean included.

Sometimes I wondered whether Dean would speak more clearly if he'd grown up in a bigger town than Colt River. Once you know the whole place calls you Stuttering Dean, it's probably tough to relax and get over something. Maybe if that wasn't how we all knew Dean, he would've had the chance to be someone different.

He was a sweet guy and it seemed like the one way you could get to know him was through writing things down. The notes were a project Chloe and I worked on together. We'd gotten Craft Shack gift vouchers for some community service prize and we spent most of them on fancy paper and crazy stickers and stuff like that. We bought a hole punch and filled one note with tiny snowflake confetti so that when Dean opened it, it would look like a miniature snowstorm. That was one of my favorites, because when we checked the school message board to see that he'd picked it up, we saw some tiny snowflakes on the floor in front of the office window.

Mostly we copied song lyrics or poems and things. We hardly used our own words at all. Later on, Chloe wrote a couple of notes by herself and posted them for him and caused one of the biggest fights we'd ever had. It just felt like she was keeping secrets, like she turned something we'd worked on together into her own thing.

Chloe and I had figured it would unfold like one of the trashy paperbacks my mom reads – finally the young hero would have the chance to pour out all his pent-up emotion in poetry. When he didn't respond to the first two notes, we realized that Dean wouldn't know who to leave messages for. It's not like he could put up some random blank note on the office window.

In our next message we left instructions to leave us notes by the old encyclopedia sets in the library. A couple of days later we found a muffin on one of the dusty shelves. We didn't think it was Dean at first, but then a week later there was a bag of homemade peanut-butter cookies. There was a carrot cake cupcake once and another muffin too. It was like Boo Radley was into baking.

He might not have left us love notes, but Dean changed a little, just in how he carried himself. When we all sat around talking before class started, Dean still sat back. But he didn't sit back like he was afraid to join in. It was more like he was so satisfied with himself that he didn't have to. One time we wrote something about his eyes and then Dean started wearing a lot of blue. He stopped slumping beneath his grey hoodie all the time.

We weren't jerks about it. We didn't write anything that wasn't true. If anything, Chloe ended up actually a little wrapped up in him. But he was still Stuttering Dean. However good he looked in a blue button-down shirt, he still went into palsied mode anytime a teacher called on him in class.

We had this demented substitute teacher at the very beginning of school. I heard that people actually complained about her. Subs are supposed to just sit there, leave us to concentrate on whatever work the teacher left. But this twitshit sat there dissecting us like we were lab rats or something. Honestly. She took notes.

And she had a blast with Dean. She called on him to read the directions on our worksheet and of course it took him a good three minutes just to work through the first two lines. So that was it. Anything we had to read, she called on Dean. Sometimes when he was struggling with a word, she'd interrupt him and coo, 'Relax. Relax. Just breathe.' It was awful. Once she brought a newspaper clipping about the genetics of stuttering. She scurried right over to Dean like a little rat, screeching, 'I've had this folded up in my purse. You have to tell me – do you have siblings that stammer? Does your father have the same impediment?'

When Dean looked up at her, it looked like he was bracing himself for execution. I saw his Adam's apple move when he swallowed. He said, 'No, Ma'am.' He faltered a little on the ma'am part, but the rest of it was clear as day.

'See? There you go – look what a little concentration can do.' Dean's jaw set harder, because it's not like the problem had just been that he was lazy. For years. 'Don't you want to communicate with others?' I wanted to raise my hand and tell her about Cam. I wanted to raise my hand and tell her about me. Dean did something kind of kickass, though. He opened his mouth to talk, twisted his lips, and started jerking his head up and down. He looked like our old dog Honey did when she had a seizure at the groomer's shop. At one point, Dean clutched at his own throat as if he was trying to physically pull out the words. And then stopped all of a sudden, stared at her, and said, 'Nope.'

And I thought, *Go Dean West*. I'm not saying we transformed him into the kind of kid who didn't take any shit from Pseudo Shrink. It seemed like that's who Dean was all along. But maybe it helped that he knew that someone noticed him for better reasons than the words he couldn't say.

* * *

They came for Dean during sixth period.

Usually they called a kid down to the office over the

loudspeaker. It didn't necessarily mean anything. Maybe someone saw you tagging a bathroom cubicle. Or maybe you had an orthodontist's appointment. But Mr. Gardener came to escort Dean out of class himself. A man I didn't recognize stood behind him in the doorway. And then I saw the blue uniforms of the two cops in the hallway. It wasn't just weird – it was wrong.

Word spread. By the time eighth period let out, most of the junior class stood clumped in clots blocking the artery of the school's main corridor. Kate threw her arms around me. 'Oh God, Finn. Can you believe it?'

No. I thought of how Chloe and I had made a to-do list, just like we did before presenting at the county fair each year. And how nothing like this had been on it.

'He's an animal.' That was Maddie's contribution. Kate looked grateful for it.

'He's a psycho,' she corrected. 'We all know he's a psycho.'

The second muffin Dean left in the library stacks was banana walnut. He left it on a napkin and on the napkin, he'd written, *Dear You – This has nuts, just in case you're allergic. Please be careful.* I remembered how Chloe's peals of laughter earned us a hushing from the librarian. Her whole face had shone. 'He's crazy!' Chloe had said. I'd agreed with her.

This wasn't what we meant. Clusters of kids stood around the hallway crafting theories about the kid most of them couldn't be bothered to listen to. 'He must have totally snapped,' I heard someone say. 'They found a bunch of pictures in his locker.'

'I heard the secretaries talking in the office – the pictures were all ripped up. He'd torn them in pieces.' The voices kept crashing around me and I felt like I was drowning. I wanted to claw my way out of the school and sprint to my grandmother's house. To take Chloe by the shoulders and shake her until she agreed to follow me up from the basement.

I knew exactly what pictures they'd found torn up in Dean's locker. I took those pictures. The notes had gone on for weeks and we thought he knew anyway. But Chloe wanted him to know for sure. So we printed out an eight by ten picture of Chloe's face and cut it out so it looked like puzzle pieces. He probably knew as soon as he saw a strand of her white-blonde hair, but we doled out the pieces over two weeks. It was when she was posing for the picture that I figured out that Dean wasn't just a game to her. She never cared what she looked like in photos, but when we took that one, Chloe posed.

The pictures couldn't have been the only reason the cops came for Dean. I tried to reassure myself, but all I kept see-ing was his puzzled face looking up at Mr. Gardener calling from the doorway. Kate rubbed my arms with her hands. 'Finn. Do you wanna sit down? You look like you're about to pass out.' I ended up sliding down to sit on the floor with my back to the lockers. 'You've been so strong, Finn.' Kate was cooing at me like she was the white Oprah. 'Let go.'

Sometime in the next twenty years, Kate was going to grow up into one of those people addicted to attending Narcotics Anonymous meetings. She was going to find some excuse to talk like this for the rest of her life.

'I gotta go,' I said.

'Finn – you don't have to be alone right now.'

Nope, I actually had to be near Chloe. We had some things we needed to make right. I heard Warren Winter talking about the men who came to clear out Dean's locker. He was practically panting. 'They were FBI guys. I could tell.' Warren spoke with authority. This was the highlight of his life. 'They were brutally efficient.'

I wondered where they'd taken Dean and forced myself to ask Warren. 'Were his parents here? Did they come get him?' That's what I was hoping for. Maybe he was suspended. And I'd go talk to Chloe and she'd just have to come back a little early. We'd hit her on the head and she could claim she didn't remember where she had been all this time. The principal would realize they made a mistake about Dean and it would just turn out that he got a day off from school.

Warren looked thrilled that I asked. His chest expanded. 'They took him away in a squad car. The FBI guys followed in their car.'

I wanted to tear Warren apart, to pick apart his bones for meat. The whole hallway buzzed and murmured. It was like some holiday. It was like none of them had known Dean at all. Or even Chloe. Both of them were only characters all of a sudden, and the whole thing was a television show that no one wanted to miss.

'I need to call my mom.' That's what I came up with. At least I didn't announce to the assembled crowd that I had to call Chloe.

Mom had already heard. She was, in fact, already in the school parking lot. 'Just come on outside, Finn,' she said. 'If you can't calm yourself down, ask one of the girls to walk with you.'

'They're wrong, Mom. There's a lot they don't know.' I was shrieking into my cell and a couple of kids were staring. Kate stopped rubbing my shoulders.

Kenneth Ryden kept hitching his pants up by the belt loop, as if he was playing Sheriff. 'I knew Dean West needed speech therapy, but not actual therapy.' He said it like my Uncle Frank tells racist jokes, with the flat pause at the end for looking around and waiting for people to appreciate his genius.

'You're brilliant, you know that, Kenneth?' I said. 'Make sure to feed that sound bite to one of the reporters. It doesn't sound at all like you've been working on drafts of it or anything.' Kenneth looked up at me and his ears went pink. I couldn't stop myself. 'It's like you're an improv god. Except not – moron— '

'Finn.' My mom said it firmly, like she meant business. 'Just come on out to the car.' I didn't say anything to Warren Winter or the girls who had swarmed around me. I stood up, picked up my backpack by one strap, and walked toward the doors.

Kate called after me, 'Finn – you don't even know Dean West. What is your problem? Chloe was your best friend.' It's funny – I knew that Kate wasn't a bad person. I was the bad person. But it was like Dean West was a skittle and they were all mad that I wouldn't pick up the ball and throw it.

'You don't know anything.' I said it to Kate, but I didn't turn back to look at her. So it sounded like I was saying it to myself. Which would have been true too.

My mom was on her cell phone when I climbed into the car, but it didn't stop me from frantically directing her as soon as I closed the door. 'We have to go right to the police station.' She held her finger up to me, motioning for one minute, but I just buckled up my seatbelt. 'We have to go straight there. There's a lot they don't know about this.' I thought I could at least tell them about the photograph and the notes we had left for Dean – maybe that would be enough to clear some things up. Maybe they would let him go home. It would look suspicious if I went in all sure that he didn't do anything and then I ended up finding and saving Chloe, but we would just have to work around that. I'd just have to be a really good liar.

My mom was still holding a hand out to me. Palm out, like a crossing guard warning me not to walk. 'We'll get to the bottom of this, Sheila. Finn's here now. We're going to come right back to the house.'

'We're not going right to the house, Mom.' I'd started arguing before she had the phone totally closed. But the look on her face turned my volume down a notch. I said more quietly, 'We have to go to the police station.' My mother maneuvered the car out of the lot and turned toward home.

'Finn – is this boy a friend of yours and Chloe's? Were the two of them seeing each other?'

'Kind of. I don't know.'

'Kind of seeing each other?'

'Well, not really. I know she liked him and he liked her. But they weren't, like, dating.'

'This didn't seem important to mention before?'

'Dean West? No. He's Stuttering Dean. He wouldn't hurt anyone. We have to go to the police station.'

'And tell them what, Finn?'

'That this is a mistake. That Dean is a good person.' I started crying then. 'He bakes muffins and he's shy and he's just starting to be a little less shy and he probably can't even explain to them.' I was losing it. 'They're not going to understand him. He's not going to be able to tell them . . .' My mom looked over at me and slowed the car down.

'We need to let the police do their job. I'm sure that they have their reasons for asking this boy questions. It's not our place to interfere with this. That's not going to help anyone.'

'But they're talking about these pict . . . these pictures.' I was stammering like Dean. 'They think Dean t-t-tore up Chloe's pic-picture, but that was us.'

'That was who?'

'Me and Chloe.'

'Why would you and Chloe tear up her picture?'

'It was a puzzle. We gave him different pieces until he could tell it was Chloe.'

'*What* was Chloe?'

'The person leaving him notes.'

'Chloe left this boy notes?'

'We left him notes. We did it together.'

'Finn.' My mom had her disappointed-in-me voice on. 'You left this mute boy notes? I thought you two knew better than to play jokes like that on people.'

'Dean West isn't mute. He stutters.'

'Oh, Finn. You girls. You have no idea how cruel—'

'No, Mom – we weren't making fun of him.'

'Chloe liked this boy? Did you like this boy?' My mom sounded almost hopeful.

'He seemed like someone we'd want to know.'

My mom sighed. It was a long-suffering sigh, like she couldn't imagine how she ended up with such a moronic daughter. 'Finn, there are only seventy-nine students in your class. How could you not know a boy in your own grade? Even if he doesn't talk.'

'He *does* talk.'

'Well, then let him speak up for himself now. I don't know what you and Chloe were thinking. Honestly, I had hoped you were kinder girls than to tease people like that.'

We pulled into the drive, but she stopped the car at the foot of the drive. 'I need to go in and sit with Sheila. I think you should go up to your room and start on your homework.'

'We haven't done anything in class since—' I stopped rather than say *since Chloe disappeared.*

'I'll tell Sheila how hard today has been on you.' My mother blew her bangs out of her eyes. She looked older. I don't know if it was just that she didn't have on make-up, but her eyes looked more worn around the corners. 'I know that several people, including your father, have asked you if Chloe has been dating anyone. I find it very surprising that you never thought to mention this Dean. If you don't have a lot of studying to do, please take some time and consider that.'

'She wasn't dating Dean.'

'Whatever was going on . . . I hope that you will positively rack your brain to come up with some details. For Chloe's sake. For Dean's sake. For everyone, really.'

The truth is I didn't know what was going on with Chloe and Dean. He started as a project we worked on together. We'd buy tiny toys out of gumball machines and glue poems out of her dad's *New Yorker* magazines on to cards. We'd check the library. But after a while, after we'd left the pieces of Chloe's pictures and Dean started writing back, Chloe stopped wanting to do those things together. Things shifted ever so slightly. When we saw Dean, he lowered his hood and looked straight at Chloe. At first he blushed and looked away. Then he stopped blushing. Then he stopped looking away.

I'd ask her and Chloe would shrug. But she stopped calling him Stuttering Dean. And once in a while, I'd be waiting for her to pick up the phone for an hour or two. Or she'd get a text message and not read it out loud to me when she read it. But I didn't know that it was Dean.

We had talked about what it would be like to have boyfriends. We would go on double dates and be in each other's weddings. And in junior high, when parties went from amusement parks to spin-the-bottle, we'd pooled anything we heard or learned. What felt good. What felt gross. It's not like it was raining men in Colt River, though. The same guys who pulled up Chloe's skirt in the days of buck teeth and Dorothy dresses were the ones trying to go up her shirt now. Different reasons maybe, but they were still the same absolute voids. We went to the prom to dress up and let some dicksmack pin a flower to our dress and then danced in a circle with other girls. Just like most people in our class.

There were a few couples at school, but they were generally football players and the girls on the dance team. There was Ashley Morecraft and Rayburn Whittier but they were pretty much married. And that had more to do with the crap going on at Ashley's house and the fact that Rayburn's mom let her sleep over. Even on weeknights. They were a couple.

I had to believe that if Chloe was serious about him, she would have told me about it. Dean was just like any of the other guys who fumbled around and, yes, stuttered and stammered when they stood next to her.

Plenty of times, guys fall for Chloe and they try to use me as a net. They talk to me first, but the whole time I can feel them leaning toward Chloe. Dean wasn't just kind to me so that she'd notice. He made me laugh. If Chloe and her family had stayed in the city and I grew up in Colt River on my own, I would have become friends with Dean West.

If we were actually friends, though, independent from Chloe, Dean and I would have been talking more over the past few days. Or even just not talking and taking some comfort in sticking close to each other. There wasn't anyone I could afford to stick close to right now. I had to watch what I said. I had to be able to get over to my grandmother's house on my own. Even up in my room, lying in my bed, I tried to position myself so that I wasn't facing the Caffrey house. I didn't want to face its windows, let alone anyone else's eyes.

Dad called up to let me know dinner was on the table, but I pretended to be asleep and didn't open my door. A little while later my mother brought up a plate fixed with food, which meant I wasn't in trouble.

'I didn't mean to snap,' she said while she made this big production of arranging a place for me to eat at my desk. 'We're just looking for answers.'

'I don't have answers.' My voice against the pillow sounded like a moan. I lifted my face but didn't look at her. 'Not about Dean.'

My mom sat down on the bed. 'I remember when your dad and I first got close – well, it was this big secret. I can't even tell you why. You know – Nana and Granddad always loved him.'

I did know. My father had worked summers on my granddad's farm. My grandfather used to say in his booming voice, 'Before he was my son-in-law, he was a son to me.' It was strange to imagine my mom keeping quiet about something that would make her parents so happy.

My mom confessed, 'I made him sneak over to pick me up. Or we'd meet by the lake.' She must have seen me looking confused because she leaned back on her elbows and looked up to the ceiling. Her eyes looked a little less worn out, gazing up that way. 'It sounds silly, but everything felt so new and I was breathless and shaky all the time. In a good way. I just wanted to keep it all to myself for a while.'

That made me panic a little. At first, I didn't know what my mom was getting at, who she was comparing herself to.

She snapped herself out of remembering and sat up a little. 'Maybe that's what it was like for Chloe.'

I didn't say anything. The corners of my eyes got hot and full. They wouldn't shift toward my mom. I knew I was supposed to meet her eyes and smile. That's what she expected from this heart-to-heart. There was a square of my quilt where the edges were unraveling a little. One of the lighter shades of blue. Chloe had the same quilt, in her bedroom down at the barn. They were expensive; we ordered them out of a catalog and I remember feeling a little guilty that maybe they were a little pricey for my parents.

'Finn, I know it's hard. All of this is hard because we're all missing Chloe. But it sounds like this would have been a hard time even if Chloe was right down the hill.'

'I don't know what you mean.' I wished my mom wouldn't look at me so closely. I felt like the quilt. I felt like I was unraveling.

'How come ravel isn't a word?'

My mom exhaled so long that I thought her bangs would blow right off of her head. 'Oh, Finn. I'm just trying to help, honey.'

'Well, haven't you always wondered that? We say unravel when something's coming apart, but we don't call it raveling when we get it all knotted together.'

'I've never wondered that, no.' My mom leaned back again, though, and her lips relaxed into a smile. 'But I have wondered about pink, though.'

'What about it?'

'Well, pink is basically light red, right? Why don't we have a word for light blue then?'

My mom just shrugged again. Leaning back on her elbows, she looked more like what I'd imagined my big sister might look like. If I'd had one. 'I think Chloe's okay.' I said it without thinking. Because I got greedy and wanted the two of us to keep acting easily around each other.

But as soon as I said it, my mom tensed up. 'What makes you think that?' She hung each word up carefully, the way we handle my grandmother's glass Christmas ornaments.

'I just feel like I'd know.' It sounded lame.

'I hope that's true.' My mom stood up. She brushed her hands over her thighs and checked the plate she had put on my desk. 'All of this is cold. You should come down and microwave it.'

'I'll eat it cold.' I didn't want to leave my room. Or warm myself with food. 'I'm really tired is all.'

'Okay, then. I finally got Sheila to take one of the pills Dr. Hilsinger prescribed. So I'm not going back over until tomorrow morning. Unless . . .' My mom trailed off.

'Unless we hear something.' I finished for her. Mom didn't shut the door behind her, which pretty much never happened, and I felt weird about running over and closing it. I waited until I heard her get all the way to the bottom of the stairs and then went to the bathroom just to close my door when I came back.

I went online and checked my email. I thought about asking around to see if anyone had heard anything about Dean, but searched instead for local news headlines. I figured even our pieceofcrap newspapers would be less insane than the

Colt River High rumor factory. Nothing in the *Hunterdon County Record*, but the *New York Times* said the police had been questioning a 'person of interest'.

That was what they were calling Dean now.

TWELVE

I set my cell phone alarm to vibrate and went to bed fully clothed. I listened for my parents moving around downstairs and heard my father in full-force snore when I stepped out into the hall. Then there was the low, whistling breathing of my mother sleeping next to him. This was the way Chloe and I would creep around together when she was staying over, back when sneaking down for ice-cream sundaes was the wildest we ever got.

When I got outside, I zipped up my hoodie and wished I'd put on a jacket. Stopped to check in on the horses because that was going to be my lameass story in case Mom or Dad woke up – I'd say I went out to feed the horses, got sad, and took a walk. Never mind the fact that if they woke up and found me gone, my parents would have the FBI dispatched to our dirt road faster than you could say *copycat killer*. It was the best I could come up with, and I had to come up with something.

I half-jogged to my grandmother's house. Because there was a cop car sitting at the bottom of our road, I had to go out the back way, which meant circling back around and trekking through the pumpkin patch. I clocked in what would have been a forty-minute walk at a little under twenty minutes. And that was through a dark patch of field.

Closer into town, where the houses are more closely spaced together and we have actual sidewalks, I tried to make myself look around and take notes. I figured there would be more cop cars circling around because of Chloe's going missing, and there were. I tried to memorize where the dark spots on each street were, where Chloe and I could stop and rest and not stand smack under a street light. I tried to notice which hedges rose tall enough to shield us from the view from the street.

If I got caught now, my parents would probably lock me up in the hayloft and never let me out. I'd be like Rapunzel, but with ratty, shoulder-length hair. If I got caught later on, though, with Chloe, Chief Kane would probably lock me up in a cell next to Dean West.

I was half scared that she had found out about Dean somehow, and that when I got to the house, it would be empty. She'd be plastered all over the paper the next morning, striding purposefully into the station, turning herself in. And another part of me was afraid that she knew about Dean and was still there, eating Pop Tarts and forgetting to feed my grandmother's plants.

When I got to the bottom of the basement steps, I found her cowered in front of the high window, with the cordless phone cord in one hand, waving my grandmother's old curling iron in the other. 'F-F-F-FFFFinn.' By the time she finally got out my name, I expected her to be saying something else.

My hands were up. Palms out, the way I'd calm a spooked horse. 'Settle down there, freakshow.'

'God.' Chloe sounded like she'd actually been praying to him. 'You didn't say you were coming. I heard someone upstairs. Oh God.' She had her hand pressed to her chest and the phone rested against her shoulder. For a split second, I got scared she would dial it.

'Just put the phone down,' I said. She just stared at me. 'Chloe, what if you accidentally call someone?' When she looked at the phone and then dropped it like it was burning, I panicked harder. 'Chloe!'

'Shhhh!' She jumped to peek out the window. 'Are you crazy? Shut up!'

We stood there, staring up at the basement window, for a full five minutes. Listened for footsteps and waited for a light to blink on next door. Nothing. Nothing. Chloe slid down to the couch and breathed out. That's when the curling iron clattered to the cement floor.

'God,' I said, 'you really can't do anything quietly, can you? It's physically impossible.'

'What's going on?' Chloe spun the flashlight toward me. 'Why are you here?' And then, frantically, 'Did something happen to Cam? Is everyone all right?'

It made me want to shake her a little. No, everyone was not all right.

'Chloe, we need to end this now. You need to come home.'

'Is Cam okay?'

Kind of. No. But instead I said, 'Yes. But your mom's a zombie, your dad's a mess. School is nuts. This was nuts. Chloe, we were nuts to do this.'

'My mom's always a zombie. Let me guess – she got someone to prescribe her something to calm down?'

'What?'

'You don't know everything about how my family works, Finn.'

But I did. I mean, I pretty much lived there. And there was no way Mrs. Caffrey could buzz around town the way she did and serve on all her committees all doped up. And even if she was, she still didn't deserve to sit around waiting for police detectives to turn up her daughter's body.

But Chloe had her chin jutted out. She'd knotted up a piece of her hair by twirling it and she glared up at me. 'My family's just fine.'

'Well, Stuttering Dean isn't.' Which is not how I meant to tell her at all. I didn't even mean to call him that. I closed my eyes, and when I reopened them, Chloe was still sitting there in front of me, looking as if she'd been raised by wolves for the past few days.

'What happened to Dean?' She asked it carefully, pronouncing each word deliberately.

'Chloe, have you been talking to Dean? After you came here, could you have called or texted and just not realized—'

'No. God, Finn – I'm not stupid. What happened?'

'Okay, but even just to say goodbye or something . . .'

'What happened to Dean, Finn?'

I tried to make my voice gentler. 'I don't know if you

watched the news tonight, but—'

'They brought in a suspect.' Chloe finished up. Her choice of words had me freaked.

'They're saying *suspect* now?'

'Yeah.'

'Earlier, they said *person of interest*.'

'Right. Same thing.'

'It's not the same thing. A person of interest . . .' I tried to remember the definitions I looked up online earlier in the night. 'I don't think they can keep you in custody unless they actually name you as a suspect.' For Dean, it meant the difference between going home with his parents or hanging around the county jail until we figured out Chloe's big reveal. I tried to tell myself that she couldn't know that. But I couldn't help it. It felt like she should know that.

Chloe actually looked bored. If I hadn't mentioned Dean she would be making fun of me for being a police geek. I pulled out the big guns.

'They came and got Dean,' I told her.

'Who?'

'The cops?'

'Why?' God.

'Because they think he had something to do with this.' I gestured around the room, at the piles of wrappers and blanket cocoons shed on to the floor. Chloe looked around at the room and back at me. I wanted to strangle her.

'Chloe, they think he hurt you.'

'But he didn't.' When Chloe gets nervous or restless, she jiggles her foot. Like part of her wants to leap up and run off the nervous energy. Her voice sounded steady, but I watched her knee bob up and down in the darkness.

'Yeah, exactly. And we need to make that clear. So you need to come home early. We'll figure out how to bring you out into the open.'

Chloe rose halfway up from the sofa and then crumpled back down. 'I can't do that now. My boyfriend gets arrested and all of a sudden I'm miraculously found. They're going to figure out exactly what happened.'

It struck me that they probably wouldn't. That would require them to imagine that girls like us could think this up. Right now that seemed unfathomable to me. Even with Chloe sitting across from me like a spoiled little kid. And so I focused on the other unbelievable part of the sentence.

'You're calling Dean West your boyfriend?'

'That's what they'd call him, right?'

'But is he?'

Chloe shrugged her shoulders. It was like I'd asked her if she wanted another Pop Tart or something. 'No. It's not like that.' But she wasn't looking at me. The couch pretty much swallowed me up when I flopped down on to it. I was so tired. My legs burned from running and I felt a blister on my heel opening up. Chloe bit her lip and looked up at me. 'I could see how someone would think that, though.'

'Does *Dean* think that?' I asked.

And then I saw something in Chloe's face. When I asked about him, she stopped looking so angry for a second. She closed her eyes and when she opened them again, her face looked softer somehow. Less bitchy. 'We've just been talking a lot,' she said. 'He's really easy to talk to.' And gave a short little laugh I'd never heard before.

'Chloe,' I said, 'they have him at the station.'

'But he didn't do anything. He'll be fine.'

'They went through his locker. They found a bunch of the stuff we left him in the library.'

She gave me the *Yeah, and?* look.

When Chloe and I swam in the lake together when we were little, we used to play this game. One person would sit up on the beach and shout orders to the person under water. And it never sounded right, so you'd have to figure out that *ham stung* meant *hand stand*. That's how I felt right now. Like Chloe was under the surface and no matter what I said, she didn't seem to hear me.

'They found the picture that we took of you, the one that we cut into pieces. They're thinking Dean did that. That it means he hurt you.'

'Dean would never hurt me.' It was like she'd gotten stupider, hanging out in my grandmother's cellar. She sounded like she did when she drank too much cough syrup.

'Chloe, you're missing. So people think someone hurt you. People are scared someone killed you. And now they think Dean did it.'

But even that didn't cut through her stupor. She stood and started picking up a bunch of the wrappers, and at first I felt this wild surge of hope. I thought she was getting ready to leave. We had maybe an hour and a half, but we could figure something, a way to get her someplace where someone would find her.

She sat down on the sofa and started braiding up her hair. 'Well, he didn't hurt me. They can't prove something that didn't happen. And what's going to happen if I go home with you now? We'll go to the police?'

'We have to.' But I already sounded unsure. She'd given me a way to back out.

'Yeah – and you think Dean's going to be grateful for that? This isn't like leaving a note in a library book. He'll hate us if he finds out.'

That would be less disastrous for me. At least I'd have Chloe back.

'Chloe, how are we going to talk to people when this is all over?' I wanted her to know what it was like to be me for a second. 'We're going to be lying to people, to everyone. This is it. It's going to be like this for the rest of our lives.' My panic grew infinite, right that moment. Realizing it was really never going to be over. Even if we came clean now. We'd just be famous in a different way. And I doubted colleges would give us scholarships based on our creativity.

Chloe reached up and tugged my hand then. She pulled me down to sit on the sofa next to her. She said, 'We'll be honest with each other.' She leaned her head on my shoulder and we both looked at the gray screen of the shut-off TV. I could see the outline of our reflection there. If we turned it on, we'd probably be on one of the channels. Or at least Chloe would be.

I realized that I didn't want to be the one who found her. Before, we had planned it that way, so that people would hear about me too. And I actually felt cast in the cooler role.

People would remember Chloe as the girl who'd gotten herself snatched. I would be the smart one, the girl detective who saved her best friend's life. But now I knew I was the one who'd fade. The minute Chloe let go of the reins of her horse and turned around and crept to this house, she had sealed her new celebrity. And that wasn't going to go away. People would know who she was at college. They'd do follow-up stories. She would apply for a job some day and someone would Google her. They would think, *She's so well-adjusted. It's like it never happened. What an amazing girl.* But then, she'd have to be amazing to pull the whole thing off.

'I'd better go,' I said.

Chloe sighed, then pointed at a stack of old paperback books. Some of the covers were torn off. The ones that weren't seemed to be variations of the same picture: a lady with long hair falling back into the arms of some muscular guy. Some of the guys were dressed like Vikings. Others were pirates.

'I've read like six of your nana's crappy books.'

'That's why you're suddenly so dumb.'

'Don't say dumb. *Dumb* is a word once used to describe mute people or stutterers. The fact that we use it as a synonym for stupid reinforces the link between clear speech and intelligence.' She sounded like she'd practiced this, the way we once practiced the single lines we'd each have in our school plays. She was speaking up for Dean then, her chin jutting out proudly. At the very least, they were fooling around.

If I outlined the ways that working to eradicate the word

dumb from the English language would fall short of making up for the fact that her apparent boyfriend had spent the night in county lock-up on our account, I'd be here until the sun rose. And I had to get home well before that. I had to slink through the lawns and hope none of my grandmother's neighbors were sitting sleepless in their living rooms. Because there's nothing nosier than an old lady without cable TV. Most of my grandmother's friends would recognize me. And the ones who wouldn't were batty enough to call the police.

'Can you find a way to tell me that he's okay?' Chloe asked as I was hugging her goodbye. I nodded. I didn't ask if I should tell her if he wasn't.

'Yeah.' I untangled myself from her. 'I'll try to get back here. We have to be really, really careful, though. Remember—'

'No lights on upstairs and only flush the toilet at night,' Chloe finished for me.

I yanked the strings of my sweatshirt so that the hood tightened around my head. I ducked out the door and walked down the street as quickly as I could without outright running. Then I kept my head down and my hands in my pocket so that they didn't pick up any light. When I turned off my grandmother's street, I jogged a little. When I hit the woods, I ran. And when I got to the ravine that signaled the edge of our property, I took a running leap over it and then pretty much hauled ass. Running through the woods at night is pretty much an exercise in faith. It's spooky to hear animals scattering in front of you and to feel saplings bending in front of your steps. It's not exactly environmentally friendly, and at one point I got all panicky that maybe I'd stepped on a sleeping bunny or something. Maybe I'd fall into a hole, but those things were less scary than imagining what my dad would do to me if I showed up and he was already awake.

The truth is I liked the feeling of the branches whipping across my face. And I already felt like I'd fallen into a hole – only I hadn't hit the bottom yet. I didn't even know where the bottom was.

I just kept falling.

THIRTEEN

Because I'm not a moron, I didn't go right inside and leap into my bed and hide under the covers, the way Chloe and I used to when we thought we'd been caught going to the kitchen for a snack after lights out.

I sat on our back steps. I had to catch my breath anyway, and the sky was lightening a little. Everything was damp and a little cold and the air smelled like wet dog. I wanted to bury my face in it.

I heard exactly when Dad scuffed down the steps. He did it kind of fast, and that made me wonder if he'd checked my room when he woke up. He must have, because I heard him call out my name while he was still on the steps. I wondered if he'd always checked on me first or if this was new. It would make sense if it had been a new thing, if parents around town were nervous. Maybe Chloe and I were responsible for that – people checking on their sleeping kids again. Feeling grateful to see them drooling on to their pillows and twisted in their sheets. That made me feel a little, tiny bit better.

But then I wondered if Dean was sleeping in his bed.

What his mother was thinking. And my stomach curdled a little.

'Finn. What the hell?'

'Couldn't sleep.'

'For how long?'

'Just a little bit. I came down to watch the sun come up.'

'We've got a big day – you should have slept.' What wasn't a big day anymore? Seriously.

He must have interpreted my grunting for interest.

'Lila Ann Price is coming out.' My stomach turned cartwheels. Lila Ann Price was this lady on TV. Her daughter disappeared at an amusement park a long time ago, before I was born. She had a show that featured a different missing kid each week. She had a regular show for Margaret Cook, an update show, and then when she came home, Margaret Cook went on and did an interview. If Lila Ann Price was coming out to Colt River, then we'd hit the big time.

'Am I going to school?' I asked, the news still unspooling in my head.

'They cancelled school.'

'What?'

Dad looked at me funny. 'You didn't hear the phone ring?'

Our town has a phone chain for snow delays or school cancellation. You get one phone call and you make one phone call and eventually the whole town gets the message. And because we're basically a speck on a map, that whole process takes about an hour. It takes sixty minutes for the whole town to hear about a snow day. How fast would it take the whole town to know if Chloe and I got caught?

'Nope.' I tried to say it casually and looked out on to the field like I was breathing like a normal person.

'Well, you must have been sleeping pretty heavily at some point.'

'Yep.' I sounded like he did, when he was trying to avoid fighting with my mom.

'But then you couldn't sleep?'

I was getting good at looking up at people and deliberately meeting their eyes. My new talent was making people believe they were finally, finally getting the truth from me.

'I had a nightmare.' I confessed it. Quietly and not at all defensively. 'It woke me up.'

'Oh.' Dad sipped his coffee. It fogged up into his face, in the cold air. 'You okay?'

'Yeah. I'm okay.' I said it like you'd say it if you weren't at all okay. Which was pretty much how I was anyway.

'Well, you might want to try to nap before Lila Price comes over.'

'Is that why they cancelled school?'

'They said it was a plumbing thing.'

'Really?'

'Yup.'

'Is there a plumbing thing?' I asked. My father shook his head, took a sip, stretched one of his legs so that it reached the metal railing. 'So why would they say that?'

'I think they worried that otherwise, people would think that something happened about Chloe.'

'Like what?' And then I got it. And freaked a little because probably that's where my mind should have leaped – and it might have, if I hadn't just left Chloe curled up on a sofa reading romance novels. 'Did they find . . .' I let my voice trail off, as if I couldn't bear to pronounce the words. But I sounded all soap-opera actressy. If the sun had been fully up, my father would have seen the phoniness shining on my face.

'No. No, nothing. But with Columbus Day on Monday, it just gives you guys a four-day weekend. And today was going to be mayhem anyway, what with this TV show and the West boy in custody—'

'He's still in custody?'

'I don't know. I hope so, for his sake. Folks are starting to get mean about this. A lot of men came out here to look for Chloe, Finn. A lot of men with daughters of their own.'

'Dean came,' I reminded him. But he just shrugged and dragged another gulp of the coffee.

'No one's forgotten that. But in this day and age . . . that doesn't mean a whole lot.'

'That doesn't make any sense.'

'There are sick people in the world, Finn. There are people who like to cause other people pain and then sit around and watch. They get . . .' I could see my dad getting uncomfortable, '. . . some kind of satisfaction from that. That's evil. We're all God's children, but that's just evil working inside a person.'

My dad wasn't trying to describe me. I kept trying to remind myself that while tears burned in my eyes. It was fine, anyway. He thought I was crying for Chloe.

We didn't hug very often, my dad and me. Sometimes we kind of chucked each other on the shoulders. He did this thing where he came up behind and wrapped one of his arms around my neck. But that morning, when he saw me start crying, he gathered me up in his arms and I cried until I got tears and snot all over his wooly flannel shirt. He petted my head near my ponytail and I cried the way you cry when you can't breathe and you get hiccups and your face stays all hot.

'I'm sorry, kiddo.' That's what my dad kept saying. Over and over.

So when I finally pulled back and rubbed my face, I asked him, 'Why are you sorry?'

'I'm sorry that the world isn't as good as I'd like to be for you.'

That is what my father said to me. Whatever seed of evil was in me began to feel like it had taken root. I was growing a tree. I don't know why I kept encouraging it. Part of me was imagining telling him, what it would feel like to explain to my dad what Chloe and I had done, that she was okay, that I had tried to somehow put the brakes on, but that this whole thing had spun out of control. I could cry and explain to him how sorry I was and beg him to help me fix it. He'd order me right into the pick-up and in minutes we'd be in my grandmother's driveway. Dad would come with me to the Caffreys' house, to the police station. He'd stand behind me with his arms folded in front of him grimly, like the time he drove me over to Cody Hameier's house and stood there while I apologized to their whole family for filling their mailbox with old eggs.

I decided it would probably feel like having a lung transplant or heart surgery. I mean afterwards – it would feel like

I could finally breathe. Someone else would take charge and they'd freak out and yell and punish, but then it would be over. This was a lot more than a dozen rotten eggs and a can of shaving cream, though. I thought about how there were maybe four or five things that would actually alter the way my parents view me as a person. And how this was one of those things.

'Do you really think something's happened to her?' I asked him like I wanted him to say no.

My father sighed and looked down into the grounds of his coffee cup. He said very carefully, 'I think we have to start preparing ourselves for that possibility.'

'But she could have run away . . .' Maybe that was going to have to be our way out after all – Chloe buckled under the pressure. She took her leftover birthday money and bought a bus ticket and this whole time she'd been riding in the back of a dingy Greyhound and buying snacks out of rest-stop vending machines, completely oblivious.

Dad shook his head. It looked like it hurt him to move it back and forth. 'It's just too long, Finn. And she would have seen something on the news and called home or sent an email. After the first press conference . . .'

The first press conference was bad. From then on, Mr. Caffrey was the only one who spoke to reporters. Most times, Chloe's mom didn't even appear. And when the reporters asked, 'How is Mrs. Caffrey holding up?', they sounded like they actually cared.

'Yeah, but she could be all the way across the country. Or someplace without a TV. Maybe she just doesn't know how bad it is. It can't be on the news all the way in California.'

Dad shot me a look and I splayed out my hands and quickly reassured him, 'No – we never, ever talked about her going to California.'

'Finn, it's pretty much a national news story.'

'Are you sure?' When my dad hesitated, I felt a surge of hope glow under my ribs like a live wire. 'See? She could be somewhere where no one's heard of Colt River. I mean, Jesus, people in Bergen County haven't heard of Colt River. Maybe she just doesn't know we're looking for her.' I wanted to sprint right back to Chloe. This was our way out. We could still work out something impressive – an older guy, someone controlling . . . he threatened her family and she was too scared not to go. I tried to keep the excitement out of my voice, but realized that Dad just thought it was some kind of poignant hope. That was fine. It was safe for him to think that.

Dad looked at me kindly. It was the aren't-you-such-a-sweet-but-vaguely-pitiful-girl look. I'd seen it before on him. Once at dinner, Chloe announced that she was going to go into neurology so that she could treat Cam. Dad's face had on the same look that creased across his face now. 'Well, then, I guess we'll have a better idea after tonight.' I looked at him, questioning. 'Maybe the show is actually a good thing,' he explained, easing himself off the step. 'Lila Ann Price is a nationally syndicated show, so chances are Chloe would have to come across it.' He looked off in the direction of the woods I'd just crawled through. 'Listen, Finn, I'll check on the animals. I want you to go upstairs and try for a little more sleep.'

'But shouldn't I get ready?' I didn't want to ask out loud if I'd be interviewed, but already I was mentally flipping through the hangers in my closet, trying to pick out the perfect tragic best friend ensemble. 'I mean – is there anything I should help with?'

'I'll make sure you don't sleep too late. But try to rest a little. And don't wake your mother when you go back upstairs. It would worry her to know you were moving around down here and she hadn't heard you.'

I crept upstairs, saying a little prayer of thanks to whatever patron saint of evil kids had helped me sneak around undetected. I skipped the third and fifth steps because they always groaned when you walked on them. I eased the doorknob to the left and stopped myself from slamming it closed.

So careful. So cautious. I could keep everything quiet. Even the doubts in my head only spoke in whispers then.

FOURTEEN

It felt like I only blinked, but when I opened my eyes, the sun had risen to the top corner of my window and a band of light crossed the wooden slats of my floor. I hadn't even untied my shoes and my feet tingled. I heard kitchen noises – pans clanging, the tap running, Mom talking.

Since Chloe left, most of my mornings had gone this way: I'd wake up, feeling a little strange and afraid, but at first I wouldn't remember why. And then all the jagged pieces would fit together – where Chloe was. What we had done. Each morning the pieces fitted together more quickly. I wondered what it would be like when that moment of not knowing didn't happen, when I woke already remembering how awful we were.

When I got down to the kitchen, I found Mom talking to Mrs. Caffrey – it was really like Chloe's mom was just sitting there and my mom had embarked on a very energetic monologue. Mrs. Caffrey sat hunched over her cup of coffee like she was trying to get warm. She didn't even make the noises people make when they're listening to someone else talking too much.

She looked skinny and yellow. She looked up at me like she didn't know who I was. When I stopped short in the doorway and managed to get out, 'Hey, Mrs. Caffrey. How are you?', she just nodded.

My mom was in desperate housewife mode. She was making bread and she kept throwing down the dough so that clouds of flour would float up into the air in front of her face. The dough squirmed and showed more expression than Mrs. Caffrey.

'Where's Cam?' I tried next, because that was a surefire hit. But Chloe's mom deflected it with a shrug.

'Sheila?' Mom asked sharply. And Mrs. Caffrey just shifted her eyes out the window.

'What?'

'Where's Cam?' Cam doesn't usually have a whole lot of unsupervised time. It's not like he's retarded. There's actually a lot of stuff he's much smarter about than most people, but day-to-day stuff is a little off his radar. If he could, he'd wear the same clothes every day. And because his mom buys him lots of the same shirts and jeans, he pretty much does. But Cam would just wear the same actual clothes. And he would have trouble figuring out how to wash them. Cam doesn't handle talking on the phone so well or getting himself food or anything. He wouldn't necessarily know to look to the stove if the smoke detector went off. Stuff like that.

'Stables.' Mrs. Caffrey issued the one word out. My mom's hand reached for the kitchen window's curtains. I could see her craning to see our horse stalls out back.

'Sheila, he's with the horses?' My mom's voice kept rising, but Mrs. Caffrey didn't really even blink. I thought about Chloe's smacktalk about her mom popping pills and wondered just a little. 'Sheila?'

Mrs. Caffrey shook her head like that would make the fog clear around her. 'No, not those stables – Brian took him to the ones at the racetrack.'

'Oh.' My mom's voice was as bright as a new quarter. 'Well, that's great. Right, Finn? Cam loves seeing horses, doesn't he? And at the racetrack – that's a great idea for a tough day.'

'Tough day?' Mrs. Caffrey said it like maybe my mother had gone crazy.

'Well – with Lila Price coming.' Mom piled the bread dough in a pan and slid it into the oven. 'That could be a circus, you know.' I could see her bite her lip, figuring out whether or not to press forward. 'How's Cam going to do with that, you think?'

'Cam?' It was like Mrs. Caffrey hadn't heard of him. I never knew my mom could be so patient. All of a sudden, Chloe and I had crossed over to the dark side and somehow my mom achieved sainthood. She was like Our Lady of Child Abductions or something.

No, that was Lila Price's title, and she was on her way to our farm with her pancake make-up and her camera crew. Like one of the local reporters, but jacked up on steroids. And I understood then what my mother was so worried about. How would Cam, with his steadfast systems and strict schedules, handle the Lila Price invasion? I mean, we couldn't even get Mrs. Caffrey to snap out of it. She was the Cam wrangler, the one person who came close to translating the world for him.

That wasn't the first time I thought about Cam, and what our brilliant plan was costing him. But it was the first time I thought of how shut down their mom was and how many steps that could set him back. His one link to the rest of us had snapped.

'Cam's not coming home,' Mrs. Caffrey said. My mother's eyes flew up. 'Today,' Mrs. Caffrey continued. 'Brian's dropping him at the tutor's on the way home from the racetrack. He's going to stay there for the night.'

'Really?' My mom asked it, but it's what I was thinking too. Cam was nineteen, but as far as I knew, he had never gone on a sleepover. Part of the reason our family always brought Chloe with us on vacation was that the Caffreys couldn't really take one. Seven years they'd lived next door to us, and I don't think Cam had ever slept anywhere else.

'Brian doesn't want to expose him—'

'Of course, it will be a madhouse—'

'To the scrutiny—'

'People can be cruel, and—'

'And if it's a ransom thing, the police think Cam would be vulnerable.'

'Oh.' My mom hadn't thought of that. 'That makes sense.'

'Does it?'

'Yeah. Doesn't it?'

'Cam raises bloody hell if someone accidentally touches his toothbrush. Do you think he'd let some stranger haul him into a van?' Mrs. Caffrey said it almost wryly. 'It's Chloe who's vulnerable that way.' She nodded to herself. 'Chloe is . . . available to people. Right, Finn? Am I right?'

And yeah, she was. Chloe smiled at everyone. Welcomed anyone. If I didn't know that I was her best friend, I'd think that everyone was her best friend.

It took me a second to realize that Mrs. Caffrey was talking again. 'I always felt that she was safe when she was with you, Finn. Brian said that was nonsense, that Chloe was still a city kid at heart and you grew up out here, but I always believed you were the more sensible one.'

'Finn and Chloe are both sensible, responsible girls.' My mother said it definitively, like she meant to shut down the conversation right then and there.

'I just never worried about Chloe when she was with Finn.' We were all quiet for a moment, the kitchen filling with the warm smell of my mom's baking bread. 'Why wasn't she with you, Finn?'

Mrs. Caffrey asked it in a small voice, so small that at first I wasn't sure if she meant for me to answer. But no one said anything. My mom coughed, and I thought she meant it as a signal.

I said, 'I was helping my dad.'

'Yeah, Finn.' Mrs. Caffrey rolled her eyes. 'You're a *great* kid.' It felt like she hit me.

I saw my mom's shoulders square back even before I heard her say, 'Now hold on there, Sheila.'

'No, it's okay,' I said. Something really sick was happening to me because I just wanted to sink into the chair beside her and let her have at me. I just wanted to hear everything she had to say.

'Go to your room, Finn.'

'No, it's okay—'

'Upstairs.' I was on the fourth step when I heard Mrs. Caffrey start crying.

'Finn!' she shouted after me. 'I'm so sorry.' And more softly, 'I'm so sorry. I don't know what came over me.' Then the sounds of weeping and my mother hushing her.

I got in the shower and ended up sitting on the tub's floor, pounded by the water. When I got out, I checked my cell phone, but there were just a stack of texts from kids wanting to know about Lila Price. My hair still fizzed with shampoo so I rinsed it in the sink. And then I set out to pick the perfect outfit for my television debut.

I settled on jeans and a deep green T-shirt that I liked to think brought out the color in my eyes. I sat at my desk with a pocket mirror and some eyeliner and tried to etch straight lines beneath my lids. I looked pretty decent. Sad, but in a tragically good-looking way. I looked better without Chloe next to me.

Figured they'd probably have plenty of pictures of her, though. Lila Price did this thing – Chloe and I noticed it during the second special about Margaret Cook. She always found a way to mention her own missing daughter. This was probably cruel to notice – I mean, the woman spent her whole life helping families going through the same personal nightmare that she'd never woken up from. I guess it made sense that the cases reminded her of her own kid. It just seemed a little gross when she did it, a little fake. But I was about to cry on national TV about my missing best friend, and Chloe was probably trying to figure out how to tape it on my grandma's ancient VCR. So I wasn't really in any position to judge.

FIFTEEN

When it was time, I saw the parade of vans and SUVs driving up to the farm. It looked like a funeral procession, except none of the cars had their headlights on. A bunch of the black SUVs turned into our drive and my knees got shaky. My legs felt watery, so I let myself fall back on to my bed. I was a puddle soaking into the sheets.

It seemed weird to run bounding down the stairs, so I waited until my mom summoned me. I cried a little when the vehicles pulled up, leaving my face all flushed and streaked, but I didn't dare turn on a tap to wash. I didn't want to miss my mom calling my name from the downstairs landing.

When she did, I checked my hair and make-up. The braid was a little loose, but I liked how a few stray strands wisped around my face. In any case, I didn't look like a monster.

No one did. My mom had even worked some kind of miracle on Mrs. Caffrey. For the first time in the past few days, Chloe's mom didn't look like you might have to restart her heart with a defibrillator. She had a shirt on that seemed ironed and even a dab of lipstick or something. She still wasn't herself – but she looked okay.

I expected Lila Price to knock on our door. But instead a younger guy did the honors, wearing a headset and a tailored suit that Ace the guidance counselor would have coveted.

'Andy Cogan, Producer.' He said it like his name was the greeting itself and stuck his hand toward each of us. With the other arm, he was already motioning the camera crew inside the house and a good, half dozen guys in coveralls started stapling cable to the ground and opening and closing the curtains in the living room.

'We'd like to take a couple of shots of Chloe's bedroom.' He had his hand on the banister, one foot on the stairs.

'Well . . . what?' Mrs. Caffrey finally turned and asked my mother. She looked like I felt. My mom was the only one who wasn't absolutely flabbergasted. This was a new trend in the world.

Mom stepped in to announce, 'I'm sorry – this isn't the Caffrey residence.'

A short woman with short hair and a short skirt stopped . . . well . . . short, and swung her head to Andy Cogan, Producer. He asked her and not my mom, 'This isn't One-oh-nine Cedar Run Lane?'

'It is, it is,' the short woman yapped, like she was worried he'd take away her food. She shuffled the papers on her clipboard. Andy warded her off with one hand.

'I need an address check,' he big-dog barked into the headset. 'I need an address check on the Caffrey house.'

'I'm Sheila Caffrey.' Chloe's mom stepped forward. She didn't look ready to run a Parents' Association meeting, but she said it like she knew the power it would command. The guys unwinding cable stopped unspooling. The short girl concentrated fiercely on her clipboard and Andy Cogan, Producer swung to look at her. For a moment, the only sound in the room was the headset's static crackle.

Andy Cogan, Producer recovered first. 'Mrs. Caffrey,' he said with reverence. 'I'm so sorry. We got a little carried away here. We're just all so pumped to play a part in helping bring your daughter home.' I wondered how many times he had to trot that line out. His voice stayed subdued. 'I'm Andrew – I'll be producing this segment of *The L. A. Price Show*. Thank you for welcoming us into your home.'

'This isn't my home. Ours is the barn out front.'

'You live in a barn?' The short girl couldn't launder the sneer out of her voice. Andy shot her a look that said she was going to be someone's assistant for the rest of her life.

'It's a renovated barn.' Mrs. Caffrey sounded apologetic.

'They used to be in a trailer,' I said.

'Finn!' Mom gasped, but Mrs. Caffrey got it and her face creased up into a slight smile.

'I'm just saying. That might have made filming hard.' No one responded to me, but Andy Cogan, Producer gestured to the assistant. She fussed with her clipboard.

'You must be Finley,' she said.

'Finn.'

'Chloe's best friend?' I just shrugged. 'I'm sure this is very hard for you.' She didn't go on to say, And that's why you're being a bitter brat. But she didn't have to. We all heard it anyway.

Mrs. Caffrey stepped in. 'The Jacobses are our closest friends and they've pretty much taken me in these last few days.' She patted my mom's hand as it squeezed her shoulder. 'The girls have grown up together.' Her voice faltered a little at that last part but she kept going. 'Chloe certainly spends a great deal of time here, but why don't I show you our home?'

The crew started spooling up all the cords and folding up all the kinds of tripods.

'Sheila, you okay?' Mom asked while she pulled our jackets from their hooks in the hall closet.

Mrs. Caffrey flashed another wry, brave smile and Andy Cogan, Producer practically licked his lips. Sheila Caffrey had some serious star power. I knew she was about to make Chloe very proud.

By the time all the cameras and sound equipment had been set up in the right house, Mr. Caffrey came bounding through the back porch. 'Sheila!' he bellowed, and for a second, I worried that someone had forgotten to tell him about the film crew.

'Brian,' she said. 'Thank God. How did it go in town?'

'Tough.' He shook his head. 'Really tough, I'm not so sure that—'

'My husband is devoted to his business.' The shrillness had started edging back into Mrs. Caffrey's voice.

'What?'

'Cam's at boarding school,' my mom told him. She sounded like she was trying to work it out in her own brain first.

'What?' Good to know that the old Caffrey lines of

communication were positively crackling.

'Cam's at boarding school.' My mom repeated it again loudly, but in the same flabbergasted tone. It wasn't enough to lead anyone to the path of clarity.

'Mrs. Caffrey thought that would be better,' I stepped in, thinking it would help.

'Better than what?'

So that was a no-go on the me-being-helpful plan. I looked to my mom to save me. She opened and closed her mouth. Twice.

'Better than discussing his autism? Really? Now we're stashing away our son?'

Mrs. Caffrey's neck snapped up and she crossed the living room to us. She glared at my mom, as if the whole thing was my mom's fault. 'How is Cam?' she asked him carefully.

'Autistic.'

'Brian, we've talked about this.'

'We talked about how the equipment and all these people would upset him.'

Mrs. Caffrey's voice dropped to a hiss. 'This isn't the time for this.'

'No, apparently it's the time to claim Cam's off at boarding school.'

Mrs. Caffrey's voice set into a hardness that at least I was afraid of. She pronounced each word like she was etching it into stainless steel. 'It's not the time to talk about Cam. We need to keep the focus on Chloe.'

'This reeks of shame, Sheila. People know about Cam. In town – his teachers – what will people at the Princeton

Center think?'

'This is our daughter's life, Brian. I don't care what people will think of us.' And then Chloe's mom tucked a loose strand of hair behind her ear and put on a bravely bright smile. 'Can I get you anything?' she asked. 'Does Lila Ann need anything?'

Andy Cogan, Producer let out an appreciative chuckle. 'No, Ma'am. Ms. Price has a battalion tending to her needs right now.'

'This must be very difficult. She must relive her own experience every time.' Mrs. Caffrey shuddered a little and brushed her hands across her lap. 'Well, the least I can do is set out a pitcher of iced tea.'

'Let me help you in the kitchen.' Mom rushed off to follow her. It was just me and Mr. Caffrey then, and a whole lot of guys with cables and cameras. And when Lila Ann Price did arrive, she just knocked on the door, like anyone else would have. Like good old Andy Cogan, Producer had an hour or two before. By the time she actually knocked, the ice cubes in the pitcher of iced tea had melted to tiny discs and the Caffreys had been sitting like guests in their own living room with my mother and me hovering in the background.

'Mr. and Mrs. Caffrey.' Her voice oozed concern and her eyes already looked a little misty. 'Thank you so much for making room for us. I know how the house feels smaller with all the police and folks in and out. And I know it feels emptier, too.'

She's good, I thought. *Lila Ann Price is very good.* I remember thinking to myself, *I'm going to have to be careful around her*. She ushered Mr. and Mrs. Caffrey back to the sofa and informed my mother and me that she'd like us to join them in twenty minutes. So we stepped back into the dining room and served as the live studio audience. Mrs. Caffrey had assembled an army of framed pictures of Chloe and they stood on alert on the coffee table.

Lila Ann Price started in immediately. 'The disappearance of Chloe has captivated the nation. What would you like to say to your daughter or the individuals holding her?' And Mrs. Caffrey crumpled on cue, bent her head into the crook of Mr. Caffrey's neck, and wept.

He spoke first. 'We've said over and over again that we believe that Chloe will come home safe. Chloe is a kind, intelligent, and generous girl, and we believe that if someone knows where she is, he or she will show the same kindness, intelligence, and generosity in helping her to return home, to her family, where Chloe belongs. We love Chloe very much and we're only interested in her safety.' It sounded a little canned and rehearsed, and maybe because it did, Lila Ann Price jolted Mrs. Caffrey again for the sake of few more tears.

'What were the last words you spoke to your daughter?'

'Oh God . . . I'd like to think I told her I loved her – that's what you mean to say, right? I mean you don't ever think . . . I would never have expected. I'm sure I told her I loved her, but the girls . . . they keep all those animals and I probably just reminded her about chores or her responsibilities or . . .' Mrs. Caffrey choked on tears and then she said defiantly, 'I must have told her I loved her.'

Mr. Caffrey stepped in again with the rehearsed lines:

'We'd like to say now that Chloe, if you're listening . . . wherever you've been or whatever you've done, it doesn't matter. We're not angry. Please just come home, and if there's something we need to talk through, we will work it out together as a family.' He looked so uncomfortable, pleading into the camera. Chloe's dad with his artfully disheveled hair and his carefully pleated tweed trousers – she had made him beg.

Lila Ann pounced. 'Do you have reason to believe that your daughter has run away on her own accord? Was Chloe experiencing difficulties?'

'She's a teenage girl,' Mr. Caffrey offered as explanation. You could tell he was a little offended. And my own mom reached out and rubbed circles across my back.

I swear to God it was calculated when Lila Ann reached up to clutch the locket dangling from her own neck. She murmured, 'I wouldn't know,' and looked up to search Mrs. Caffrey's face with brimming eyes.

'I'm so sorry.' Bingo. Mrs. Caffrey grabbed Lila Ann Price's hands and held them with her own. 'Brian didn't mean to . . .'

'Of course not. And I didn't mean . . . it's just not . . .' and here she slipped in a rueful chuckle. 'I'm sure the teenage years are a trying time. But in all of these photographs . . .' You could see the cameraman's hand reach toward a dial to zoom in. 'Your Chloe just strikes me as such a happy and confident young woman.'

Out of the corner of my eye, I saw my mom watching me carefully. It's not like I was going to dart out on to the set and object. Chloe *was* happy. Until the whole Margaret Cook thing, I would have said that Chloe saw her own life as perfect. Except for maybe Cam.

'She is a very happy girl.' Mrs. Caffrey nodded. 'Especially when surrounded by all of us who love her.' And I wondered then. Mrs. Caffrey didn't miss as much as I thought. Because that's exactly what I would have said: As long as she's encircled by people, Chloe's fine. And really who wouldn't be? Chloe travels in a sea of adoration. But when she was on her own, when there wasn't anything planned on a Saturday except for cleaning stalls or working through the Blockbuster list, she was different. Lately, I'd seen her looking out on the stretch of land around our houses almost hatefully.

Mrs. Caffrey continued to prove she might actually be familiar with the individual who was her daughter. 'I don't know any teenage girl who's exactly confident.' And she deflected the inevitable tug on the locket when she said, 'I remember how it was – do you? Chloe puts on a good show of it, but I imagine she has the same self-doubts any of us did. She can be very hard on herself.'

'That's a lot of pressure – could Chloe have made a poor decision because of all of it?' Lila Ann fixed her face into a look of sympathetic wisdom.

'No.' That was Mr. Caffrey. Abruptly. He might as well have finished by declaring, Case closed.

Now Mrs. Caffrey reached over to squeeze his hand. Chloe's dad continued, 'That's impossible to imagine. Chloe is devoted to our family. She's very close to her brother.'

'Will we have a chance to meet Cameron?'

'It's important to us that he focuses on his schoolwork.'

And aside from the swift grimace across Mr. Caffrey's face, no one skipped a beat. *Well-played, Mrs. Caffrey.*

'Do the police have any leads?'

At first, when Mr. Caffrey said yes, it felt like I'd swallowed a jagged rock.

But I could tell by his carefully composed expression that he wasn't talking about Dean West – it was just one of the answers they'd prepared beforehand. He said it with dead eyes.

Lila Ann Price cocked her head slightly, and then let it slide. 'Well, we won't ask you what those leads are, Mr. Caffrey – I'd never want to interfere with a police investigation. Let me take this opportunity, however, to offer our assistance. If any of our viewers at home have any information about Chloe's whereabouts, please call *The L. A. Price Show*'s toll-free hotline. Dial 1-800-LAP-INFO. Mr. and Mrs. Caffrey, as a showing of our support, *The L. A. Price Show* would like to offer a one hundred thousand dollar reward for any information leading to the return of your daughter.'

Mrs. Caffrey's hands flew to her face. 'Thank you so much. Thank you, Ms. Price. We appreciate . . .'

And then because her mom was crying so hard, Chloe's dad finished, 'Our whole family appreciates your help.'

'Cut.' A guy in a similar suit as Andy Cogan, Producer barked, and Mr. Caffrey looked startled.

'That's it?' I cringed when the question came out of my mouth – I sounded desperate for camera time, but the Caffreys looked confused too. A woman swooped in with a make-up brush and Lila Ann Price tipped her face up as she spoke. 'Oh no – I'm afraid we've just started. Is everyone okay with that? We'd like to see Chloe's bedroom, maybe the family around the dinner table. We'd really love to walk out to the stables if that would be all right. Andy, I thought you covered this?'

'I did, but there's a lot to remember, right, Finley?' He sounded like a camp counselor. 'We like to film the closing session first on *The L. A. Price Show*.'

'Why?'

'Finn – we don't need to question how these people do their job,' Mom interrupted.

'No, it's okay.' Chloe's mom spoke up. The make-up lady was back with a new brush, but this time she was going to town on Mrs. Caffrey. 'Finn, honey, they filmed his part first so that I would cry.' The make-up brush stilled in the air. 'Well, I'm right, aren't I?'

'Sheila—' Mr. Caffrey said her name like a warning.

'No, it's okay. It's Hollywood, right? You know we're out in the sticks, and here I am a housewife living in a barn, but I'm not stupid, you know. I went to Vassar, for christsakes. I know how media works.'

'Sheila.' The warning was lower now, a hissing whisper.

'What is the problem? What? Because Amy didn't go to college?' I heard my mom's sharp intake of breath behind me. All of a sudden it hit me that Mrs. Caffrey might have taken a few too many pills this morning.

'Amy – I'm so sorry,' Mr. Caffrey apologized to my mom. 'I don't know what's come over—'

'It's fine, Brian,' Mom said. 'Of course it's fine. No one's themselves right now.'

Lila Ann Price walked over. 'Mrs. Caffrey, is everything okay? I thought that segment went very smoothly.' Her voice dripped with honey.

'Of course you did – I cried right on cue for you.'

'Sheila—'

'What, I can't say that out loud? No one has the decency to admit they're manipulating us? Did I tell my daughter I loved her the last time I saw her? Did you? Come on, I played my part – we were all professionals. I am now a professional bad mother.'

It was amazing to see Lila Ann Price just check out. She sat back, popped a stick of gum in her mouth, and gazed at Mrs. Caffrey like she was a chihuaha who'd crapped on the carpet. Apparently, it was Andy Cogan, Producer, who was on damage control.

'No one believes that, Mrs. Caffrey,' he said. 'Really. Chloe had an idyllic life. That's part of what makes your daughter's story so compelling.'

'Has a life.' Mr. Caffrey coughed apologetically. 'Chloe *has* an idyllic life here in Colt River.'

'Of course. Absolutely.' Andy Cogan looked from the Caffreys to Lila Ann. Mrs. Caffrey glared at Lila Ann, and Lila Ann glared at the sweating pitcher of iced tea.

'Well, what else do we need to do here?' Mrs. Caffrey went on. 'Just tell us what part of that idyllic life you want to showcase.' I wanted to tell her to shut up. It was like she was daring them to leave.

Andy Cogan, Producer clapped his hands together. 'The horses? We'd love to get a few shots of Chloe's horse.'

Mr. Caffrey pressed his lips together. 'Sure thing.'

Andy looked as shocked as I was. 'Great. Should we go out?'

'Do you need me for this?' Mrs. Caffrey sounded bored. I wanted to tell my mom to go get her enough pills to knock her out for an hour.

'Do you normally work beside Chloe caring for the horses?' Lila Ann Price asked.

And Mrs. Caffrey stood up and snatched the iced tea off the table. 'No, I just take care of the rest of the family.'

'Well, then. We should be fine.' The sugar was back in Lila Ann Price's voice, but it sounded a little bit like artificial sweetener. My mom turned to me and zipped up my jacket.

'Sheila and I are going to stay back and regroup. You okay?' I felt the eyes of all the adults in the room on me and shrugged her hands away from straightening my collar.

'I'm fine.' It sounded like a whine. The camera guy looked up as he unwound more cord. Andy Cogan walked backwards through the kitchen like he had grown up there too. I realized he was a pretty young guy. A little older than college maybe. He stopped by the back door.

'Through here, Mr. Caffrey?'

'Right out back.' We all stomped through the mudroom and out the back door. It wasn't the first time that I'd stepped out of the Caffreys' porch and looked past the stables to our house. I thought about how it might look to a stranger. We had a nice house. It looked cared for. It had to, now that houses were my dad's business. The Caffreys' place dwarfed it, though. Our house looked old and I know that was supposed to be charming, but it didn't look old in the *Better Homes & Gardens* magazine way. I knew that Andy Cogan, Producer was looking at me and seeing the poor friend. Part of me wanted to hand him my grandmother's address and demand that he write me a cheque for the hundred grand reward right there.

'Can you lead Chloe's horse on to the grass for us? The horse's name is Caraway, am I right?' Andy Cogan, Producer was clearly showing off his research. As Mr. Caffrey coaxed the gelding out of the stall, he turned to me. 'Maybe you can show us what the horse looks like when you guys get ready to ride?'

But Chloe's dad wasn't having it. 'No saddle.' Andy nodded quickly in the way that said, *It was worth a try.* 'If it's okay, I'm just going to set up Lila Ann for this shot.' He reached out to me and ruffled my hair. Awkwardly. 'Besides, I know she'll want to meet Caraway.'

Lila Ann Price looked like she was interested in no such thing. But she'd clearly given herself a pep talk back in the frosty living room. Maybe she figured that she shouldn't alienate every member of the Caffrey family. She cooed at Mr. Caffrey.

'Brian – it's Brian, right? What a gorgeous animal! Brian, I'm going to ask you to lead the horse right behind me. I'll stay on this side of the fence so I don't alarm the animal.'

'Oh no . . .' Mr. Caffrey started to explain that the horse couldn't care less, but Lila Ann Price wasn't having it.

'No, please, we really don't mean to disrupt your lives. We're really just trying to help bring Chloe home.'

'Yes, of course.' Mr. Caffrey's eyes brimmed with apologies.

'What a wonderful provider you are. A horse right in her backyard – that's every little girl's dream.' And then she asked, 'Is that what it was like, Finn?'

'Once Chloe moved here.' I surprised myself with the truth a little bit. 'We took care of all the animals together.'

Lila Ann ducked her head toward me. 'You're being so strong for Chloe and her family. She's lucky to have you.'

'Thanks.' I knew she was working me, but I still blushed.

'Let's walk him out slowly.' Lila Ann Price shook out her hair a little and leaned back on the fence.

One of the camera guys raised a hand over his head and Lila Ann started the same riff we'd seen every local reporter do about the horse.

'I'm standing here on the Caffrey family farm . . .' It's not like I could interrupt a Lila Ann Price broadcast to point out that it was *our* family farm. Mr. Caffrey looked at me a little perplexed, like it was up to me to fix it. It wasn't the first time that I wanted to tell him to grow some balls. Honestly, I was getting a little tired of the adults looking to me for the answers. If for no other reason than I was nervous that I might let one slip out.

'This handsome gelding Caraway might be one of the last creatures to see Chloe Caffrey.' It was hard not to snicker at this one. I kept waiting for someone to bring in animal psychics or something.

If only we could find an expert to translate this horse's perplexing pattern of neighs into an exact location. No one said that, but I wished someone would. Or that someone would bring Caraway into the Windsor County police station for some kind of equestrian interrogation. The Lila Ann Price horse segment was so weird because they had Mr. Caffrey just stand there, holding the horse's reins. All, *This man has lost his daughter so now he's keeping a really tight hold on his horse.* It's not like the horses were on his chore chart or anything. So instead of the even speeches of the living room interview, Chloe's dad just stood there baffled, his too-expensive loafers sinking into the muck. He looked like he had meant to walk the family dog but grabbed the wrong leash on the way out the door.

Lila Ann Price didn't seem to notice. She asked Camera Guy to zoom in on the horse's face. 'He has such wise eyes.' Only people who don't like animals say crap like that. 'Can we get a shot of the horse walking away? Like maybe toward the road?'

Mr. Caffrey nodded, dropped the reins, and stepped back, 'Go on, Caraway.' We all stood watching, while the horse dropped his head to nibble the grass.

'He doesn't go by remote control.' I was sorry that I said it, because it really wasn't Mr. Caffrey's fault he was out there. He was being more of a sport about the whole thing than I would ever have imagined. One of the assistants snorted a little, though, and the corners of Lila Ann Price's mouth turned up slightly – in a real smile, not just a camera-ready jackal grin.

'Finn, maybe you could lead him? Thank you so much, dear.' I took the reins and brought Caraway out of the gate and on to the gravel of the drive.

'Do us a favor and get a little farther ahead of him, sweetheart? Right?' she asked Camera Guy. 'Does that give you a clear shot?' It took me a second to realize she wanted to make sure they could cut me out of the picture. Mr. Caffrey got it first because he sighed really loudly, like he was disgusted. And then Lila Ann made me start back from the beginning, and asked for 'quiet on the set'.

'Just give the horse some breathing room, there, Finn' – in other words, I didn't even get to share the frame with a horse.

I bit my lip and thought of what the interview would be like when Lila Ann Price brought me back on the show. After. Chloe would remember nothing about her ordeal except slipping in and out of consciousness and reassuring herself that her resourceful best friend would find a way to track her down and bring her home. 'To think that even then, when we filmed our first segment, you were busy tracking down leads – taking a break from investigating to support Chloe's parents. We had no idea how brave you are, Finn. Maybe if we had asked you what you thought of the case, we could have lent our resources to help you rescue Chloe sooner.' Lila Ann Price would be contrite. At first I'd think she was just hamming it up for the cameras, but during the interview, when we broke for commercial, she'd wave off the make-up crew. She'd shake her head at the memory and say,

'You know what I keep going back to, Finn? That afternoon when we were trying to get the shot of the horse . . . we just overlooked—'

And right then I would stop her and say, 'Lila Ann, what's important here is that we have Chloe back home.' And then Lila Ann Price would insist on paying my college tuition. She'd say, 'I hope you'll consider pursuing a degree in law enforcement.' And I'd shake my head, let her wallow a little in the disappointment. Then I'd smile and announce, 'What I'm most interested in is political science. I want to legislate stronger protective measures to keep kids across America safe.'

I remember thinking, *That's how it will be when they stop cutting me out of the frame.*

'God, that's great. And we're even getting a little bit of the sunlight in the trees there. Someone upstairs is looking out for Chloe, too, Mr. Caffrey. Isn't that a great image?' I bet Lila Ann Price was just used to heads around her nodding. She and Chloe weren't so different, really. 'God, that's heaven. I think we'll have to close the segment with that shot.'

'So are we ready to wrap things up?' Mr. Caffrey sounded hopeful. 'Thank you so much for the help here today.' He stepped forward to shake Andy Cogan, Producer's hand.

'If it's all right – I know this afternoon has turned into quite an imposition for your family – but I would still love to film in Chloe's bedroom. I'm looking around this beautiful home, Mr. Caffrey, and I'm sure that your daughter has a girl's dream room, right? Let's show America what we're all hoping Chloe will come home to.'

And then it was like the heavens opened up. Because Lila Ann Price turned and shined her perfectly capped teeth on to me. 'Finn,' she asked, 'do you think you could give us a tour of Chloe's room?' And I couldn't help it. I knew that she was working me over. I just stood there and watched while she worked Mrs. Caffrey and Mr. Caffrey, but as soon as she focused on me, all I wanted was Lila Ann to keep beaming in my direction. Had she known what question to ask, I would have brought her right to Chloe's little hideout. I would have pedaled her there on the handlebars of my bike.

I couldn't even pretend to stay calm. 'Okay, sure,' I stammered. I sounded like Stuttering Dean. 'I mean, if that's okay with Mr. Caffrey.'

'Of course.' He looked kindly at me, and it made me feel bad that in my head I'd been mocking his cheesy loafers. 'I think that's a great idea. Finn knows where everything is. She knows what's important to Chloe.'

'That's how best friends are, right?' Lila Ann Price said. I searched around for Mrs. Caffrey and my mom when we went inside. Nowhere. 'I still speak to my best friend every day.' Lila Ann said it proudly, like I should know who her best friend was.

'Wow. I hope Chloe and I are like that someday.' I said it because I meant it. But it came out as a killer tragic line, and you could tell that Lila Ann Price wished that she had a sound bite of it. She reached up and patted me on the back.

'I hope so too.'

SIXTEEN

Chloe's door was at the end of the hall, and as we walked past the framed photos on the wall, I wondered whether the camera would pan across them, whether Lila Ann would latch on to the pictures of Cam and shake out the story in them. 'Here it is,' I said. 'Right down the hall. Chloe's room is all the way at the end.' I pretty much just kept up the chatter until we go to the door.

I wondered how many kids' bedroom doors Lila Ann Price had been led to. It felt like those shows on the true crime network, where they led the goofy psychic lady in and let her sniff around the missing person's pillow and clothes. But Lila Ann Price never spoke in any kind of far-away, dreamy voice. She was warm and all, but also all business. I was more scared talking to her than talking to anyone – the Caffreys, the cops, Dr. Ace, because Lila Ann Price was a pro. And I figured she had a finely tuned mechanism to monitor bullshit.

But it turned out, no. I showed her the windows overlooking the stables and pointed out that you could see my room from Chloe's. She asked me about our hobbies and I talked about the livestock a little. Then I blanked about anything else we did and ended up describing the hours we spent baking and knitting. Which was untrue. And kind of bizarre.

The truth was that Chloe and I didn't do a lot of regular girl stuff. We were far enough from town that Girl Scout meetings had been a foreign concept. We never took dance or gymnastics or karate or any of the other classes that most people sign their kids up for. Lila Ann Price might have written that tidbit down in her notebook and used it later on Mrs. Caffrey, but we wouldn't have wanted to tumble around in leotards with a bunch of other girls. It took a few years for us to blend in with them, for one thing.

Chloe and I had our games and some of them were sicker than others. Mostly I guess we played like any two little girls played – dolls and school, and when we played house, we pretended we'd married twin brothers and lived together in a condo split down the middle. When we hit junior high, we stopped calling it 'playing'. By then, we called it 'imagining'.

That's how we did it. One of us would start, 'Imagine if . . .' and then we'd keep going. We played Paparazzi and filled memory cards with images of each other ducking into doorways. We interviewed each other for *People* magazine and *Vanity Fair*. We pretended to be famous for being pretty. We acted like actresses and introduced each other as starlets. But it wasn't like I was going to sit there and tell Lila Ann Price these things.

Especially because once in a while, we imagined being

famous for other, stranger reasons. For escaping burning cars and collapsing buildings. At the start of ninth grade, when we first had to practice lockdown drills, there was a while when Chloe and I got into surviving school shootings. But the one we did a lot, the one we could do anywhere, was the dead body.

We'd be on the school bus, looking out into the ravine alongside the road. Or sailing with her dad – Chloe and I would sit on deck and point out shapes bobbing in the water. We'd describe the corpses to each other, as if we were giving newscasters' interviews. We knew it was weird. We must have, because we were careful to not let anyone overhear us.

One of us would hold the hairbrush like a microphone as the other said, 'At first, I didn't know what I was looking at. It looked like a doll hand, sticking out from under the wet leaves.' I could defend it to Lila Ann Price and explain that it wasn't a game about being famous. It's not like you ever remember the names of those people. It was more about being important, maybe temporarily, but still crucial, just for keeping your eyes open.

We'd even talk about what you did, what you had to do when you found one. If you called and stayed, waiting to show the cops. Or if you reported it anonymously and then hid nearby, waiting until help arrived. We went over it so often it was like we were training for the dead body Olympics or something.

It's not so far from what ended up happening after all. When news of Chloe's disappearance first hit the city tabloids, I looked for dead body stories running alongside the short little columns about Chloe. There was a drowning, some capsized boat off Long Island. One day there was a hit and run. None of those people got a visit from Lila Ann Price, though. Our little columns stretched longer and longer each day. It would have been easier, is what I thought, to just have found a corpse. You got in, made a phone call, and got out; you could even go into school the same day and tell people about it. It's not like you'd be marked for life, but maybe it would lead to a little self-reflection, a discussion of mortality and human fragility. You could write a kickass college essay about that.

Now, after being mixed up in the whole Chloe Caffrey Case, finding a body might be all sorts of trouble for me. It would look a little nutso to find her and then it. Even if it happened years later, they'd probably look at me like they were looking at Dean now. I'd be a suspect.

Ushering a reporter into Chloe's bedroom with a camera in my face, I wasn't a suspect or even a person of interest. But I was interesting – I was downright intriguing to Lila Ann Price. 'Tell me about what a typical day is like for you girls,' she gently prodded. 'What has school been like without your best friend?' And 'Chloe must have confided in you – what are her dreams for the future?'

So I sat there on Chloe's bed, clutching her pillow in my lap and telling Lila Ann Price how hard it had been to get through each day, how empty the room felt without Chloe. It got a little embarrassing. But the thing was, it had to be. Everyone else focused on the rest of the story – Mrs. Caffrey's bloodshot eyes, the horse. Lila Ann Price was our chance to sell Chloe as a missing kid with star power – an extraordinary case worth coming back to for a follow-up.

The next night I cleared the dishes from the table and tried to stop looking up at the kitchen clock. My mom had walked a lasagna over to the Caffreys and rushed inside, saw me scraping plates and my dad at the sink. 'Will you get a move on, you guys?' she asked. 'It's almost on.'

Dad and I glanced at each other as she shook off her coat and headed towards the den. Dad called out, 'We're going to watch the episode?'

'Well, of course we're going to watch it. Why not?'

'It just seems kind of indulgent to sit around watching ourselves on TV.' Even my dad's voice was embarrassed.

But Mom insisted, 'We're watching for Chloe's sake.' She clucked through the interview with Mrs. Caffrey and dabbed her eyes at the shots of the horse. When I came on screen though, my mother reached across and patted my thigh. 'Finn, you look lovely. And so poised too. Look at her, Bart.'

Dad cleared his throat and then nodded. 'We're really proud of you, Finn.' Their tender looks seared me. I wished we'd actually popped popcorn so I could drown myself in burning kernels.

Chloe was not nearly as impressed. I snuck out to watch the late-night rerun with her. She said, 'That's sick. God, Finn – it's so over-the-top. You sound a little creepy. It sounds like you're obsessed with me or something.'

'Well, we said we had to do that. You said—'

'I know, I know, I just didn't realize how it would sound, I mean—'

'And it's edited. They edit the segments. I had to talk about your volunteer work and how gentle you are with the animals—'

'That's it! That's the creepiest part. That's my special quality? That I'm gentle with animals? You couldn't have said I'm really smart or creative or I have leadership potential? It's not like Wesleyan University's going to call up and say, 'You're home – that's great, because we were just remarking about the shortage of teenage girls in our admissions pool who are REALLY GOOD WITH ANIMALS.'

'I said you were funny and kind. And that people love being around you.'

She calmed down a little. 'I know, and that was nice and all, but it's nothing special, really. I mean, people would say the same thing about you.'

We were both quiet for a little bit. Until I finally said, 'Um . . . thanks?'

'Oh, don't be mad. You know what I mean. She's Lila Ann Price. We just needed to make an impression, is all.'

'We *did* make an impression.' She didn't look up at me. 'Chloe.' Still nothing. 'I made an impression.' And then I dug into my jeans and pulled the card out of my pocket. I flicked it on to my grandmother's slate coffee table.

She barely even glanced at it. 'I didn't screw it up, Chloe.' I just wanted her to acknowledge it. I had done the hard part. And when I got done talking about how great and smart Chloe was and how even the light bulb in her bedside lamp seemed dimmer without her nearby, the original celebrity of tragedy actually seemed moved. Even beyond the usual sympathetic outrage you see in her commercials. And after that I listened while Lila Ann Price told me that her daughter loved animals and had gotten a little pet rabbit the Easter right before she disappeared.

Before she left, right as all the techs were winding up the cords and packing microphones and cameras into hard cases, Lila Ann Price put her hand on my shoulder and called Andy Cogan, Producer over. 'Andy, I want you to give Finn here your business card.' She was talking to him but mostly looking at me. 'Andy's my right-hand man in this fight. And he's on call twenty-four hours a day. So if you need anything, or if you think of anything that might help us bring Chloe home, I want you to call Andy. And Andy will get you right in touch with me.' It wasn't so different from the spiel I got from the police officer who first came to question us or even from Dr. Ace at the counseling center. The card itself was just as plain, with careful text that you could feel raised against the tips of your fingers. But it felt like that card could get more done. At least Lila Ann Price believed that, and Andy Cogan, Producer believed that, and by the time they left, I believed it too.

Chloe wasn't as convinced. 'That's just part of the show.'

'No – I'm telling you – the camera guy wasn't even in the room right then.'

'There doesn't have to be a camera guy for there to be a show.' But Chloe traced her finger along the writing on the card. For a second, I thought she was going to grab it, but then she lifted her hand and I picked it up and swiftly tucked it back in my pocket.

'Don't run it through the laundry.' Chloe said it wryly and we laughed and the tension drifted away a little. 'You can't be the one who finds me, you know.' When she said that, I felt my throat close up a little, a lump in the back that hurt. It wasn't that Chloe was wrong or that I hadn't already had the same thought. But it was how casually she said it – my chance to step forward into the light that we rigged up around her, and she yanked it away like it was nothing. 'Come on, Finn – you have to see that. I mean, after this?' She gestured at the television. 'Just a couple days after you go on network TV and discuss how you would trade yourself in to whoever had taken me? Then suddenly you're going to rescue me from my pit of kidnap despair? Do you get how crazy that would seem?'

Yes. I got it. My voice rose . . . it gave out a little and I felt exposed, embarrassed. 'We knew that. You and I both said that. But we said that's what would make the story so extra-ordinary – that people would eat it up. It would become about the Friendship That Overcame Everything.' Even if my voice hadn't been shaking, it would have sounded stupid.

'I just think it's unrealistic, is all.' Chloe shrugged.

'Well, yeah – you going missing is unrealistic. The way the whole town acts like you're already dead is unrealistic.'

'What's going to happen, Finn? Really? I'm going to sneak up on to some hunting blind, that the search parties have probably already covered by now? I'll hang out on the plat-form for a night and then you'll wander out to the woods and suddenly just happen to look up?'

It hadn't sounded so ridiculous the week before. Lots of people hunted in Colt River; more importantly, even more used to hunt. That meant that all over the woods around our houses, rickety platforms were perched up in trees. Some people still used them and probably more than one had been transformed into a smoke shack by local potheads. Our dads were pretty militant, though – you didn't play in hunting blinds. Some were rotting out of branches and the others . . . well, people used those. People with guns used those, and hunters tended to get territorial.

'Well, yeah – that's what we said.'

'No one's going to believe that, Finn. No one's going to believe that I spent all week up in one of those, that I didn't scream for help—'

'We'll gag you.'

'Or that I didn't have food or water.'

'Your abductor moved you. We said—'

'It's not going to work, Finn!' I heard the panic in her voice. 'I'm not going to be able to lie like you. And they're going to be asking for descriptions – they might make me take a lie detector test.'

'Why would they make you take a lie detector test? You're not going to be the suspect. You're the victim.'

'I think that people can switch off from the victim to the suspect pretty quickly.' I thought of Dean, wondered if Chloe was picturing Dean hooked up to some monitor, answering questions while some techie decided if he was honest and good.

'People live in trees all the time.'

'Do you hear yourself?' Chloe looked incredulous.

'No, they do. People out in California – you know those hippies that protest on behalf of redwoods. They climb up and live on platforms so that the loggers can't cut down the tallest of the trees. People have spent years up in trees.' I kept talking faster, as if my voice could outrun Chloe's laughter, but by the end I felt myself smile and she was dabbing at her eyes, wheezing and giggling.

'Could you imagine? You could leave me up there with bongos AND a bong. I could write my college essay about being a real-life tree-hugger.'

But whatever silliness had snuck up on us disappeared again. 'Oh my God, Chlo – what were we thinking? How are we going to get you back home?' I tried to picture sitting on a sofa on *The L. A. Price Show*, explaining how I had spotted Chloe's blond braid glinting in the sunlight filtering through the hunting blind. I wasn't even halfway through all the lying yet. And Chloe couldn't even forge passes out of study hall . . . how was she going to get through police questioning, the media interviews? My chest constricted. I felt the basement walls close around me and squeeze.

'But see, that's just it. I have to get myself back home – you can't find me.' Chloe sounded less bitchy this time – or maybe I was just more afraid. In my head, I had played the images like scenes from a horror movie. I'd hold her up, half-carry, half-drag her toward the road. I would flag a passing car down, screaming, 'Somebody help us! Please, someone help!'

'You can't just show up on your back porch like nothing happened.'

'Yeah, well. I figured I'd just take off my boots in the mudroom and wash up for supper.' Chloe's sarcasm wasn't reassuring. And then she got less reassuring when she said. 'I think I'd have to be injured.' I must have blinked. When she kept going, it didn't get better. 'I'd need a head injury. That way it would make sense for me to be hazy on details.'

'Chloe, you can't fake a head injury. The first thing they'll do is take you for a medical evaluation.'

'I'm not talking about faking.' She stood up then and started pacing in front of me in the way that she always did when she was planning something. Or planning to convince me of something. 'I've been thinking a lot about it. And it's the only way. I mean, we're really in trouble.' She stopped then and looked straight at me. 'I'm in serious trouble.' At first when she knelt down, I thought she was going to beg me for something but really she was getting something from underneath my grandmother's old sofa. 'I've been looking around and I found these.' Chloe pulled out a wrench and a pipe and then a long, wide piece of wood. She left one hand on the piece of wood. 'I think this is our best bet, because the others are metal and that might be too dangerous, right? It's actually a shelf I took down from the wall. You'd have to put it back up afterwards.'

'After what?' I swear to God, even then I had no idea what she was talking about.

'After you hit me with it.' I waited for Chloe to laugh

after she said it, but she just kind of looked up at me with a lop-sided smile. 'I think it's our only shot. I need to have a real head injury.'

'No way.' Standing up, I reached down for her, tried to pull her to her feet. 'Chloe. You've lost it.' She shook my hands off her and grabbed the wooden plank like it was a banister. 'This is enough, Chloe – you're just nuts from being in the basement. We made a mistake. We made a really stupid mistake, but we're just kids and people will eventually understand.' But Chloe just looked up at me. It was like she was waiting for me to imagine telling my parents, her parents, the police, all those men who searched for her – in the woods, in the lake. Forget about Lila Ann Price – how would we buy gum at Mr. Donahue's little grocery down the street? Who would we sit with at lunch? What would we say to Dean West? By the time I got through imagining all of it, I couldn't even look Chloe in the eye. She just stared at me, waiting.

'I'm telling you I can't do it,' I told her. Chloe said nothing. 'I mean, what if something goes wrong?' She rolled the pipe back under the sofa. It had flakes of rust dusting one side. I didn't even know where she'd gotten it from. She pushed the wrench under, away. She kept rubbing the shelf like it was the head of a restless animal. 'I could really hurt you.' Chloe shoved the shelf under the sofa with the rest of the collection.

'Tell me what else to do.' She looked at me expectantly. 'Seriously, because I'd love for there to be an alternative.' My lips pursed together. I had nothing. 'Exactly. People get hit in the head all the time.' She gestured to my face. 'They get into car accidents. They fall down.'

'When?'

'Two days.' Chloe nodded at me, like my agreement confirmed something. 'That's long enough after tonight's *L. A. Price* episode. Otherwise, it looks too convenient.' She'd already decided, even before I climbed down the basement steps. 'We'll do it in the middle of the night, and I get myself home. You can run ahead and listen for me. That way, you can still be the one to call 911.' Chloe offered it up like a consolation prize.

'And what if you can't make it home?'

'We'll do it in the middle of the woods. Plan B, you come up with an excuse to find me there.'

'I'm not saying I'll do it.'

'If you come up with a better idea, we'll do that. Otherwise, you need to come by and help me with the trash from this place and then we can go into the woods behind the farm.' I looked around the basement at the wrappers and water bottles and soda cans. It was so stupid, but at first I thought, *We're not going to be able to recycle.* Like that's what would clinch our status as bad citizens. I picked up a bottle and a few cans and packed them in my backpack.

'And you should take this.' She pulled her shirt over her head in one motion and handed it over. Chloe was always getting naked like it was nothing. She walked to the corner and wriggled into a sports bra. 'On your way home, you can bury it and then I can put it on before we do the other thing. Then I'll be all filthy and it'll help throw people off.'

'I can't take this.' I wanted to the throw the shirt back at her.

'I'll use a blanket.'

'Chloe, I can't bury this in the woods. Do you know what would happen if someone saw me?'

'Nobody's looking through the woods anymore. They wouldn't have released Dean if they thought there was a body out there.'

'You don't get it. Do you want them to bring me in for questioning? Then you'd have to hit yourself with a two by four.'

'How hard is it to bury a shirt under a pile of leaves? Thirty seconds. Maybe forty-five. If someone finds it, well then, they find it. It'll just throw people farther off the trail.' I pictured seeing Chloe stagger toward the back door of the Caffreys' place. I would run out to her. I'd tear off my jacket and wrap it around her shoulders. I'd scream for my mom. I'd yell out for them to call 911. I shoved the shirt into my backpack with the soda cans and started up the stairs.

'What, no goodbye?' Chloe reached up toward me.

'You're not wearing any clothes, for God's sake.'

'Finn, are you mad at me?' She sounded so worried, like it would be the worst thing in the world if I were. 'It's all going to be over soon.'

'It's never going to be over.' I almost cried when I said it, because I knew it was true. 'This is really hard. You have no idea. You should start practicing.'

'Yeah, whatevs.' Because really, what could Chloe practice? 'You should practice your swing.'

'Not at all funny,' I called out behind me. But she had already bounced back on to the sofa, searching for the news networks on the remote. I pulled the cellar door closed behind me, checked around my grandmother's first floor, and headed out the front door.

SEVENTEEN

It took forty-six seconds to bury Chloe's sweatshirt beneath dead leaves and wet dirt. And the whole time, I was ready for a helicopter to swoop down, a searchlight to capture me in its wide beam. I dug a little hole and brushed aside the leaves. Stuck in the shirt, covered it up and then stamped on the whole pile. Then I worried that somehow my footprints could be matched if they left marks on the shirt. So then I threw a pretty sturdy rock on the pile and covered that up with more leaves. And the whole process was about twenty times worse than I had expected it would be. By the time I got to our fence, my eyes ached from darting around.

There were lights on at the Caffreys', but not our house, so I went straight to chores. Stepped into the big hip waders we used for muck work and started cleaning out the stalls in the stable. I dumped the old water from the troughs and set up the hoses to fill them. I made the rounds, feeling for weird lumps and hoping to ease the hurt feelings of the past week or two of neglect. Took out a tennis ball and started tossing it around for Chauncey. Quietly and all – I made sure that Mrs. Caffrey wouldn't step out on her porch and see me prancing around with a dog. The sky was graying and it smelled like someone was burning leaves.

It was my mom who stepped outside into the porch. 'I have to talk to you. Hold up, let me come over there.' I could see her tying her sneakers. I felt sick of the sick feeling I got every time someone else acknowledged my existence. Even Chauncey dropped the ball in front of me and looked up at me like he was waiting for an explanation. My mom hadn't tailed me back and forth from Grandma's, though. She just said, 'Mr. West called.'

I had been in the middle of launching a real good toss for Chauncey, but when my mom said that, I clutched the ball reflexively, so it only looked like I'd thrown it into the darkening night. But he took off running anyway, snuffling through the tall grass for a ball that was still in my hand.

'Dean Jr. would like to speak with you. Now, if you're not comfortable with that, I understand, but you did sound so worried about Dean in the car the other day that I thought maybe.'

'Of course.' I thought I said it out loud, but my mom kept talking.

'Your father and I have known Mr. West for a very long time. He's reached out to us, and your father especially would like him to feel supported. I'd imagine they must feel very much alone in Dean West's house tonight.' Mom was looking toward the yellow windows of the Caffreys' kitchen, though. She wasn't really trying to convince me – it was weird to think of adults feeling guilty, forcing each other to choose sides like Lizbette and Katie fighting at a school dance.

'Mom, of course I want to talk to Dean. Why didn't he email me? Or text?'

'Oh, I don't know . . . maybe there are legal reasons for that.' Before I could ask, she explained. 'Maybe his lawyer told him not to put anything in writing. I don't know. I've probably just watched too many *Law & Order* episodes . . .'

'No, that makes sense. That's really smart.'

'You think so? It sounds so far-fetched.' It bugs me that my mom doesn't give herself enough credit. I remembered what Mrs. Caffrey said to Lila Ann Price about my mom never heading off to college and it blistered me. What the hell did she know? Her A grade student's hiding out in a basement, waiting for me to hit her with a wooden plank. No wonder Chloe was so obsessed with getting into a good school. She'd grown up listening to her mom work her four years at Vassar College into every possible conversation. My mom could at least control herself and have a discussion without a prescription.

'Well, why don't you call Dean Jr. then? I wrote down their land line. The police kept Dean's cell—'

'Really? Can they do that? Doesn't that interfere with his civil rights or something?'

'Oh, Finley. Everyone's just trying to find Chloe. There's no bad guy here.'

I said nothing. I threw Chauncey's ball into the dark yard and went to get his bowl for supper. My mom went to go get the number and I called after her, 'Do I invite him over?'

'Finn. Use some common sense.' I did not want to go over to Stuttering Dean's house. Pretty much the only house I wanted to be at less was the Caffreys'.

'Well, it's not like I can meet him out in public.'

'You're damn right you're going to meet him out in public.' The screen door slapped closed behind my dad and he kicked his muddy boots off next to mine. I looked at Mom, all *What is this?*, but she looked just as lost as me.

'Bart – we talked about this – you're the one who wanted Finn to call.'

'I want her to call him. I don't want her to be alone with him.'

'Dad, that's crazy.'

'Bart—'

'Absolutely not. This isn't up for discussion.'

'Bart, I'd like to talk to you in the parlor, please.' My mom only calls the living room 'the parlor' when she's angry. It's like she reverts back to some kind of repressed Victorian fury. But my dad didn't meekly follow her in like he usually did. He took off ranting and I even heard him bang the top of my grandmother's old piano.

I heard her hiss, 'What has gotten into you? Here I'm telling her how important this is to her father—'

'I said it would be nice if she talked to the kid.'

'Yes and—'

'Talk to the kid, not set herself up like some kind of bait.'

'Oh, for Pete's sake, Bart – you have got to be kidding. Where would you even get something like that?'

'What happened to a kid just calling another kid on the phone?'

'What happened to that? I'll tell you what happened to that – the Wests are scared to death. Their son spent the night in jail. How do they know we're not going to tape the call?'

'Why would they worry about that? If there's nothing for us to worry about, then there's nothing for them to worry about. I'll tell you something, Amy – innocent people don't worry whether or not someone's going to tape their calls.'

'We don't know what they're worried about. I can't imagine. The way people are talking about this poor boy – I understand them wanting to protect their son.'

'Exactly!' My dad banged the piano again. This time the keys moaned. 'We have to protect our daughter, just like they're doing.'

I wanted to storm into the living room and yell too. I'd say, *You don't have to protect me from Stuttering Dean.* But our house wasn't like the Caffreys' – we didn't resolve things at family meetings. I sat down at the kitchen table and waited.

When they came back in, my mom was walking ahead and my dad had her shoulders gripped in her hands. Like he was steering her, but she was smiling. My mom liked to be steered. 'Finn, your father and I both agree it would be best if you asked Dean to meet you at the library.'

'Well, that's just stupid.'

'Finn—' My dad was a siren, warning me.

'You can't talk at the library.'

'Plenty of people talk at the library.'

'And people give you dirty looks. And if it's Dean talking,

they'll find a way to arrest us for disturbing the peace or something.'

My mother sighed, like this was so hard for her. 'Fine. You can meet him at Slave to the Grind or at the diner.'

'I don't understand why he can't just come over here. It's going to cause all sorts of trouble for me to go out with Dean West while Chloe's missing.'

'For Pete's sake, Finn – you're afraid people are going to think you're trying to steal Chloe's boyfriend?'

'He's not her boyfriend!' It killed me to think that days before I had sat up there in my bedroom eating up my mom's girl talk session like it was cake and ice cream and she was just going to throw the whole thing in my face. She might as well have pointed out the impossibility of anyone dumping Chloe for me. And it wasn't really other people that worried me. But Chloe was coming home in two days and she'd hear about it. 'The only reason you won't let him come here is because you're afraid of Mrs. Caffrey.' I looked toward Dad, hoping to swing him to my side. 'You're always so worried about her and what she thinks.'

'Right now I *am* worried about Mrs. Caffrey, yes. Mrs. Caffrey's daughter is missing and I don't think we're being too accommodating by not hosting the only suspect in Chloe's disappearance.'

'He was just a person of interest!' I yelled it loud enough that offending the Caffreys was now beside the point, because they probably heard me. My dad looked back and forth between my mom and me. He stepped forward, and for a second I thought he'd call a family huddle.

'You know there's an easy solution for this.' Dad held his hands up, like he was calming wild animals. My mother motioned for him to talk on. 'I can just drive Finn over to your mom's house,' he told her, and I bit my tongue hard. 'I can check out the yard and the thermostat and the kids can sit in the kitchen and talk.' My mom sighed and sank into a chair. My mouth filled with blood. At least that's what it felt like. I couldn't get myself to speak. My dad turned expectantly to me. 'Okay?'

There's no way Chloe would just sit quietly in the basement while I had a heart-to-heart with Dean. And even if by some miracle she did, then the whole time we spoke, my dad would be puttering around the house. I swallowed, touched the sore spot on my tongue against my back teeth. 'I'm sorry – this is silly. I can just meet him at the diner.' I tried to say it casually, like none of it was any kind of big deal.

Leave it to my mom. 'No, honey, I think Daddy's dug up a great solution.'

'But I want to be careful about Dean too.' I tried to match my mom's tone of voice. 'Meeting at Grandma's would be easier for me, but Dean's going to figure out why we didn't want him here. That's really obvious. I just think it'll hurt his feelings. We can meet at the diner – that's not so weird. And I'll make sure we get a booth so it seems private.' One of the things I've learned is it's important to stop talking when you're lying. People sound fake when they try to fill up silence. I stood up, as if everything was settled, and headed back toward the kitchen with the Wests' phone number clutched in my hand. 'I'll call Dean now.'

Because I was so worried my parents would stop me, it didn't even occur to me to be nervous about calling Dean West. Dialing the number, I kept waiting to hear them call my name. But instead a woman's voice answered, 'Hello?' so suspiciously that it made me wonder what kind of calls the Wests had been getting over the past few days. I guessed it was his mom because when I asked for Dean, she asked, 'Dean or Dean Jr.?'

It must feel a little bit invisible to go through life with someone else's name. I mean, I have my mom's last name and that's weird sometimes, but to just be a total sequel to someone else? 'Ma'am – this is Finley Jacobs calling to speak to Dean Jr.' I turned to see my own mom leaning against the kitchen doorframe, nodding her head approvingly.

The voice on the phone lost its edge. 'Oh, Finley, I'm happy you've called. Let me get Dean for you.' I heard the phone clank against something hard. In my house, my mom would have just hollered up for me. But then again, the only person who called me on the land line was my grandmother.

I heard muffled speaking and then Dean said 'Hello?' without a hitch in his voice or anything. 'Hello?' He said it again, because I had blanked out on what to say to him.

'Dean? It's Finn. Hi. Um . . .' I looked at my mom. 'How are you?' I felt my face crinkle saying it because, well, what was he supposed to say to that?

But Dean was Dean. He just said, 'Fine, thank you,' as if I'd called to tell him a reading assignment or something. He cleared his throat, then asked, 'How are you? I mean, are you okay?'

And I wasn't, hearing Dean West ask me that. Because I'd never be able to know the kind of trouble we'd caused him and him asking me – it wasn't like Maddy or Kate asking me. Dean sounded like he actually cared.

'I'm okay. It just feels like everything's gone crazy.' I looked up at the doorway, but Mom had turned to head back to the living room. Maybe she meant to give me some privacy.

Dean exhaled. 'Yeah it does.' Silence. 'Li-listen. Woo-woo-would you want to meet somewhere? Just hang out?'

'Yeah. Yeah, that'd be great. Do you want to meet at the diner?' I tried to stop myself from talking fast. It must feel awful to hear everyone always rushing to talk so that you don't have to stammer through a whole sentence. 'We could meet there in an hour or two?' I made myself say it slowly, but then it only sounded like maybe I thought Dean didn't speak English.

'Sure.'

'Sure?'

'Yeah.' So obviously Dean had switched to the one-word strategy.

'Okay, I'll meet you at seven then, okay? That's an hour and a half.'

'See you there.'

Dean hung up before I could reply. For a second, I thought, *He knows. He hates me.* But Dean West probably hated talking on the phone. Maybe he hadn't even ever called Chloe. Maybe that was the deal with all the texts.

My parents stopped talking when I ducked through the

room. I got halfway up the stairs before my mom called up, 'Whoa. Hold on there, Finn.'

'I'm going to meet him in an hour and a half. We're going to the diner.'

'Well, do you want your dad to take you?' She jutted her chin at him and he stopped stacking the pile of newspapers by his chair.

'Yeah, I'll take you. I'll just have a cup of coffee or two up at the counter.'

'I'll just take the van.'

My mom shot a look at my dad and my dad stood up, brushing imaginary dust from his thighs.

'Nah.' At least he tried to say it casually. 'I'll take you, poundcake.' I looked down at the two of them. 'Just to make sure everyone minds their manners.'

In my head, I saw Dean West stand, squared up to Jeff McHale or Craig Davelman.

'Yeah, okay. Fine.' Headed back up the steps.

'Finn.' My mom called up.

'What?' I felt like *enough already, whatever you say.*

But my mom said, 'I'm really proud of you. This is a kind thing.'

EIGHTEEN

I kept thinking: *The next time I do something like fake a kidnapping, I'm going to make sure to work out my issues with guilt and shame first.* Because it was getting hard to drag myself up the steps. In my room, I realized there wasn't even music I wanted to hear. I went to CNN on my laptop and clicked on the Crime section. There was Chloe and her little lamb smiling out of the screen. I shut that and then slid open the doors of my closet. It was time to pick out an outfit to wear to meet Dean West.

I went with jeans and then the big debate was a crewneck or a v-neck. The v-neck was a deep one – not the kind of thing I'd risk wearing to school, where there was always some perv like Cody Hameier throwing balled-up paper down your shirt. Or worse. Chloe would take issue with it, but whatever, I was wearing jeans. It wasn't like anyone could say I was dressing up for Stuttering Dean. I brushed out my hair and put on a little make-up. I mean, I did my eyes. Lately I'd been wearing a lot of mascara so that it was really obvious when I cried.

I was ready about forty-five minutes sooner than we need-ed to leave. I stuck on a cami under the v-neck at the last minute and shook out my hair from the braid I'd tied it back in. If necessary, I could hide behind it. I stopped myself from going down the stairs twice until finally it was 6:30 and my mom yelled up from the kitchen.

'Finley – you want an early supper before you go off?'

I headed down the stairs and reminded her, 'We're going to a diner. It's customary to order food there.' Yep, I would order a grilled cheese and discuss Chloe's disappearance with the main suspect in the crime.

My mom looked up – I assumed to tell me to quit it. Instead said, 'Finn – you look so nice, honey.' Too loudly. Too enthusiastically.

'I'm just wearing jeans.' I sounded defensive to myself. 'It's not like it's a date or anything.'

'No, of course not.' Too quickly. Too knowingly. 'But your make-up looks nice – it looks so natural.'

'Thanks.' I tried to say it in a way that established that she should shut up. But sometimes my mom picks up on clues more slowly than Cam.

'Really, Finn. You look great.'

'It's nothing. I'm just going to meet him and hear him out. You wanted me to go.'

'Oh, I know – you just look so lovely when you put in the effort.'

'What is that supposed to mean?'

My dad came stomping in. He reached past me for the hook where we hang our keys. 'What is what supposed to mean?'

But I stared my mom down. 'Like I don't normally put in the effort.'

My mom sighed. 'Finn, I don't know why you're so sensitive. You've never been one to dress up. That's all I meant.'

'Just because I don't dress up doesn't mean I don't put in the effort.'

My mom met my dad's eyes and shrugged. 'Okay. That's fine.' She said it like she was placating a crazy person. 'Obviously I don't know what I'm talking about. I've just noticed that lately, you've seemed to spend more time on yourself. And while I wouldn't want you to be any different, you've looked really pretty lately.'

I just stood there. She swooped in to kiss my cheek, and I stiffened. She kissed it anyway. She stood there for a second and I almost told her the truth. Well, part of the truth. I almost said, *It's easier to work on being pretty when I don't have to stand next to Chloe all the time. Because when I do, well, what's the point of that?* But my mom just said, 'Tell Dean we said hello and that he and his folks should call us if they need anything at all.'

'Got it.'

'Good.'

In the truck, Dad and I laid out the ground rules for the diner. 'You're just going to sit at the counter, right?' I asked.

He said, 'Well, yeah, except . . .' and trailed off.

'Dad!'

He cackled. 'Well, except that I might have to use the little boys' room.'

'God.' I leaned back and stared out the window. 'Jesus.'

'Any other lords' names you want to take in vain?'

I laughed. 'Yeah – Ganesh. Ganesh damn it.'

'Who's Ganesh?'

'He's a Hindu god. He's the Remover of Obstacles.'

'Oh yeah?' My dad switched his toothpick from one side of his mouth to the other. 'They got a god for that? We could use a Remover of Obstacles. Well, I don't care if you take a Hindu god's name in vain – just lay off Jesus.'

'Okay, Dad. I'll lay off Jesus.'

'What's this Remover of Obstacles look like?'

'I think he's an elephant.'

'Yeah? An elephant. Jesus Christ, can you believe that?'

'Dad!' But he had me laughing, even as I was praying to any god possible. Mostly to just stop feeling. It was one thing to lie to someone who didn't matter, but Dean was one of the kindest people I knew. And Chloe and I had changed him a little. I remembered the feeling of seeing him strut around a little after he first started getting our notes. Like all of a sudden he mattered more.

If I thought that had been stomped out of him over the past few days of interrogations and innuendos, then I was right. Dad and I had left early to make sure to get a booth in the back. But when I got there, Teddy Selander's older sister was hostessing and she said, 'You're meeting Dean West? He's sitting right over here,' loud enough for everyone to hear. I heard the bells on top of the door jangle and turned to see my dad coming in behind me.

'You're sitting down too?' Teddy's sister asked.

'No, I think I'll just grab a seat at the counter, thanks.'

Teddy's sister looked my dad up and down and I remembered that a teacher from the vocational college got fired last year and everyone said his wife had caught him in a car with her on his lap. Chloe would die when I told her it was probably true.

'Everything okay?' My dad shot me a look that said he didn't mind hitting someone with a stool.

'Everything's fine.' I followed Teddy's sister into the dining room and saw Dean sitting with his back to the wall. He rushed to stand up when I got there, and it reminded me that he was old Colt River too, just like me. He'd probably grow up to be a lot like my dad.

Teddy's sister cracked her gum when she talked, even when she talked in a stage whisper. 'How are you?' she asked me now, right in front of Dean. 'Has anyone heard anything about Chloe?'

I shook my head, waited for her to be done.

'Oh my God. That's so horrible. Well, you tell her mom and dad we've been praying for them. Everyone in here's been talking about it.' She shot a slow look toward Dean. 'No one can get over it.'

'Thanks.'

'No problem.' Gum crack. 'Tanya's going to be taking care of you two today. I'll go make sure your dad's got everything he needs.'

I wanted to call out *Stay off his lap* or something as she left. But I never had the guts to say those things. I just thought those things.

Dean coughed into his closed hand and I realized he was

still standing there, waiting for me to sit down. 'Oh, sorry.' I slid into the bench and shook off my jacket.

'Your dad's here? Is he – is he going to sit with us?' Dean seemed terrified by the prospect.

'No. He's up at the counter.' And then, so he didn't think it was just about him, I added, 'My parents have been crazy – they don't let me out of the house without one of them. It's like total lockdown.' And all of a sudden, I wondered if lockdown was a prison term. 'I mean – they're just so paranoid. It's crazy.'

'No, it makes sense.' Dean nodded to himself. 'I mean, most times you would have been with her, right? It could have been the two of you disappeared together.'

I wished. But I said, 'Yeah . . . or the two of you, apparently.' Dean looked like I'd slapped him. I hadn't meant for it to come out sounding mean.

'It hadn't gotten that serious.' Dean looked up and then past me at the approaching waitress. 'May I have a Coke, please?' he asked her calmly, and then his eyes fell back down to me. 'Would you like something to drink?'

'Sure. A Coke.'

'Two C-Cokes, please.' It was the first time a boy had ever ordered for me. Sitting there in my v-neck sweater and heavy mascara, it occurred to me that this was the closest I'd ever come to a date.

I heard Dean say, 'Thank you.' He said it slowly and carefully.

'Is it hard?' I asked him before even thinking about whether or not it was polite. 'Talking to strangers – is it hard when they might not know . . .'

'Nahh,' Dean said. 'P-people c-c-call me Stuttering Dean, right? Most p-people know already.' And then he actually talked to me about it. His grandfather had stuttered, but had grown out of it. Dean just shrugged when he said that, but I think he meant that he was hoping. And there were specific sounds that he got hung up on more often than others. He called them 'triggers', and the reason he spoke slowly was that sometimes he was looking for ways around them. Like 'c's and 'k's were hard so that at home, he'd call it a Pepsi even when he wanted Coke.

'Then why didn't you call it a Pepsi here?'

'Bec-cause I don't like Pepsi.' He smiled then a little. I tried to smile back, but it was too hard.

'Cam does something a little like that,' I told him. 'About certain words. Except we're the ones who can't say them. If you say them, he makes this noise – it sounds like the way Ernie laughs on *Sesame Street*.'

'Like a raspberry?'

'Kind of.'

'What words?'

'That's the thing. They're words like *sleep* and *quiet* and *please*.

'You can't say *please* at C-C-Chloe's house?'

'You can't say a bunch of things. For a while, Cam did it when anyone said Chloe's name. She couldn't say her own name. She never told you about that?'

'Chloe doesn't really talk about her brother.' Dean took a long swallow from his soda. 'Listen, Finn, you know that I don't know where she is, right?'

'Yeah. I know.' I said it quickly. It would have been slicker to make him convince me. But I wasn't going to sit there and make Dean West do that.

'W-w-well, I figured that maybe you and I c-could p-p-put our heads together. Maybe we don't think w-we know something, but maybe going over it together . . .'

'I've already gone over it with everyone,' I told him.

Dean pressed his lips together and creased the paper wrapper shed from the straw.

'Sure. It w-was a long shot. Sorry.'

'No, I mean – we can try.'

Dean looked up. 'Yeah?'

'Yeah. I mean, it's worth a try, right? Anything's worth a try.'

He nodded. I asked him then, 'What was it like? I mean, people said you spent two nights in jail.'

It seemed like Dean sighed for ten minutes. Just one, long, continuous exhale. He said, 'No. They have to arrest you in order for them to k-k-keep you overnight.'

'Yeah. I thought—'

'I wasn't arrested.' Dean said it flatly.

'Oh.'

'They'd have to have evidence to arrest me. Like, actual evidence.'

In my head, pieces of Chloe's photographs fluttered to the floor. 'Dean, I'm really sorry about—'

But he interrupted me. 'Don't be. It wasn't your fault.' I sat there with my straw in my mouth, without taking a sip.

'It's harder on my parents than anyone, I guess.'

'Were they mad?'

'Not at me.' Dean knocked a bunch of sugar packets out of the ceramic container. He started stacking them, one on top of the other. 'They've spent their wh-wh-ole lives in this town. My great-grandfather was born in our house. The other day Trudy Williams refused to serve my mom at the supermarket.'

'What?'

'Yeah, she just stepped out of the register and said she didn't feel comfortable h-he-helping her.' Dean articulated each syllable. 'Some freshman kid who was bagging groceries had to do it. My parents don't let me answer the phone anymore or pick up the mail. My aunt lives up in Bergen County and someone sent her pictures of a girl getting autopsied.'

'Jesus.'

'My mom thought maybe we should move, you know? Not sell off, but maybe rent and live somewhere else for a while. But my dad says that I might as well turn myself in and plead guilty. That eventually we'll all know what h-ha-happened.' Dean's voice hitched, even beneath the stutter. 'Then I think – what if it's something . . . that you'd never want to know.' He swallowed hard. 'Are you afraid?'

God. Christ. Ganesh. If Dean West only knew. I blinked, made myself wait before I answered. But when I did, when I said, 'I'm so afraid,' I said it honestly.

* * *

We talked through three refills and two orders of disco fries. After a while, I stopped worrying about who came into the diner. We mostly talked about Chloe, and some of that was hard to hear. She'd been meeting him. Sometimes she'd even been skipping student council meetings to see him.

I didn't think about that too much. I didn't wonder whether some of the afternoons I'd sat in the school library waiting for Chloe, she was actually off somewhere with Dean West. He said she'd seemed distant lately, but that made sense. There were a lot of plans being put into place, after all.

'I never thought of something bad happening in C-C-Colt River,' Dean said at one point.

'That's what everyone's saying,' I told him.

'But doesn't that make you feel better?' Dean asked me. 'It makes me think that Chloe took off. You know, all the p-p-pressure she's under.'

'Everyone's under pressure though, right? What would make Chloe crack and not, say, Kenny Ryden?'

Dean shrugged and cocked his head to the side. 'I don't know. M-maybe we should be looking out for K-K-Kenny Ryden.'

'Why not you? Or me?' Because that's what I'd really meant.

Dean seemed to take that in his stride. 'Because we're from here. Our p-p-parents are from here. If I never left this place . . .' he gestured around the dining room '. . . no one would think twice. Hell, wouldn't yours rather you stuck around? Do you think the Caffreys are c-c-counting on that for Chloe? No – they want her in some university town. It doesn't have to be a big town, right? It just has to have prestige.'

'Well, they're not really Colt River people.' I felt guilty, like I was airing their business. 'The Caffreys moved out here for Cam.'

'Exactly.' Dean announced his need for another refill with a loud slurp. The waitress descended. 'Thank you.' He met her eyes. I noticed Dean West always said thank you. When she came back with a fresh Coke, Dean leaned in to talk softly to me. 'Don't you see that makes it harder for Chloe? Because of C-C-Cam, she's their only shot?'

I really hadn't seen it like that. I wondered what it must feel like to be studied by someone like Dean West. For him to consider you fascinating.

'Where would you go?' I asked. 'If you're going – where would you want to end up?'

'You're going to laugh.'

'I won't laugh.'

'Swear.'

'Sure.'

'The C.I.A.'

I tried really hard not to laugh. In a way, it disappointed me, because I thought, *Jesus, Dean West is just like every other guy who wants to be a secret agent. Now he's going to tell me that if he doesn't make it into the C.I.A, he wants to be a fireman.* 'Good for you,' I said in my best I-believe-in-you voice.

'Yeah, well, I have to sell my dad on it.'

'Because he'd worry about you getting hurt?'

'What?' Dean looked puzzled. 'No, not the CIA, the C.I.A.' The only difference was that he said the letters more slowly the second time. I just looked at him.

'The C-C-C-Culinary Institute of America.' That one took him a little bit because he was so excited.

'Oh.' I thought of the muffins and cookies Dean had left for us. 'Oh! You want to be a cook?'

He smiled to himself. 'I want to be a chef.'

'Because that doesn't start with a k sound?'

He laughed. 'No, because I don't want to work in a diner.' Dean nodded toward the back, where the kitchen was. 'I want to own my own p-p-place some day.' He sat back a little, straighter. 'I want to serve innovative cuisine. And you know, I'd use regional foods. Jersey corn, heirloom tomatoes – we've got the best produce right here and yet you don't really see serious chefs coming out of N.J. The way I figure it, my dad's going to want to sell off most of the farm eventually, but if we keep the house and a couple of the surrounding acres, then my mom and dad could retire there and just keep a few small sustenance crops going. Then I'd always have access to fresh organics. You know, I'd use my contacts around town.' He grinned. 'Like for lamb. I'd essentially put Colt River on a plate.'

It was the longest stretch Dean had gone without stuttering. 'It sounds like you have it all figured out,' I said.

'Well, it's a plan.' Dean splayed his hands on the table like *Who knows?*

'No,' I told him. 'It's a really good plan.'

'What about you, Finn?'

'Oh – I don't know.' What was I supposed to tell him? That I hoped to get in whatever college Chloe did or, barring that, a respectable state college nearby? That I hadn't thought past college. That I hadn't really thought past my triumphant return to *The L. A. Price Show*?

'There has to be something – what's your dream job? What would you do if you could do absolutely anything?'

It might be sick, but right then, I pretty much had my dream job. I got to take care of Chloe. We could hang out for a couple of hours every day if I planned it right, and around town most people knew who I was. Or maybe I'd just graduated from being Bart and Amy's Girl to being Chloe Caffrey's Friend. People stopped to talk to me. I made occasional appearances on nationally syndicated talk shows.

Instead of all that, I put on my best tragic friend voice and said, 'It's just hard to think of the future right now when who knows if Chloe . . .'

'Yeah. Of course.' Dean sagged in the leather diner seat. 'You must think I'm a real bastard.'

'No, not at all.' There was going to be a time when Chloe came home and maybe the three of us would be sitting in this booth or the next one down. We'd all be talking but I'd feel like the outsider. However privileged I felt to hear Dean's secrets or whatever covert operations Chloe and I kept between us, that wouldn't matter so much. That would just be something I used to make myself feel better. 'Chloe would be happy that we were hanging out, that we had each other in the middle of all this mess.'

Lie. And when Dean looked up at me, I could tell that I'd overplayed it, that he knew it was a lie.

'Well, that's what I'd hope, anyway,' I added, aiming for wry, but landing on bitter.

'Chloe's kind of funny that way, huh? I w-w-w-worried that she was embarrassed or something.' Dean looked out the window.

'No, she just holds on to some things for herself. She'd have told me, if it was just about being embarrassed.'

'You didn't know anything?'

I tried to remember what I knew before I knew. Chloe flipping her phone open and closed, over and over. Her random grins.

'I knew she was really happy,' I said. 'You know, at first I helped with the notes. So I knew she thought you were cute and all. And it's Chloe. Who could resist Chloe?'

That didn't make Dean West smile. If anything, he tensed up. 'I keep thinking that she wouldn't just have taken off without saying anything, you know? She'd never want to just disappear from me, no matter how much everything else was pressing down. But then the alternative . . .' His voice faded and caught. 'You're kind of caught between hoping she cared about you and then hoping she didn't, you know what I mean?' We sat in silence for a second, imagining. Then Dean said, 'I figured you'd know what I mean.'

I couldn't say anything. The script dictated I should insist that Chloe would never willingly vanish, but that was tanta-mount to saying, Yeah, dude, they'll probably find your girlfriend dismembered in some parolee's crawl space. And I couldn't be too reassuring either, knowing that Chloe planned to literally come crawling back in two days, after I bricked her in the head. Dean wasn't simple, like people liked to think. He'd put it together. He might never say anything – to anyone – but he'd know.

So I just nodded. I bit my lip and looked up, and Dean looked at me and said, 'You guys are a lot alike. You have the same man-man-mannerisms.'

And I said, 'Not really,' and left it at that. Dean paid up at the register after a supremely awkward conversation about whether or not we should split the bill. I didn't say, 'But this isn't a date.' But I almost did, and I said enough that Dean got it and stammered out something about his dad and then he just stopped walking and turned and said, 'Hey, Finn, I really appreciate you coming out here and meeting me to talk.' He said it loudly enough for the several diners who recognized us and were craning their necks to hear. 'You didn't have to, but it really helped.'

For all the trouble Dean had talking to people, he usually knew exactly what to say. I thought about Chloe's ease moving back and forth between crowds of people at school, how she never seemed out of place. And how at home, alone on the farm, even there she didn't flit around like a moth looking for light. She kind of was the light.

The two of them, Dean and Chloe, would be so easy together. So I wondered what had gotten into her, that she had to go ahead and make this year so hard. My dad had gotten through a good chunk of a Tom Clancy book, waiting for us to finish. He left money on the counter and sidled up to us by the door.

'Dean,' he said.

'Mr. Jacobs.'

'You kids had a lot to talk about. How are you, Dean?'

'Been better, thanks, but you get by.' Dean rocked back on his heels.

And my dad nodded at him. 'I hear you there.'

We walked through the first set of doors together, but Dean stopped in the foyer and stood by the pay phone. It was the first time I'd seen anyone actually move to use the phone – it was in one of those old-fashioned wooden booths, right next to a machine that sold peanuts and one that sold stickers. 'I'm just going to c-c-call my mom and let her know I'm on the way.' I wanted to ask Dean when he'd get his cell phone back, but that was another thing you didn't talk about. I stopped myself just in time. 'Thank you, Finn, for speaking with me.' Dean turned to my dad. 'Thanks sir, for taking the time.'

'Any time.' Dad declared it, like he was handing Dean our land, and not just giving him permission to communicate with us.

Dad and I were in the car all of four seconds before he said, 'Good kid.'

'Yeah.'

'Manners.'

'Yeah.'

'He's had a hard time of it, huh?'

'Lately, yeah. He didn't really talk too much about it.'

'No? You were there for a while. Jack Ryan got through

three missions while you were yakking.'

I asked 'What?' and my dad tapped the cover of his book. 'Oh – sorry,' I said. 'No, he mostly just wanted to talk about Chloe.'

'Poor kid.'

'Yeah.'

'Anything you want to talk about?'

I looked up but my dad was navigating through the parking lot; he wasn't watching me.

'Not really. It's just sad.' And it *was* sad. I wondered if Chloe would ever understand what we were putting Dean through.

Dad turned out of the lot. 'We're just going to make a stop at your grandma's place real quick. I promised your mother.'

If I'd followed my instincts, I would have opened the door and dropped out of the moving truck. Instead, I closed my eyes to concentrate and filled my voice with weariness.

'Dad,' I said, 'I really just want to go home. Lie down, be by myself for while.'

'Yeah, I know, and you can do that in half an hour. But your grandmother's coming back next week and we've hardly been by the place. What's going to happen if another raccoon got in through the chimney?'

I didn't laugh. 'I've been checking in.'

'Your mother and I appreciate that, Finn. It's going to take fifteen minutes.' There wasn't anything to do. Every time he turned on his blinker, the pain in my stomach ratcheted up a notch. *Chloe will see the truck,* I tried to convince myself.

She'd never believe that my dad let me drive his truck. She'd know it was him.

By the time we pulled in the drive, I felt like I was dissolving in the seat.

My legs shook as I got out and headed to the house.

NINETEEN

Dad unlocked the back door, off the kitchen. Following him in, I yelled, 'All right, Dad – what do we have to do?' and hoped Chloe would hear me through the vents.

'All you have to do is calm down.' He opened the fridge door. 'We should have brought over milk and eggs so that your grandmother had them fresh when she got home.'

'Yeah, if you want to kill her with cholesterol.'

'Finn, sometimes you do things for your mother-in-law, because it's like taking vitamins. It's preventive medicine.'

I made myself smile. Dad's making mother-in-law jokes – hilarity ensues. 'I can stop by Donahue's Grocery after school,' I volunteered. 'That way, they'll be super fresh. You can even take credit.'

My dad clapped me on the back. 'That's what I'm talking about.' I tried to trail him without clinging to him. 'The plants look great, kiddo.' He checked the thermostat and headed for the first floor bath. 'Aw, jeez – I hope this faucet hasn't been dripping for ten days.' My belly clenched. 'Huhh.'

'What's up?' I attempted to sound bored.

'These towels are damp,' Dad said. I wanted to yell down the cellar steps: *Jesus Christ, Chloe. You were supposed to stop showering a couple of days ago.*

'Oh – I spilled the watering can,' I explained. 'I just grabbed what I could find. It's okay. It didn't seep into the carpet.' My grandfather shipped home the carpets when he was in the Navy. Nothing could seep into that carpet. Not even feet.

'Finley.' It amazed me that when they were mad, my mom and dad could pronounce my name in the exact same annoying way.

'It was an accident.'

'Well, you don't sop messes up with your grandmother's good hand towels.' Dad stopped in front of the basement door. My ribs started aching from my heart throwing itself against them.

Impatient: 'Now what are you doing?'

'I'm just going to check the basement; we had a heavy rain the other day.'

Whiny: 'Daaa-aaad . . .'

'Finn, give it a rest.' He was irritated now. He flicked on the light at the top of the steps.

Brat: 'Fine.' I stomped down the steps past him. 'I'll do it.' Then I kept stomping, praying he wouldn't follow me.

'I didn't mean for you—'

'You can check the attic. There's spiders up there.'

'Whooooooaaa – spiders. Good heavens.' But I heard his steps cross the floor, then the stairs to the second floor creak.

Chloe was crouched in the corner of the room, by the water heater. She had a blanket wrapped around her, so I could only see her pale hair and paler face. The TV was on mute and the litter strewn in front of it glittered in the light. I crossed over to her with my hand clamped over my own mouth, shaking my head, trying to stop her from saying anything. Her mouth kept opening and closing though, like she wanted to yell.

'SHUT. UP.' I hissed it, but hugged her so she knew I wasn't mad.

She started babbling. 'I would just say you didn't know, that I broke in and you didn't know a thing about it.'

'Like they'd believe that. Shut up.' But I couldn't help asking, 'Why are you showering, anyway? We said you had to be all grimy. What if he'd opened the shower curtain and seen wet tiles?'

'I didn't.' Chloe whispered. She still looked terrified. 'I just washed my hands after I peed.'

'You're crazy,' I said. I put either of my hands on the sides of her head. Pressed my forehead against hers. 'Listen, I gotta go. I'll be back tomorrow. Don't move for at least twenty minutes, okay?'

When she nodded, I felt her face move against mine, her scalp move against my hands. I heard the slam of the attic ladder swinging up, my dad's footsteps clomping overhead. 'No kittens down here!' I called out and started up the steps, waving to the light face in the dark corner.

'Kittens?' Dad called back.

'Yeah, I was hoping. Bella Livingston said she's got a

bunch of barn cats so I was hoping maybe a few snuck in here.'

'That's all we need: a few more animals.' Back in the kitchen, Dad checked the light switches. He steered me out and then locked the door behind him.

Keep it light. Keep it light, I kept telling myself. Out loud, I said, 'We could always use more animals.'

'Yeah? And who's going to care for all these creatures while you're away at your fancypants college?'

'Yeah, yeah, yeah. That's only if I get into a fancypants college.' I stopped and squirmed in my seat. It was funny – I knew Chloe was alive. I knew she sat a couple feet away from us, probably debating whether it was safe to unmute the TV. And still I felt weird talking about the future. I didn't know how people really managed to lose people and then go on with their lives. At least, I didn't know then.

When I went to latch my seat belt, I smelled Chloe's shampoo on my hands.

TWENTY

It was late by the time we finally pulled up our drive and my mom was in the kitchen, stirring something on the stove. I could see through the screens on the back porch and then the glass of the back door. I remembered her critique of my appearance, how I'd been so angry at her, but now it hardly mattered. All that mattered was that Chloe had stayed hidden. We were thirty-six hours from the whole thing being over. I thought about Dean, and wished there was a way to let him know.

My mom looked pretty in the warm kitchen light. She's younger than most moms, about fifteen years younger than Mrs. Caffrey and she looked like a girl, standing there looking out at us. It was easy to see her sitting across from my dad at the diner, blushing while she tried to figure out if she should offer to pay for her food. It felt like Dean said my name differently from anyone else. He said it carefully, and even though it was probably him just concentrating on getting all the sounds out smoothly, it felt gentle.

My mom and dad grew up together, so there probably

wasn't a time when he said 'Amy' and she believed no one had ever pronounced her name with such care. It wasn't the kind of thing I'd ask her anyway. It wasn't the kind of thing I'd ask anyone, except maybe Chloe.

'Something smells good!' Dad bellowed on the way through the porch. He stood behind her and crooked his arm around her neck. She craned her neck to kiss him.

'Uggghhh,' I said. 'Get a room.'

'Heads up, peanut – we have a room. We have a whole house.' Dad started to spoon rice straight into his mouth. 'If your mom and I wanted to have at it right here in the middle of the kitchen, there'd be nothing you could do about it.'

'Bart!' Mom's face flushed. 'What's gotten into you?' She swatted him away.

Dad leaned back against the counter. 'It must have been that hot little hostess, swishing around in front of me. Whoa, Nelly. No one's paid me that much attention since . . . well, I don't know. When was the last time you paid me some attention, honey?'

Mom laughed, and adjusted the heat on the stove. She spooned half the rice into the serving dish.

'He's talking about Teddy Selander's sister,' I said.

'Oooooooh, I heard she's trouble,' Mom said. 'The reverend at St. Luke's warns about her in his sermons.'

'Really?' I tried to picture being so trashy, a minister would preach about me.

'No, I'm kidding. Go set the table.'

'No dinner for me. I just ate a ton of cheese fries. Do

people really talk about her, though? What did you hear?'

'I heard enough. Let's just say she's not famous in a good way. You're going to want to sit down and eat with us – it's paella.'

'It smells terrific, but really I just want to go to bed.'

'Already?' She examined me. 'You okay?'

'Yeah, I'm just beat.'

'Fine. But before you go up, can you just run this over to the Caffreys'?'

'What? No, Mom. I just want to go to my room.'

'Finn. Please. It's rice. It'll dry out if it gets cold.'

'I don't want to go over there.' My voice sounded louder than I meant it to. The party in our kitchen kind of fizzled. My dad went to the cupboard, pulled out two plates.

'Help your mother.' His voice was quiet. He'd switched from frat boy to funeral director. 'It'll take you five minutes.' I zipped my coat back up and Mom handed me the oven mitts.

On my way out, I heard her say to him, 'Well, that was a little bit harsh.'

'I'm tired of the teenage thing,' I heard my dad say. That stung. It's not like I could help the teenage thing.

'Bart, it's a tough time.'

'She needs to realize it's a tough time for other people too . . .' My dad's voice faded behind me. I trudged through the yard with the casserole, arguing with him in my head. Of course it was a tough time for other people – I didn't need to go over the Caffreys' to figure that out. Seeing Dean was enough – if I thought any more about the tough time that

Chloe and I had ushered in, I'd have to hit myself with a piece of wood.

At Chloe's house, Cam was sitting in the kitchen, drawing. A plastic model of a horse stood in the center of the table. It was one of those science models. Half of it looked like a regular horse and then, on the other side, you could see the bands of muscles in some places, the skeletal structure on the other. I knocked on the door and he made the noise that meant you weren't allowed to say a particular word.

'Cam, I'm just knocking.' Way before I even understood what was different about Cam, Chloe taught me to speak to him like anyone else.

'He's smarter than both of us,' I remembered her insisting. She told me, 'Don't use babytalk like he doesn't understand you. He just doesn't know how to connect to you.'

'Cam, this dish is kind of hot.' Nothing. 'Hey, Cam?' And that got the noise again. When I rang the bell, Cam didn't even look up. His pencil never stopped moving across the page.

Mr. Caffrey came scuffing in from his library, calling out, 'One second.' He saw me through the window and asked, 'What's this? Dinner? You tell that mother of yours she doesn't have to do this. We really appreciate it, but—'

'It's paella.'

'Well then,' Mr. Caffrey eked out a sheepish smile. 'Keep it coming.'

'How are you guys?'

Cam blared his noise as I asked it.

Mr. Caffrey blinked, then lowered his voice. 'It's *guys*.'

Cam blared. 'It's been a rough couple of days around here. We shifted some routines and sometimes that causes trouble.'

I nodded. 'Mom said to eat it while it's hot, because it might dry out otherwise.'

'We'll do that, thank you.' Another blare. Mr. Caffrey shut his eyes for a second and rubbed his temples.

'Okay then.' Cam's horse had one eye and one empty socket.

'Thanks again.' One last blast from the Cam alarm and I backed out the door. The windows on the second floor sat dark and I wondered if Mrs. Caffrey was lying down in her room. Maybe she had gone into Chloe's. In the kitchen, Mr. Caffrey leaned over Cam's drawing, pointing out parts.

My mom and dad had sat down at the dining room table and left a plate set there for me. I started to shake my head, but Mom spoke before I could. 'We just wanted you to feel welcome – it's fine if you'd rather rest.' She looked toward my dad and he looked at me, then nodded.

'Thank you.' I paused, half-expecting to hear Cam's odd blurt. 'I'm going to just head upstairs.' All that was left of their dinnertime conversation was the sound of their forks and knives sliding across the plates. It was like the sadness from the Caffreys' house had spread.

Once I closed my bedroom door, I felt restless. I wasn't tired so much as I was tired of performing. I checked my email, just in case Dean had tried to get in touch. There wasn't anything, but the cops probably had his laptop too. Word had apparently reached the masses about the diplomatic breakthrough of me and Dean meeting over cheese fries, because it looked like someone had just dumped the names of the most obnoxious girls from school in my inbox. I just checked them all and hit delete. I even emptied my trash folder right after so that I couldn't go back and read them later.

Probably some were sent right after last night's Lila Ann Price broadcast, but even that didn't matter. What was anyone going to say? I didn't have anything left to say back. Besides, in two days Chloe would be back and then that would be total chaos. The whole planet would be reaching out to us. I had to make sure there was space.

When we had first started planning, we made lists for everything. Food to pack, sparse clues to be left behind. In the week before, we'd had to-do lists two pages long. It's how we dealt with stress – we felt more brave once we'd made back-up plans for all the things that could go wrong. And then one of the last things on our to-do list was to burn all our to-do lists.

With thirty hours left, my fingers were actually cramping – I wanted so desperately to sit at my desk and write down the dozens of things we needed to remember. Chloe and I had promised each other though, and those rules had gotten us this far. Really close. So I wouldn't even let myself catalog the tasks we needed to complete out loud to myself just in case my parents came upstairs and stood outside my bedroom door. But I thought them. I burrowed under the covers and tried to keep track by counting on my fingers.

1) Trash.
2) Chloe's shirt in the woods.

3) Take down the towels we'd stretched across the two basement windows.

4) Make sure we left Grandma's TV on channel 7 and a taped recording of *Days of Our Lives* in the VCR.

5) Check the bathroom, carefully. Bring a towel in case you need to dry off the shower or the faucets.

6) Put back in the old roll of toilet paper. (We'd taken it out in case my grandmother remembered how much was left.)

7) Take the roll Chloe had used in my backpack.

And also I had to hit Chloe, hard. That was the one I kept going back to in my head. I'd have to take her into the woods, and then hit her really hard.

Then I'd have to leave her to find her own way home.

TWENTY-ONE

The alarm on my phone rang at three-thirty in the morning, and I silenced it on the first ring. I almost groaned, but then remembered to be quiet and carry my shoes downstairs. I felt bad for just walking past the stables, for not checking on the horses or the sheep or Chauncey. My dad had taken up a lot of that slack lately and that comment about too many animals had been the first time he'd mentioned it. With Dad, things had a way of percolating. He had said it once now, so there would be more coming.

It was dark outside but I saved the penlight for the woods. And even then, I used it sparingly – the last thing I needed was some cop to follow me to my grandmother's house. At some point in the past week, I had stopped worrying about the vague assailants that Stranger Patrol and McGruff the Crime Dog had taught us about when we were little kids. I'd become more worried about cops than robbers. And really, most of the time, since Chloe left, I would have welcomed some crazy coming out of the brush to snatch me up. Not some pervert or anything. But someone who would hide me until I gathered my strength and fought him off. And then it would be like I'd rose from the dead. Like it would be for Chloe.

I let myself into my grandmother's house. I felt my way to the cellar stairs so that crazy Bella Livingston didn't see a light on and come snooping around. Chloe didn't call out even when I eased my way down the steps. For a second, I saw her stretched out across the sofa and thought, *She's dead.* And I didn't even think about it in terms of never seeing her again or lying on our backs in the field behind our houses. I just thought, *There's no way out of this, now* and inched closer to her on my knees. When I saw her chest rising, falling, relief lapped over me and I thought, *This is a tenth of what it will be like when Mrs. Caffrey sees her tomorrow.* I tried to imagine what Dean would say to her, the first time he saw her again. I wondered how he would say her name.

Chloe still had her hair braided. I remembered being so angry earlier, realizing she'd lied to me about the shower. Sure enough, when I touched it, in the back, behind her neck, it was damp. The sides, the feathery parts right near her temples, were really soft, like silk threads.

I don't like remembering what happened next. I mean, it was confusing, for one thing. It felt like me, kneeling there, and also not me. I'd been so stressed out all week, and even the weeks before, really. Everything had gotten so complicated. I was thinking about how happy everyone would feel when Chloe came home, and how I felt happy to just see her eyes flickering under her lids and know she was okay. She was dreaming. The strands of hair tucked behind her ear felt so soft. So I'd just reached out my hand, to brush the soft piece of her hair with my fingers. Like you rub a rabbit's foot – for reassurance maybe. Chloe woke up and she didn't even move at first. Her eyes widened and she grabbed my wrist.

Chloe had just woken up; she didn't know it was me, and that scared her. But when she reached for me, I thought that she felt happy too. The whole thing was almost over and we'd executed it. Ourselves. Together.

I just reacted and it must have seemed to her that my hands held her down. Chloe had grabbed my wrist and it seemed like she was trying to hold my hand against her face. Maybe she moved to sit up, but I thought she leaned up into me. I thought she was craning her neck toward me. She never screamed or shoved me away or anything like that. She must have just been struggling to sit up but I'd tried to check on her, so my body was crouched over her body. And then, I guess it was like some instinct misfired. I'd never kissed anyone before. I remember thinking that her lips were as soft as her hair.

Chloe would say that she screamed and that I covered her mouth with my hand. We needed to be quiet in the basement. That's all. We had said that. She bit my hand, hard, and I didn't cry out even then. She kept yelling, 'Are you crazy?' I remember that was what she yelled first because I felt crazy. I almost told her yes because in those seconds, everything had seemed so sure. And then nothing was.

She'd stood up and she held her hand to her lips, like I had been the one to bite her. 'What are you doing?' Everything she said, she said so ugly. She didn't sound like herself at all.

She tried to tell me to get out, but it's not like I had any place to go. She wouldn't sit down on the couch and calm down. She wouldn't sit anywhere near me. She kept saying, 'Finn – what the hell?' She walked toward the stairs and I thought, *She's just going to walk upstairs and leave. She'll flag down a car. She'll go home.* But then she pivoted and almost rushed at me, asking questions. It wasn't even two days after I had told Lila Ann Price, 'Chloe and I – we can talk to each other about anything.' But that wasn't true anymore. She asked me again, 'What the hell?'

And I said, 'What do you mean?' And she just shook her head and kept pacing.

After a while, she just faded. She sat in the corner with her arms clasped around her knees and wouldn't really look at me. I tried to find something to offer up and finally told her that I'd seen Cam, that he'd been drawing a horse with her dad.

'Cam probably hasn't realized I'm gone,' she said blankly. She was like Chloe, but with the lights out.

'When I came down the steps, it was scary because you didn't say anything,' I explained. 'Usually you'd call out to me or something. So I thought something had happened, I mean that you'd been hurt or sick.'

'I don't really care what you thought.' But as coldly as she said it, she stood up then and said, 'Before I fell asleep, I was trying to figure out all the things we had to remember.'

'I did the exact same thing!' But it rang out fake.

Chloe kept going as if I hadn't said anything at all. 'You should take back your sleeping bag on this trip. There's also still a lot of trash here.' She picked up a packed yellow plastic bag. 'I think this is all of it but maybe if you could just check around . . . that way we'll have a second set of eyes.'

We just started knocking things off the checklist, working side-by-side like usual. Each time one of us completed a task, the tension in the room dissolved a little bit more. I almost didn't leave on time – I figured that if I stayed a little bit longer, eventually we'd have to go back to normal. But we had one more day. If my parents woke up and found me missing, the whole thing would unravel pretty quickly. I packed up the trash, looped my hand under the cord of the sleeping bag. I tried to tell Chloe that I was sorry – that the whole thing was just a weird short circuit and everything would be fine, but she just said, 'Let's leave it alone. It was a strange moment; this is a strange time.'

And I said, 'Great,' but didn't feel relieved. 'I should be back here tonight at two?'

'That should give us enough time. But listen – I think we should just meet in the woods.'

'Can you handle that?' I asked. In response, Chloe glared at me. 'No – I'm serious. It's probably going to be nuts tomorrow. You're taking your first steps outside of this basement.' Her eyes rolled. 'Don't underestimate that. You might get disoriented. It's not like you'll have a cell phone to call me if you need backup.'

'I'll be okay,' she said to me. 'And if I'm not, it's better if I'm on my own.' I let that sit for a second and tried not to let it sting. But then Chloe kept going. 'If someone sees me, if they find me – I'll just say I had a copy of your key made. I'll tell them that you never knew I was here.'

Nobody would ever buy that. But that didn't erase the fact that Chloe had thought of it. It felt like a gift she'd wrapped for me. When I left the basement, I remembered, *This is the last time that we'll exist in this hidden corner of the world together.* Even then, I thought that we'd be closer than ever because of the secret between us.

The next time I came down to my grandmother's basement, it would just be my grandmother's basement – damp and smelling like newsprint and jars of homemade jam. When Chloe called out, 'Wait!' I thought she had realized it too. But she held the wooden shelf in her hand.

'No way,' I said. It wasn't like we had just veered in a weird direction anymore. We'd derailed. Into a foreign country whose name neither of us could even pronounce.

Chloe just shook her head. 'It's not a big deal. We said we'd do this yesterday.' Meaning: before. I wondered if everything from now on would be split like that. She sighed. 'Could you please just take it?' I just stood there, dumbly. 'We'll figure out what to do later on.'

I lifted it out of her hands and tried to fit it under my arm. Balanced everything carefully and then tried to take one of the stairs. The shelf slid and clunked down. Chloe's giggles started slowly and built up into a full fit. 'It's not funny!' I told her. I was tired of trying to balance everything, trying to say the right things and keep all the stories straight.

'Oh come on,' Chloe said. 'You should see what you look like. You've got the sleeping bag in one arm and then the backpack full of wrappers and cans and now a big wooden beam. You look like some crazy homicidal camper.'

I laughed, relieved that Chloe could still make jokes, could still find me funny. 'I can't take this,' I said and lifted the shelf a little ways off the floor. I meant the shelf, but I meant other things too.

Chloe shook her head. 'I guess not. Besides, where would you stash it from Bart and Amy?' I used to think it was funny when Chloe called my mom and dad by their first names. But she was living in a basement, while my mom cooked for their family and kept her mom doped up. Maybe that deserved a little respect. She came forward and picked up the wood.

'Thanks,' I said.

'No, it was a stupid idea. If someone saw you with it, they'd ask all kinds of questions.'

I wondered if other people ever felt like this talking to Chloe, like they were diffusing a bomb. Tugging one wire was harmless, but if they said the wrong thing, if they snipped the wrong line, then the whole thing would explode.

'Do you want me to bring food tonight, so that you can have a real meal? Before . . .' I meant before the absolute chaos that would be her return.

'I think it's better if I get myself good and hungry,' Chloe said. 'Could you imagine if you called the cops and my breath smelled like cheese steak?'

I still couldn't imagine calling the cops at all. 'It's going to be a rough few days,' I said. I meant: *We have to stick together on this.*

Chloe always heard both the things I did and didn't say.

'It's going to be fine,' she told me, saying it with enough certainty in her voice that it felt okay to keep walking up the steps, to step out into the sunrise, and go back to one more day of acting like the saddest seventeen-year-old girl in Colt River. At that moment, though, I might have qualified as the most desperate.

It was almost six a.m. and there was no way my dad hadn't woken up yet. The one saving grace was that it was Columbus Day. We had it off and the neighborhood had the sleepy feel of a bank holiday. I forced myself to walk the couple of blocks through my grandma's little development slowly, deliberately. I'd gone past maybe five houses when I noticed a white van creeping up the street behind me. The closer it got, the harder it was for me to breathe, to swallow. I thought *that's it*, trying out all the cop show phrases in my head: *sting operation, perp, I've been tailed*. And when I heard the thump behind me, I just about dropped to the ground, waving my hands in the air. I turned, and it was just the newspaper, packed in plastic. The yellow bundles dotted the driveways along the street, but it didn't even occur to me then to steal one. For the first time in a week, I didn't care whether or not Chloe was in the paper.

I hit the woods sprinting and tried to outrun the flashes of Chloe and me on the sofa. By the time I reached the edge of our property, my parents' bathroom window was lit up, but I'd pretty much expected that.

I gambled. I figured that Dad hadn't been downstairs yet, so I'd just get to work in the barn. I gave the sheep their grain first, because otherwise they'd make a racket and tip off my dad, time-wise. I stashed the backpack and sleeping bag beneath some old leather saddles we rarely used anymore, then poured some dry food into Chauncey's bowl and led the horses out to the west pasture. I carried bales of hay over there in case the grass was too sparse. After the sheep ate, I turned them out to the paddock and started in on the barn. I got the foul straw piled into a wheelbarrow and took it over to spread over the dead spot in my mom's garden. Then I spread new straw over the wooden planks of the barn's floor and tossed in some pine shavings.

I'd started on the water pails next and was uncoiling the hose when I heard my dad call in, 'What is this?'

I made myself busy. I was tired of looking my mom and dad in the eye while I lied.

'Just figured I'd get an early start,' I explained.

'I'll say.' My dad blew over his cup of coffee. 'You want some help with the heavy lifting?'

'Heavy lifting's already done,' I told him.

'That's my girl.' I felt him tousle my hair. 'How about I go in and get some breakfast going? We'll do it up . . . eggs and sausage, cornbread . . .'

I thought of Chloe getting herself good and hungry. 'Nah – I'll just grab a bowl of cereal or something.'

'Well, I'm going in to make a real breakfast. If you smell something good, you should just grab a plate.' But I was busy thinking to myself, *Tomorrow we probably wouldn't eat breakfast. I'd run out to meet Chloe in the fields behind my house, dragging her, and screaming. The cops would be out here in seconds. We'll probably call the rescue squad. Then the press conference. Maybe we'd have to do some interviews.*

By the time I sat down on the porch steps, my arms ached and my hands were raw and red – blisters threatened to bloom on my palms. But the animals seemed content as they milled around. I led the horses back to their stalls and they kicked up, whinnied at the fresh hay. It was almost done. That's really all I kept thinking. I leaned back on my elbows, and tried to pretend the dry leaves under me were grains of white sand. Instead of the low murmur of the sheep mingling around, I made myself hear ocean waves crest and break against an imaginary shore. But it wasn't really working – I'd hear my dad slam a pan on the range or the radio go loud. Somewhere from up in the house, I heard my mom's blow dryer whir on, eventually click off.

It felt like nap time – I figured on resting up, so that later on I'd be careful and alert. I dodged Dad and his full skillet and went upstairs to run a bath. I sat there until my fingertips pruned and then afterwards shut myself up in my room. The sheets felt cool against my warm body. The pain in my back and shoulders reassured me; it felt good to ache from pure, hard work. It didn't stop me from worrying about what had gone on with Chloe and me, but I only replayed the worst moments nine or ten times before falling asleep.

I'd set my phone to ring at noon, but then slept through it, so it wasn't until two in the afternoon that I finally rolled myself out of bed and found fresh clothes. I checked my email, but no one particularly exciting had written me. I wondered what Chloe was doing, how she was getting ready. Downstairs, Dad watched football and Mom sat on the window seat in the den, reading a paperback. The day seemed so normal, a little bit subdued. If Chloe had really been abducted, then this would have been the first day that it seemed a little bit like my family was getting back to normal. It hurt me a little, for Chloe's sake. She'd practically grown up here and it took us about a week to adjust ourselves to her absence.

And then another part of me . . . I don't know . . . my parents were mine. We moved around the house quietly and gratefully. Before all this, once in a while, especially when I was mad at them, I'd pretend to be Mr. and Mrs. Caffrey's second daughter. My parents were stricter about most things and they talked mostly about the money they worried about spending and what Colt River had changed into. The Caffreys talked about books and took us into the city to visit galleries, to see shows. The one thing they were strict about was schoolwork and grades, but Chloe and I never had much trouble with that anyway. Except for Advanced Bio, when Chloe and I both tanked the first test. Mr. Caffrey went in for a meeting with a list of ways that he felt Dr. Bryson could adjust his teaching. He even met with the principal. The Caffreys hired a tutor and Chloe ended up with an A-. My parents had me drop down to regular biology.

Right then, my dad looked pretty snug under a plaid wool blanket watching his Jets get their asses handed to them. He might never have gone to see the principal for the sake of my grades, but he'd kept me safe in a warm house. He'd raised an obedient girl, a good girl. A normal, uncomplicated girl who knew how to work hard and be kind. I would give anything to make sure he never thought anything different.

Around four, my mom came into the den and sat down on the rocker. 'I was just going to go check on things next door. You want to come?'

It might have looked strange if I didn't. I ran upstairs to grab my jacket and snuck a peek out my window to Chloe's bedroom across the way. The curtains were closed. Downstairs, Mom had packed up a bunch of those earth-friendly grocery bags with some tupperwares of food. Mostly casseroles, but there was a loaf of her homemade bread there and a whole bag jammed with rolls of paper towel and toilet paper. I understood that they were a mess and all and that it was partly my fault, but still it seemed to me like Mr. or Mrs. Caffrey could probably have purchased their own toilet paper. But Mom shrugged when she saw me looking in the bag. 'One less thing for them to worry about,' she said.

My parents probably expected that I'd grow up to be a good person because they were. They probably never even imagined that I could construct an elaborate, diabolical scheme and lie, almost constantly, for weeks on end. I mean, who thinks that about their kid?

If our house felt warm and cozy, then Chloe's felt stifling. It seriously seemed like the thermostat had been jacked up to eighty. My mom knocked on our way in, called out, 'Brian? Sheila? We're here.' I wondered if I'd go back to doing that when Chloe came home. It seemed doubtful.

Mr. Caffrey appeared in the doorway. 'Ah, the Jacobs women!' he said. 'A sight to behold!' For a second, I wondered if he was a little drunk, but decided it was more that he was trying to act happy and jovial.

My mom could compete in jovial. 'Well, we brought some goodies!' She tipped her head a little and flashed a smile. She looked like a lady in a paper towel commercial. She unzipped her coat and I groaned inside. That meant we'd be staying awhile. 'Is something up with your radiator, Bri?'

'No, no — we just needed some tropical weather, we decided.'

My mom looked at him, mystified. After we set down all the bags and dumped the tupperware into the fridge, we followed Mr. Caffrey into the great room. The Caffreys called their living room 'the great room' because it was so big. Or, my dad liked to joke, because it was so expensive. Everything in it was huge — huge sofa, wide beams in the ceilings. Tall windows and this enormous stone fireplace that takes up a good share of one whole wall. Like when the settlers first founded Colt River, I bet that fireplace would have taken care of the entire town. Mrs. Caffrey usually referred to it as the hearth. I guessed if you had a fireplace large enough to fit a human being on a rotisserie, you were allowed to call it whatever you'd like.

Cam had constructed a tee-pee in front of the fireplace. It was the canvas kind that you can buy at toy stores. A dozen horse models stood in a row along the firehouse bricks. That wasn't so weird, but Cam was sitting in front of the whole collection in his swimming trunks.

'What's going on there, Cam?' my mom asked in her soothing voice. He shifted his eyes to her briefly.

'We just felt strongly that it was a bathing suit kind of

day.' Mr. Caffrey said it like they'd voted on it or something. Obviously, Cam had been the main lobbyist. Mr. Caffrey had on shorts and a T-shirt and sweat beaded his forehead. It had collected on his upper lip. 'It's pretty warm in here, huh?' he asked my mom a little sheepishly.

'It's definitely toasty,' she replied. Cam sat there, arranging the horses in various order across the stone fireplace. 'Where's Sheila?'

'Oh, she's just resting.' He sounded a little lost, as if he'd been telling himself that all day.

Mom brushed off her hands and reached out like she was going to tousle Cam's hair, then changed her mind. 'Why don't I go up and see if she'll come down to visit with us?'

Mr. Caffrey actually looked relieved. 'I'm sure she'd love to see you, Amy. We're so grateful.'

'Don't say another word.' Mom started up the wide, wooden steps. 'Sheila, it's Amy – I'm coming up.'

I watched Mr. Caffrey watch my mom ascend their staircase, her hands on the carved banister. It occurred to me that he liked my mother, probably more than he was supposed to. Maybe he'd begun to appreciate her cooking or how kind she was to Cam, but probably it had to do with the fact that my mom was so capable. I remembered what Chloe had said, that I didn't know everything about her family. Anyway, it was weird to see her dad look at my mom like that. Especially since I'd always suspected Mr. Caffrey looked down on my parents. Oh, he'd drink a beer on the porch with my dad all right. But when he'd take Chloe and me to the city, Mr.

Caffrey would talk to me about art or theater or books in a tone of voice that told me he thought it was a real shame I didn't already know about them.

He never called it charity, but that's how he meant it. But for all her stupid art history courses and the thick books with weird titles on her bookshelf, Mrs. Caffrey had turned out to be pretty brittle. I remembered how she had lashed out at me, my mom, even Lila Ann Price. I couldn't imagine that Mr. Caffrey hadn't felt those fangs too. And now it was his turn to feel grateful.

Standing there in the great room, I felt a little bit like Santa on December 24th. I knew that early the next morning, Mr. Caffrey would tumble down the stairs, trying to adjust his eyes to the lights. He'd find me struggling through our back field, tugging along Chloe. Maybe Mrs. Caffrey would be like Sleeping Beauty – she'd come floating down to the back porch and the color would flush back into her cheeks. Cam would take a break from lining up his horses over and over again, because all the people in the house would be safe and accounted for. I almost couldn't take it – I wanted to say: *It's going to be okay.* Or *Just a few more hours – hold on for just a few more hours.*

Instead I said, 'I should really go back home and get to work on my homework.' Mr. Caffrey looked startled, like he'd just remembered I was still in the room.

'Sure thing, Finn. Thanks again for all the help.' Cam blurted his alarm sound and I smiled at Mr. Caffrey. 'What can you do?' he asked, bending down to gently squeeze Cam's shoulder. He wasn't a bad guy, Mr. Caffrey. I felt crappy for thinking he was actually a better guy after he lost his daughter.

I got back to our house and checked my phone but there weren't any missed calls, just a bunch of texts from people I didn't want to talk to anyway. I tried to start homework, but it seemed pointless – it's not like I would actually be going to school the next day. I looked around in my closet because I figured that there would probably be cameras around. At one point, I saw the red lights of a squad car pull into the Caffreys' drive. They didn't use the siren, though, and it had become almost normal for a policeman to stop by and give Mr. and Mrs. Caffrey an update. I talked myself out of panicking and running downstairs and confessing from the back porch. I played computer Scrabble for a while. I heard my mom come in at around six or seven. When I went to check out the window again, the squad car had gone.

It was the knock on the door that shocked me. It was my mom's face, the shaky tone of her voice. She asked me to come downstairs. She didn't say, 'Finley,' so I knew I wasn't in trouble, but when she said, 'Finn, your father and I need to talk with you about something, please,' there was obviously something wrong. She'd been crying, for one. And Dad stood at the bottom of the steps waiting for us. He wasn't even in a chair. Mom looked down at him and murmured, 'Bart – turn it off.'

'Turn off what?' I asked. Dad stepped toward the den, and reached for the remote. 'What is it?' I was asking my mom, but I'd already brushed past her. On the television, they had Dean's school picture back up. I asked, 'Is he dead? Did

someone hurt him?' But the TV cut to footage of police officers leading Dean out of his house. His hands hung cuffed in
front of him and his mom ran alongside, trying to hold a
jacket over his face. From each side of the walkway up to the
Wests' house, a throng of people leaned in toward Dean, the
cops, and Dean's mom. It was like they were trying to get a
better glimpse of the sad parade.

'Dean's great-grandfather was born in that house.' My
voice was hollow. Everything felt hollow.

The woman sitting at the news desk looked satisfied with
herself. 'Tragic new developments in the case of missing New
Jersey teen, Chloe Marie Caffrey. Local police have charged a
classmate of Miss Caffrey's, eighteen-year-old Dean West,
with her murder. The Caffrey family issued a brief statement
thanking the community for their thoughts and prayers and
requesting privacy during this difficult time. Police are still
combing the area for the remains of the popular A grade
student. They urge anyone with any information to come
forward.' The camera cut to a uniformed man in a mustache,
but my dad had regained his motor skills by then. He shut
the TV off.

Nobody said anything for the longest time. I guess my
parents were trying to figure out what to say. I was, anyway.
It even ran through my head that it was a trap – somehow our
parents had figured it out and rigged up an elaborate trap to see
if Chloe and I would come forward. But my mom's streaked
face was as real as Mrs. West's agonized face on the TV.

Finally I asked, 'Why do they think she's dead?' My mom
shook her head.

'I don't know. From what the police officer told Mr. and Mrs. Caffrey . . .' My mom looked helplessly at my dad and started again. 'It sounded like they might have a confession.' She paused again, swallowed. 'Or some kind of evidence.'

'Dean didn't do this,' I said. Mom shut her eyes, rubbed the bridge of her nose.

Dad spoke up and said, 'That's not for us to say, Finn.'

'But you just met him – you called him a good—'

Mom spoke up then, enunciating each word clearly. 'As a family, we do not have an opinion. Our concern is supporting the Caffreys.' I opened my mouth to argue, but my mom spoke again. 'I know you cared for this boy, Finn, but the fact is that police don't arrest innocent people for no reason. The truth might turn out to be slightly more complicated, but he's obviously involved.'

Dad was studying my reaction, so I tried to compose my face – but at the same time I kept seeing Dean being propelled across his lawn. He'd looked so resigned. And then the jacket going up to shroud him . . .

'Finn,' my dad spoke carefully. 'You realize what this means for Chloe?'

Our script could go to hell. 'She's not dead. I don't care what they say.' We'd planned to meet that night in the woods. 'Where do they think she is?'

My mom studied her fingernails. 'The officer indicated to the Caffreys that they'd be focusing in the area behind the high school.' So at least that was clear.

'It's not true.'

'It's hard to believe any of it.'

'Why do they think he hurt her?' The pictures of Chloe, the notes between them – he must have explained those because they released him the first time. I racked my brain, trying to pinpoint anything that had changed. 'Is it because we met at the diner?'

'No, sweetheart.' Mom put her hand on my arm. It felt cold and clammy. 'You can't let yourself feel guilty for that – you were trying to do a kind thing. And the Caffreys will understand that. I'm sorry for making it seem like we should hide that.'

'I don't care what the Caffreys think about me. I'm telling you Dean didn't do anything wrong—'

'They found some of Chloe's clothing, Finn. He had some of her clothing.' Dad looked surprised at his own angry voice. He looked at my mom and said, 'I'm sorry, but I think she should know what we're dealing with here.' And then back to me, 'It's perfectly natural to have a tough time accepting this. It's a terrible thing. But you just can't ignore reality either. We're going to face this and we'll get through this.'

I forced myself to nod. 'May I go back upstairs, please? I just really want to be alone.' Dad's eyes shifted toward Mom's.

She answered, 'Go ahead.' I backed toward the steps. I felt like a cornered animal. 'We'll be right down here, if you need anything. At some point, I might go to check in on Brian and Sheila, but then Daddy will be here.'

'Are there going to be reporters all over the place?' At least the dread in my voice was real. I still had to get to the woods to bring home Chloe.

My mom shook her head. 'They've planned a press conference for tomorrow afternoon. And they've set up a blockade down at the bottom of our road. The police have been very kind in recognizing we'd all need some time to ourselves – the Caffreys especially. But I imagine that tomorrow it'll be pretty busy around here.'

Upstairs, I sat on my bed and tried to make sense of it. I lay back, pulled the covers up around me, and tried to fall back asleep. All I wanted to do was wake up and find out that none of it had happened. Chloe would be asleep under the window across from mine. Maybe we'd stayed up all night watching movies or working on some project for school. We'd crawl back out of bed, have Sunday supper with our folks, and then watch movies on our computers or something. We'd talk about being famous someday, but we'd mean later, after we'd grown up and did something to earn it.

With my head under my comforter, that other life seemed so perfect. It seemed inconceivable that I had ever decided it was somehow not enough. But the truth is, I don't know if it was me who decided that. I think I was the one who just followed along.

I wondered what they were doing to Dean, if his mom had gone to the police station with him, if they'd let him call a lawyer right away. In the movies, cops beat people during interrogations, but I didn't know if that happened in real life. At least in Colt River, where Dean's mom and the cop's wife probably sang in the church choir together or the cop once coached Dean in Little League or something, odds were that they'd treat him okay. When my mom knocked on my door, I was crying, and that was probably a good thing. She didn't have to know that I was crying for Dean West and what Chloe and I had done to him.

'Honeybear . . .' She hadn't called me that since I was really little. 'I'm going next door for just a little bit.'

'Okay.' It was hard to breathe – I was gasping and hiccupping.

'Would you like to come with me?'

'No thank you.'

'I think it would really mean a lot to Mr. and Mrs. Caffrey, just to see you. They're worried about you.'

Probably I was the last person the Caffreys were worried about. 'I'm not ready to do that,' I said. No human being could actually do that. I didn't care what Chloe said about making sure we didn't act suspiciously and acting like I really believed she was gone too. I was not going to sit there while her parents planned her funeral or tried to explain death to Cam when I knew she'd be back before the quart of milk in their fridge ran out. 'Please.' I was openly begging my mom now. 'I just want to be alone right now.'

'I just don't know that you should be.'

'Can I bring Chauncey up here?'

'What?' Chauncey usually slept outside or, in the winter, the kitchen. But there were some nights – when I had the chicken pox, the night of my grandfather's funeral – that my mom let me lead him upstairs to my room. 'Okay. Yeah, you can bring Chauncey up. But, Finn, you need to be around people, too.'

'I know. But I'm just not ready yet.' I almost said, *Give me a few hours. I'll be ready at, oh, maybe four in the morning.* 'Please?'

'Well, okay.' I climbed out of bed and followed her down the stairs. She stopped halfway down. 'Have you eaten anything today?' I just gave her dead eyes. 'All right, but when I come back we'll sit down together, I'll make French toast. Or have a bowl of cereal or something.'

Dad was staring out the window toward the Caffrey house. He spun when Mom and I came down the steps and looked embarrassed to be caught. 'You guys are going over?'

'I am.' Mom wound a scarf around her neck. 'Finn's just going out to grab Chauncey.'

'Ahh. Well, he'll be pleased. I've got a busy bone you can give him.'

'Thanks.' We all just stood in the middle of the living room, though. No one seemed to understand how to move.

Then Dad said, 'I was just thinking about that Margaret Cook girl.' He might as well have kicked me in the chest. 'Chloe followed that story so closely. Remember how happy we all were when the newspapers said that girl had returned home?' For one excruciating second, I thought my dad was going to cry.

Mom smiled. 'She was so preoccupied with that story.'

'Chloe was always like that about news stories, though,' I said. 'It wasn't just Margaret Cook.'

'Oh.' Dad shrugged and smiled. 'I guess it just crossed my mind because of what is going on.'

'Oh, sweetheart.' Mom hugged him and then said, 'Call

over if you need me. Either of you.' She grabbed her purse and headed out the back door.

I didn't want to follow her out the back and have the Caffreys see me go into the barn instead. I sat down on the edge of the sofa and Dad came over and put his hand on the top of my head.

'So, we're bringing out the big guns, right?' he said. 'Chauncey's coming inside?'

'Is that okay? I'll clean up after him and everything.'

'Of course it's okay. He's been pretty excited about that freshly swept stable, though. You might have to drag him out fighting.'

It felt like I cleaned out the barns years ago. 'Yeah, but fresh hay's nothing compared to a bed with two quilts and a bunch of pillows.' That came out too light, too jokey. I shoved my hands in my pockets and looked down at my socks. Dad tousled my hair again.

'Well, I'll leave the busy bones on the counter. You should fill up a water dish before you bring him up, too. I don't want him drinking out of the toilets.'

'Okay.'

'You're just going to be up in your room? We could watch a movie in the den. I could fix you something . . .'

'No, it's okay. I just really want to be in my room right now, by myself.' I got halfway to the kitchen and then turned back. Dad was back to staring out the window, looking so baffled.

'I'm sorry,' I said.

'Oh, it's fine. I'll just be puttering around here if you need anything.'

I filled one of Chauncey's big metal bowls with water and laid a couple of towels over my bedspread in case he had muddy paws. When I got outside he was lying on the porch steps, basking in a patch of light. He lifted his head and thumped his tail against the weathered wood. If someone came to arrest me right now, maybe they'd notice how much Chauncey loved me. They'd think, *She can't possibly have done this terrible thing – she's so good with animals.* You always read in books how serial killers often started off abusing animals. They shot squirrels or pets started disappearing from the neighborhood. There had to be some kind of opposite rule – people who grew up caring for animals ended up more charitable or something. Maybe I was just the exception to that rule.

TWENTY-TWO

Chauncey knew something was up, because he mouthed my arm the whole way into the house. He wasn't biting, he just kept his big retriever's jaw softly closed around my forearm as we walked back to the house. It's sort of his way of holding hands. In the house, he got excited and I let him sniff around the kitchen and check in with my dad in the living room before I bribed him upstairs with a bone.

One year, when Chloe and I were racing each other to win the community service award, I suggested we train Chauncey to be a therapy dog. We'd take him to hospitals and retirement homes to visit with the patients. He had to get special shots and go through even more obedience training. And then when we were finally ready, I groomed him and tied a jaunty little kerchief around his neck and everything. Mom and I got him in the car and through the hospital lobby – only to have him pee as soon as the elevator started climbing. We tried three different times, and each time he peed in the elevator.

He was a good dog, though; he hopped right up on the

foot of the bed and gazed expectantly at me, waiting for his busy bone. Chauncey wasn't like most dogs – he didn't snap or bite. I could even reach in and steal his bone back and he'd just look at me like he wanted to say, *Excuse me, but I'd like to chomp down on that again, please.* I spent the next couple of hours lying on my bed, listening to the dog smack his lips and occasionally rubbing his belly. I dozed and woke. He dozed and woke. It helped because I didn't have to be alone, but I also didn't have to worry about reacting the right way in front of Chauncey.

I lay there, stretched out on my bed, petting and petting, waiting to calm down. I'd meet Chloe in the woods and explain to her what happened. Chances were she'd been watching TV all day and knew everything that had unfolded.

I'd find her and we would walk back to the houses together. We would wake up all our parents and explain what we had done. It would be awful – so awful that I really couldn't even imagine how they would look at us, but they would have to go with us to the police station. The police would sit us in separate interrogation rooms and make us explain, in detail, exactly what we'd done.

It would be worse for me, I knew. Everyone would be overjoyed to see Chloe, in spite of themselves. They'd be angry at her, but they'd also be so thankful she was home safe. Her parents would have to pay a lot of money probably, for the cost of all the hours spent searching for her, but it wasn't like they didn't have it to spend.

I didn't know what they would do to me. They'd charge me with something. Probably interfering in an investigation.

But the town, our parents, Dean West . . . it would be worse for me because I did all the lying. Chloe dismounted her horse, turned him around, and then sent him back in the direction of our stables. Then she hid in a basement for almost eight days. She lied by omission.

I'd watched the whole town comb the woods. I'd helped staple up flyers. I'd let them drag the lake, and I'd said nothing. I'd toured Lila Ann Price through Chloe's bedroom. I'd watched them lead Dean away. Twice. And I'd said nothing.

Chauncey looked up at me with his wet, trusting eyes. I kept petting and he rolled over, kicked his legs a little, and gave me his belly to rub. His tail wagged because he thought I was a good person who'd never hurt him. I heard the back door slam a couple of times, realized my mom was probably going back and forth. I kept my door closed.

One time, I figured it was safe to go to the bathroom. This is hard to admit, but for a couple of tense minutes I stood in front of the medicine cabinet, imagining how much I'd have to swallow to close my eyes and just drift away. I could just lay there with the lights off and the dog at my feet. When they found me, they'd think I was overwhelmed with grief for Chloe. And when they found Chloe, she'd be the one who would have to explain everything.

There wasn't a lot there though. There was an antibiotic, Mom's allergy meds, and some aspirin. Slim pickings on the suicide shelf. So I went back to my room. I didn't turn on the TV or my computer, or even check my phone. I just lay there. At around ten-thirty, I zombie-walked downstairs, with Chauncey close to my side. I felt guilty. Half of his busy bone sat in its wrapper on top of my desk, but I needed to save it for later so that I could slip out the back door without him creating a fuss.

My parents sat at the kitchen table. Mom had a yellow legal pad in front of her and the two of them were listing tasks they could take care of for the Caffreys. I went to the fridge to retrieve the water pitcher and poured myself a glass. Mom practically leaped up.

'Why don't I make you a sandwich?' she asked.

'No thank you.'

'Really – it'll take me two minutes.' She was already pulling crap out of the fridge – wax paper packets, jars of mayonnaise and mustard.

'I'm not really hungry—'

'Let your mother make you a sandwich, Finn,' Dad chimed in. 'It'll make her feel better.'

So I sat there while she cut off the crusts and poured me a glass of milk.

'Thanks,' I said. She set the plate on the table next to my dad. 'I can sit in the dining room if you guys need to be alone.'

'Don't be silly.' I knew she was just going to sit there hawkeyed, making sure I ate. 'Would you like some chips?'

Chloe and I had this thing we loved – we put plain potato chips on tuna fish. Chloe would explain in her weirdly accented gourmet voice, *The crisp of the potato ideally augments the tuna's soggy tendencies.*

'Finn?' Mom broke into my thoughts.

'No.' I looked up at my dad next to me, my mom at the

pantry. 'No, thank you. I don't care for potato chips.' I ate while they discussed the next day.

My mom ticked through the events. 'They're sending out a representative from the police force to explain what to expect over the next few days. She'll get here at nine.'

'A woman?' Dad asked.

'Yes, a woman.' Mom's voice clicked with warning.

'Hmm. I guess that makes sense, that a woman cop would come out and deal with the victim's family. Comforting, right?'

'For Pete's sakes, Bart!'

'What? I just think it's interesting. What's wrong with noticing something like that?'

'Well, maybe she's coming out, not because she's a woman, but because it's her job to coordinate aspects of the investigation with the family. That sounds like a difficult job to me.'

'Yeah, but an easier job for a woman.' I thought my mom was going to pick up the uneaten half of my sandwich and throw it at him.

'I don't understand why it would be an easier job for a woman.' She glanced at me. 'Nor should we assume she is the only female police officer working the case.'

'I never said that. But you know, you've been really good at dealing with the Caffreys and all. You know what they need, what to say. I get over there . . . I just want to pour Brian a drink. That's about all I can think of to do . . .' He trailed off.

'Oh, honey.'

'Seriously. I'm sorry. I didn't mean to imply—'

'Well, you just have to be careful how you word things. You're the father of a daughter, you know.' I felt like piping up that probably he was the father of a daughter who had disqualified herself from any future forays into the world of law enforcement, but instead I just kept quiet and started on the second half of the sandwich. My parents didn't usually fight in front of me. Usually they closed themselves up in the den or the bedroom and doors slammed and voices rose, but I didn't hear details. This was like watching a sitcom where there's a big misunderstanding and the audience knows the fight is silly and then they just have to wait for the characters to catch up.

But then my dad said, 'I'm very aware that I'm the father of a daughter and, frankly, it seems like an unimaginable responsibility right now.' His voice caught and my mom gasped a little. She bent down to hug him and she whispered, 'Oh, Bart.' And just as I was ready to pretty much sink through the kitchen tiles, they both reached out for me. I sort of leaned toward them, across the table, and let them hug me. They probably thought it was a Big Moment. I was thinking it might be the last time they hugged me for a long while.

TWENTY-THREE

Because I had stayed upstairs most of the evening, it was pretty easy to avoid going up to bed when my parents turned in. Instead, I brought down a huge box of photos of Chloe and me from the past few years and three different albums. I made a big production of setting up a workstation in the dining room. My mom totally ate it up.

'I think that's a really good idea, Finn,' she said. 'Would you like help picking out some pictures?'

'No, it's really something I think I should do by myself.'

'That's fine. Whatever you need.' She tipped her head, considering something. 'I'm not sure if you know this, but it's common at wakes or memorial services to display collections of photographs of the . . . person . . . being mourned. I'm sure that the Caffreys are going to want to do that, but Sheila and Brian might not be up for that right now. I bet they'd appreciate—'

'Yeah, okay.' My mom looked a little stricken, so I followed it up with, 'I'm glad that would help out.'

She rubbed circles on my back and kissed the top of my

head. Again I thought, *Will this be the last time?*

'I'm sure it would help a lot,' Mom said. And that's how I got started working on my Chloe Marie Caffrey Memorial Vision Board. At around quarter to eleven, Dad came by and collected Chauncey for a walk, but then the dog trotted right back to his spot at my feet, under the table. Maybe ten minutes later, my parents drifted through the doorway of the dining room. Mom asked, 'How long are you going to be up, do you think?'

I looked up at them both and summoned one last tragic look. 'Um, not sure. I never expected this to help so much, but . . . it just makes me feel closer to her.'

'Oh, that's good, sweetheart. Just try not to get hung up on finishing it tonight, okay? Tomorrow will be busy, but we'll all have some downtime, and I'd rather you not try to deal with everything without having slept.'

'I slept all day, though.'

'That's right, but it doesn't always work like that. Just try to listen to your body.'

She bent down to kiss the top of my head, and said, 'We love you.'

And Dad echoed, 'Love you, kiddo.'

I said, 'Love you too,' and I thought *last time, last time, last time* the whole while it took them to climb the stairs to the second floor. I waited through the toilet's flushing, the softer rush of pipes which meant someone upstairs had turned on the sink. By the time I could convince myself that my parents were asleep, I'd filled fifteen pages with photographs of Chloe – first days of school, county fairs, birthday parties. I found the pictures of the two of us dressed as Super Mario Brothers for Halloween. I made some pretty good progress on my weird fake memorial to my undead best friend. And then I dug out the bone from the bottom of one of the boxes of photos and gave it to Chauncey. I put on my jacket, then slipped out the back door. There were still lights on upstairs at the Caffreys', so I was relieved that I'd remembered to wear my black tracksuit.

I ran off to bring Chloe home.

I had decided not to use the penlight, since I didn't know if there were really cops parked at the bottom of the hill, protecting the Caffreys from the press. The moon was out, though, and my eyes adjusted to the dark pretty quickly. I tracked down Chloe's sweatshirt first. At first, I had trouble finding it and thought maybe Dean had come across it, and that was the clothing the police claimed was evidence. But it just took some raking the ground and then Chloe's sleeve peeked out from the dead leaves and mud. Digging it up creeped me out – it felt like I was unearthing a body.

It took me even longer to find Chloe – long enough that I was starting to panic and think that maybe she had just decided to hop on a bus instead. Or maybe she'd gone straight to the police. But I heard her before I saw her. I heard twigs snap. I whispered her name and figured that if it turned out to be someone else, I'd just pretend to be mad with grief.

But she answered. I could see her frosting breath before I could make her out in the dark. She had the stupid shelf in her hand and it seemed so ridiculous. She'd tugged most of her braid out of her hair and it looked like she had rolled in mud and dirt. She went to hug me and then stopped. I thought she was remembering what had happened that morning. But instead she said, 'I shouldn't get you dirty.' She grabbed her sweatshirt out of my hands and whimpered, 'It's cold. Finn, it's wet.'

While she tugged her arms through the sleeves, I asked her, 'Did you watch any of the news?'

'You told me to leave the TV off.' She sounded bored.

'I know, but did you turn it on? It's okay – we can talk about it.' But she just looked up at me, so I knew she hadn't.

'You told me not to, and I was going crazy all day trying to make sure that every little thing was back in the exact same spot. I didn't use the sink or the shower and I fluffed out the cushions of the sofa, in case you could see my outline sunken into it. I checked the stations of the TV and the radio but I couldn't figure out if it smelled like me in the basement. Maybe we should have left potpourri or something.' She was rambling, and I wondered if she was okay, if being out in the wide night for the first time in so long was screwing with her head.

'It's okay, Chloe.' I tried to figure out how to say it. I thought of how it would feel from her side – she hadn't even gotten on TV. She'd sat in a cellar for days, for nothing. I tried to be really clear. 'Chloe, we can't do this. We have to go home and wake up our parents.' She went to speak but I shook my head, kept going. 'They arrested Dean today. Really arrested him – last time they brought him in for questioning or something. But today it was all over the news – they charged him with murder.'

'Well, they can't do that.'

'Chloe – I saw it. It was like a mob scene.'

'There's no body.'

I took a deep breath, made myself keep going. 'The cops came to your house today. They said they had evidence, that they found your clothes – why did Dean have your clothes?' I saw Chloe and Dean in my head, sitting across from each other on his bed. He'd pull her shirt over her head, reach behind her back. He would have cupped her chin with his fingers and tipped her face up to his. But that wasn't the point. 'We knew we'd be doing this, Chloe. How could you risk letting him keep your clothes?'

For a moment, I had the awful thought that maybe she'd done it on purpose, that maybe Dean was really convenient that way. But Chloe didn't say that. She rubbed her eyes and then her temples. And then, 'Well, when I come home, everyone will know there hasn't been a murder. They'll just release him again.'

'Not if you say you can't remember anything. You can't be sure it wasn't Dean and be so unsure about everything else. Honestly, the timing looks awful anyway. He's arrested and then you magically appear. People are going to suspect. We might as well just come forward before—'

'People aren't going to suspect.' Chloe's voice had gone cold, like when she'd spoken about her mom. 'And if you tell them, they'll never believe you. It's too insane.'

'So we have to go in together.' I couldn't believe I needed to convince her. I expected that she'd cry, that she'd be angry. But I figured on just telling her that we would face it together, that no one could hate us indefinitely. Especially her. No one could be angry with Chloe for long.

'You don't get it. This is the kind of thing that will follow us forever. I can't go home and tell my parents I did this. You can't either—'

'Of course I can't. But I will.'

'No. You won't.' She tossed the wooden shelf from one hand to another. 'We have to go forward, just how we said we would. They'll let Dean go. They can't convict him with jeans and underwear.' She saw my stricken face. 'And the times won't match up. It'll never even get to trial.' She kept going. 'You have to just hit me with this like we said. Because otherwise, the only other option is for me to go back and say I broke out of your grandmother's basement. I'll say that you tricked me and kept me locked down there.' My skin crawled, but Chloe kept talking. 'I'll tell them that you scared me, that you're weirdly obsessed with me.' She shrugged like it meant nothing. 'I'll tell them about this morning.'

I didn't know when I had started crying. My face was wet and it was hard to breathe and I said, 'Chloe?'

'It's okay.' She said it kindly. All of a sudden, her voice went really gentle. 'Just think about it. People might eventually decide I'm lying, but they'll know I'm not lying about all of it.'

I couldn't make it make sense. 'What's happened to you? It's his whole future, for christsakes.'

She sobbed a little and I thought I could maybe snap her out of it, but she just stepped back from me. She said, 'I know how horrible it sounds, but we said one of us would probably want to back out. We said the other had to stay strong. Remember? We said we had to be resolved.'

'That was before we got Dean arrested. Chloe, we can't do this. It's the rest of his life.'

And then Chloe started shrieking. 'It's the rest of *our* lives. Don't you get what people will do to us? We'll be a joke for years. You can't just back out of this. You don't get to just bail.' And when I hushed her, I realized that I had lost. Because if I were really ready to turn myself in, I wouldn't have cared who heard her screaming. I would have felt relieved that we were about to be caught.

And I could lie and say that I didn't know what we were doing to Dean West the minute my fingers closed around that piece of wood. That I hadn't noticed how kids had talked about him at school after the police had come to get him. Or how people had openly stared at him in the diner. The minute Chloe showed up bleeding, Dean's chance for full exoneration evaporated. It didn't even matter if they could prove that he was in custody when she was injured. People would just call him an accomplice. And worse. There would always be doubts, phone calls, hate mail. I knew all that. 'It's his whole future.' I said it again, pleading with her.

Chloe nodded at me. 'You're really just trading his for ours.'

I felt myself shaking and gripped the plank in both hands. Stepped back and twisted my body away from hers. For a second, when I swung back, I pictured letting the piece of wood sail out of my hands. It would disappear into the dark trees. Maybe that's what Chloe thought would happen too. But I didn't do that. I held on and turned back toward her and aimed for her temple, for the place near her ear, where her hair felt like silk. I hit her hard.

At first, she just stood there and I thought I'd messed it up. The woods sat silently around us. 'Chloe?' My voice shook. She went to take a step toward me and staggered a little. She sank down to her knees. I went to reach for her and she waved me away. Her hand was dark with blood. 'You shouldn't touch me,' she said, kind of laughing a little, kind of singing.

'Oh God, Chloe. Oh God, I'm so sorry.' I backed away, felt sick.

'Don't throw up,' she said. 'It's okay, but you can't throw up.'

'Chloe . . .' The blood ran down her cheek and ear.

'You should go.' She tried to stand and then stumbled, fell forward. 'It's okay. You have to get back to the house. It's okay.' She moaned a little.

'I don't think you should be alone. I don't know that you can make it back. '

'Now you're so worried about me.' Her voice rose up and fell down.

'Chloe.'

'You'll come and find me if I'm not back in an hour.' Her hair was matted and the right side of her face was already swelling. She sat down fully on the ground and put her head between her knees. 'I can't believe you really did it. It's okay. It's okay. Finn, you have to go back to the house.'

'Chloe, I'm so sorry. I'm really sorry.' It was hard to look at her. I started to back away, in the direction of our fields.

'Wait – you have to take that.' I followed her hand to see she was gesturing toward the plank. I felt sick again. 'We can't just leave it here.' I thought about what Chloe had said, that she could claim I'd kept her in the cellar like some insane person. She caught me staring at it and then her. 'Hide it. I won't know where.'

I nodded, picked it up, and looked down at her.

'It's okay,' she told me. 'We're going to be okay.' She said it one last time before I left her there and sprinted home.

TWENTY-FOUR

I figured the lake was the safest place. It's not like they would drag it again. And once the piece of wood sank into the muck, that'd be it anyway. I hurled it as far as I could and then heard the deep splash in the dark. I ran the rest of the way back to our stables. Pumped some water out of the spigot and washed my hands, dried them on my jeans. The lights were off at the Caffreys' and only our porch light glowed. I slipped inside the house and the dog rushed up and knocked me back a bit. So I knelt down, pressed my face into his wheat-colored fur, and tried to stop shaking.

I forced myself to open up another box of pictures and spread them out over most of the table. Later on, when everyone told the story, my mom would probably say in her breathless hippie way, *It must have been like looking up and seeing another photograph of Chloe, hung in the window.* The truth was that mostly I sat with my face pressed close to the window so that the glass kept fogging up and I'd have to wipe it with my sleeve.

It was hard to think about anything else than how hard I

had hit Chloe, of how I had even kind of hated her when I did it, so maybe that meant I had hit her too hard. She could have been crawling around the pine-needled floor, trying to make sense of where she had found herself. She could have been bleeding to death, I guess.

It didn't matter that the whole thing was her idea or that she was the one who dragged the stupid plank into the woods. If we found her the next day curled up near a fallen tree trunk frozen and smeared with her own blood, then I would be responsible. I kept remembering how the board had stiffened in my hands, the sick crunch it made when it connected. I almost went back out, thought about letting Chauncey out, so that I could chase him to the edge of our property and find Chloe on the outskirts, just in time. But then I rubbed the window clear again.

Even though I'd been sitting there waiting, at first I thought she was a deer. She was crouched on all fours, off in the distance, and moving so slowly, it looked like she'd stilled in fear. I stopped myself from screaming before realizing that I didn't have to stop myself from screaming anymore. And then I took off running, again, letting the screen door slam loudly behind me.

'Chloe!' I called out. 'Chloe!' The shadows shifted in front of me and I turned back to see lights winking on in both houses. I ran to meet my best friend, who had galloped off through this pasture a little over a week before. I promised myself that as long as she could find her way back to normal, then I would let her. We'd never fight about the past few days, the decisions we'd made. They were lousy ones all around, but Chloe had been closed up in a dark cellar for days. She had the right to lose her mind a little.

Even knowing what to expect, I stopped a couple feet from her and gasped. Her head was still bleeding – it streaked down her face and neck and some of it had even spattered across the collar of her shirt. But she'd also been busy. Her whole right arm was scraped. Her jeans were torn at the knees. 'Jesus, Chloe. What did you do?'

She sort of lunged forward into me, clung to my shoulders and leaned in. 'Does it look good?'

'Yeah, you look terrible.' I wrapped my arm around her waist and she clung to my neck and we just inched our way across the field, staring out at our houses. I saw my mom step on to the back porch and then my dad follow. Chauncey circled my parents in excited loops, barking.

'Where are my parents?' Chloe whimpered. 'Where are my mom and dad?' She started crying then, really crying. It was hard to keep us standing upright.

Then I heard my mom yell her name and then yell, 'Oh my God. Sheila . . . Sheila!' We could see my mom run to the Caffreys' door, frantically knocking and trying the locked door. 'Help them, Bart. Help them.' And then again, 'Sheila!' I thought of what Chloe had said about her mom, wondered if she was too doped up to react. But then we saw the Caffreys' back door swing open. My mom waved her arms and then the three tentative figures stepped out into the floodlights.

Mrs. Caffrey screamed Chloe's name. She knelt down for a second like she'd been knocked down and then she ran toward us. Her white nightgown billowed and she screamed Chloe's name again and again. By the time she reached us, I glanced past her and saw Mr. Caffrey halfway there. I slid out from under the loop of Chloe's arms and stepped away, watched them swoop in and gather her up. Both Chloe's eyes were closed – one of them looked swollen shut – but her smile split her face and tears seeped from both eyes. I thought back to all the times that I'd believed she hadn't understood what her family was going through above ground.

My parents stood together on the grass between the Caffreys' place and ours. Cam stood next to my mom, and my dad kept stepping forward and then turning back to my mom. I reached and realized my mom wasn't just waving her arms; she was making the sign of the cross, over and over again. I tried to arrange my face to look like I'd just seen a miracle. But when I asked my parents, 'Do you believe it?' I meant *Are you buying this?* And judging from the tears in their eyes and my mom's fluttering hands, they thought it was an act of God and not us.

We all ended up in the Caffreys' great room, and in the lamp light, Chloe's injuries looked even worse. What had looked like a scrape on her arm was actually closer to a gash. It gaped when she moved her arm and I almost got sick, imagining her doing it to herself. I couldn't force myself to look at her head. My mom had the Caffreys' cordless phone in her hand and she kept saying they needed to call an ambulance, but Mrs. Caffrey kept alternating between holding Chloe close to her and then asking, 'Where have you been?' And 'Oh God – what happened?' over and over again. Chloe just kept shaking her head and then groaning because it must have hurt to shake her head. By this time her speech was slurred, so none of us could really understand much. She got out, 'It was dark and cold.' Which wasn't necessarily untrue. A few times I also heard her say, 'I woke up and my head was all bloody.' Also probably accurate.

'She's so cold.' Mrs. Caffrey rubbed Chloe's good arm, wrapped her in the blanket that had been folded on the top of the sofa. 'Her clothes are soaked. Amy, look at what they did to her face.' Mrs. Caffrey's voice sounded panicked, like she thought someone would break in and take her daughter away.

My mom looked at me. 'Finn – why don't you go get a warm washcloth and a fresh change of clothes for Chloe?' I nodded and hopped up, happy to have something to do. From Chloe's drawers, I grabbed a set of flannel pajamas, socks, and a sweater in case she wanted to wear it over her clothes. I ran back out and looked down at the scene in the great room. Mr. Caffrey and my dad were setting Cam up at the coffee table with a drawing pad and some charcoal pencils. Our moms hovered over the sofa where Chloe was stretched out. My dad called over to my mom, 'Honey, I think you need to call 911.'

I ran to the linen closet outside the hall bath, grabbed a washcloth. I figured it could only be good for us if Mrs. Caffrey helped Chloe change out of her clothes, so I was trying to be helpful enough that we got it done before one of the adults finally pulled it together enough to call the police. I took the stairs down two at a time and handed off the pajamas to Mrs. Caffrey.

Chloe's dad squinted and wrinkled his brow. 'Sheila,' he said, 'I don't know if we should do that yet. He knelt down to Chloe. 'Is it just her head? What if she has other injuries?' His voice choked off.

Mrs. Caffrey sobbed and asked, 'Chloe – did someone hurt you, honey?' I almost said, *Look at her head, for God's sake.* But then I realized – Chloe's mom was talking about rape.

But Chloe piped up from her concussion country and said, 'I'm so cold,' so pathetically that her dad nodded at her mom and Mrs. Caffrey gently tugged her left arm through the sleeve. When she went to free up the other arm, Chloe moaned.

Her mom looked up at me and said, 'There should be some kitchen shears in the butcher block.' I scuttled off to get those, but when I went to hand them to her, Mrs. Caffrey said, 'You know what? I'm shaking so much.' So my mom took them and cut Chloe's clothes off her body.

I ran the kitchen sink until the water steamed and then brought the wet washcloth in. Mrs. Caffrey sponged off the blood from Chloe's shoulder, neck, and face. She held open the pajama shirt while Chloe wriggled in one arm and then the other, but Chloe's breath hissed with the shirt brushed up against the cuts. 'I'm sorry, darling,' she said, then tugged the blanket more tightly around Chloe's shoulders.

My mom stood up, went to the kitchen, and returned with a plastic bag from the grocery store. 'Here – let's just put everything in here in case anyone needs to take a look at them later on. Chloe, can you hear me? When was the last time you had any water? Are you hungry?'

And then I guess my dad figured he'd step in before they sat Chloe down to a five-course meal. 'We need to contact the authorities. If you don't want her in an ambulance, that's fine. But it looks like she needs stitches and medical attention, and, well, people need to know that Chloe's home.'

Everyone stopped. Except for Cam's pencils scratching across the page, no one made a sound. My dad looked embarrassed. But Mr. Caffrey stepped forward and said, 'Jesus, Bart, you're absolutely correct.' He flipped open his cell phone. 'I'm going to call Detective Stewart.' His voice boomed through the huge room. Mrs. Caffrey nodded. I reached down to squeeze Chloe's shoulder. We'd done a really good job. The next part would be pretty hard and she would be on her own for it.

It was a long night. The police cars showed up first and then the first aid squad. Chloe's mom and dad rode with her, and my parents and I stayed back at the Caffreys' with Cam. Seeing them lift her up and into the ambulance scared me. The doors closed and I knew that she could tell them whatever she wanted.

The police questioned me that night too. Not formally or anything. Just sitting in the Caffreys' kitchen. What was I doing up so late? *Working on a photo memorial.* What made me look out the window? *The dog must have barked – I got scared.* How did I know it was Chloe? *I didn't.* What was she doing when I found her? She was on her knees, trying to crawl. Most of it, I didn't even have to lie about. They asked me if I'd heard anything, though. And I said it sounded like it might have been a bunch of deer or maybe a black bear in the area, because I heard a lot of twigs snapping, like something was moving through the woods.

Detective Stewart looked at the other cop. 'You heard someone moving in the woods?'

'You know, like animals or something.' I acted like it had just occurred to me. 'Oh my God. You don't think the guy who hurt Chloe was there? Why would he bring her back to the woods near our farm?'

'Why do you think a guy hurt Chloe?' Oh, this Detective Stewart thought he was so slick. He'd probably been utterly certain that Dean had killed Chloe because she made fun of how he talked or something. It probably screwed up his whole game if I heard someone in the woods.

I erased my face, so that it was blank and open. 'Well, Chloe's face was . . .' I bit my lip like it hurt me to remember. It wasn't acting so much anymore – it was more like just leaving key pieces out. 'Chloe's face was really banged up, so I thought it had to be a guy, a man.'

Detective Stewart looked up at my parents. 'Anything odd over the course of the night? Unfamiliar sounds around the property?'

Dad slowly shook his head. 'We would have called it in. Last night was rough around here. It wasn't exactly a normal day.'

The other cop nodded, straightened his back. Dad forced the issue. 'Must be a tough thing to tell a mother that her daughter's been murdered.' He worked his jaw back and forth.

'Yes, sir.' Other Cop folded his arms in front of his chest. Mom sat up, like she'd just taken the room temperature or something and was thinking of keeping it home from school.

'Bart?' she asked, alarmed.

'I'd just figure that you'd want to make sure the girl was actually dead.'

My mother gasped out loud.

'We appreciate that, sir.'

'Are you going to be releasing the West boy?'

Detective Stewart stepped between my father and the other police officer. 'Mr. Jacobs, unfortunately we can't comment on an ongoing police investigation.' Dad turned his full gaze toward him. 'I will say that we still have a young lady who has obviously been subjected to some harm. Let's hope the head injury is the extent of it.' My dad looked down. 'Now, no one's jumping to any conclusions here. But we brought Dean West in for a reason. And we're going to see this through.'

I honestly couldn't tell if my dad wanted to make sure they let Dean go or kept him locked up.

'Is Dean still a suspect?' I asked.

'Finley!' My mother scolded me and glared at my dad.

Detective Stewart raised his hands as if to calm everyone down. 'That's fine, ma'am.' He smiled a little at me. 'We're just working hard to keep this town safe for you and your friends.'

If I were any kind of decent person, I would have said *Dean is my friend.* But my mother was looking steadily at me so I stepped back into the great room to check on Cam. I heard the cop say, 'We just have a couple routine questions for you, Mr. and Mrs. Jacobs.' Cam was bent over his sketchpad, shadowing in the flank of thoroughbred.

'That's an amazing animal, Cam,' I said. 'Can you imagine racing him?' Cam didn't look up, but he clucked happily. Chloe had been so sure that he wouldn't even notice that she was gone, but Cam seemed glad that she was back. Relieved. I wondered what the past week had been like for him.

Chloe once told me that she knew that Cam didn't always absorb conversations but that he totally tuned into the mood of the house. And I'd seen it too. If I showed up and Chloe was losing it, stressed out about a Chem test or something, Cam would be the one rocking and pacing. If Mr. and Mrs. Caffrey were fighting, Cam would be in the kitchen slamming cupboards or going nuts with his blurting noise.

Chloe's mom called the house, and while my mom spoke to her, my dad led the police officers out the door. Detective Stewart said, 'We're going to have a couple guys out here, combing the area, as soon as it's fully light.'

And Dad said, 'We'll keep an eye out,' as if the cop had asked him for the help.

I heard Mom say, 'Well, it's expected that they keep her overnight for observation, right? You tell them you want a cot set up right into the room. That's right. Well, Sheila, it's not special treatment – any parent who has a kid getting her tonsils out is asking for the same thing.' And then I heard Mom say, 'Well, thank God for that. Really. I know. It's not the worst thing in the world, but she's going to have enough to deal with.' And then, 'Let us know how that turns out. And how we can help.' She crossed over to peek at Cam. 'He's fine, Sheila. I think he senses that we all have a reason to celebrate right now. Tell Chloe we all love her very much.'

She clicked off the phone and saw me watching her expectantly. 'Chloe's going in for a CAT scan soon. They're keeping her for a few hours, just to keep an eye on her.'

I nodded. 'Is she okay?'

'They have her on intravenous fluids, monitors – they're just covering all the bases.' I didn't say anything. My mom opened her mouth to speak and then closed it again. She tried once more. 'Sweetheart, Chloe wasn't attacked . . . sexually.' Mom looked startled that she'd been able to say it. 'They didn't find any evidence of that.'

I just nodded, managed to say, 'That's good.' But then Cam let out a whooping yawn from the great room, and that saved me from having to fake concern that Chloe had been molested. I asked, 'Are we staying here?', thinking we'd have to put Cam to bed and wondering how we could possibly manage that.

But Mom said, 'Brian should be back soon.' And then, 'If you're tired, though, why don't you go back to the house, take a nap?'

Right at that moment, I wanted to sleep as much as Chloe wanted to be on a magazine cover. But I didn't know if I was still supposed to be coasting on adrenaline. What would the girl who had just discovered her best friend bleeding in the woods do?

'I want to be here when Chloe comes home,' I said.

'Well, go on up to Chloe's room then.' And so I climbed

the stairs up to the second floor. I fixed the clothes that I'd left tumbled out of the drawers. I sat on the bed and remembered touring Lila Ann Price through. All those things I'd said about how amazing Chloe was, how she made people happier just by settling her wide smile on them – I'd meant them. I was trying to sell Chloe to the Lila Ann Price audience, sure, but I'd meant them, too.

That night, you could have interviewed me and I wouldn't have known what to say. You wouldn't have even been able to get a sound bite from me. I stood at Chloe's window and looked across to mine and wondered, *What does she really think about me?* I wondered, *What do I think about her?*

TWENTY-FIVE

That night, the night I found Chloe, was actually one of the last times I was up there. We still spent a lot of time together. We had Sunday dinners and breakfasts before band practice. Our parents seemed closer for a while afterwards, especially during all the madness of the immediate aftermath.

For a while, it was total anarchy. For one thing, for most of the first week, Mr. Caffrey and my dad had to chase tabloid reporters off the property. They installed an alarm system and finally the cops stationed a patrol car at the bottom of our hill again. Chloe and I both stayed home from school for the first few days. The police were there every other day, asking Chloe pretty much the same questions over and over again. I never heard her give them more than the same few flimsy threads she had unwound that first night. They questioned me a couple more times too, and every time they closed their notebooks, I expected them to whip out a warrant for my arrest.

Chloe and I never spoke about it. Maybe we figured that it was best not to talk about the details – we'd already planned everything so carefully. We just had to follow it through. Or maybe we were trying so hard to be convincing and the only people we couldn't convince were each other. We spent less and less time alone together anyway – there wouldn't have been many opportunities to talk it through.

They postponed the press conference until Chloe's face faded to pinks and lavenders. My family stood there too. The police department's media specialist planted us off to the side with Cam while the three of them – Mr. and Mrs. Caffrey, with Chloe balanced between them – thanked the town and the state and even the country for their support. Sometime between climbing up into Chloe's ambulance and helping her up the walk to the front door of the farmhouse, Mrs. Caffrey had been transformed back into the single most capable woman alive. She did most of the talking up on the podium. Mr. Caffrey stood there like a man whose daughter had been snatched off his own property.

I remember that Mrs. Caffrey announced that the family appreciated the opportunity to share their joy. But then she added, 'I will not allow my daughter's life to be defined by this experience.' Which was sort of funny because that, after all, had been Chloe's whole plan. The Caffreys still did a few interviews after that, though. And the newslady I met in the girls' bathroom came back to school and did a feature on the two of us together.

Colt River went a little crazy in those first few weeks after. It took three days for them to drop the charges and release Dean, but even then it wasn't over. People picketed and threatened to pull their kids out of school. He came to classes for about a week and then someone said he dropped out. I wrote him a lot of emails that I never sent. I called once, but when his mom answered, she sounded so afraid and weary that I hung up. And then I hated myself, because she probably thought the crank calls had started up again.

Chloe and I didn't speak about Dean. Once I came late to lunch and caught her telling Maddie and Kate what a relief it was to not have to see him in school everyday. She said, 'I'm sure it's just me being paranoid, but every time I see him, the hairs on the back of my neck stand up. It's like I'm afraid, but I don't know why – like my memory is afraid.'

I stared at her, but she just stared right back. It's not like I was going to open my mouth in the middle of the school cafeteria. After Chloe and I went back to school, we didn't turn out to have so many days left to sit across from each other at lunchtime. First Mrs. Caffrey appealed the school board's decision to allow Dean to attend school with us. She lost that round and kept Chloe home for a few days in protest.

And then December hit and a lot seemed to shift at Chloe's house. Mr. Caffrey didn't put up all the Christmas lights – which sounds like a small thing, but the Caffreys always went nuts with the lights at the holidays. My mom used to cluck that she thought Mrs. Caffrey had more taste than that and my dad used to fake clutch his heart at the thought of their power bill, but people used to come from all over town to see the display they put up. At first, I figured they were aiming to avoid attention.

No one said anything. I didn't bring it up to my parents

and I wasn't about to mention it to Chloe. It felt like the time we had together kept shrinking. She stopped going to local tutoring and instead took SATs classes all the way in the city. Her mom went with her, so that Chloe wouldn't have to navigate the trains and the subways alone. And then Chloe came over for waffles one morning and started chattering about this little apartment she and her mom were decorating. I remember staring at her, my brain moving as slowly at the pitcher of syrup in my hands. My mom finally asked – all breezily, like she'd just been wondering, but I caught the look she passed my dad first, 'What's this about an apartment, Chloe?'

'Oh, we just rented a little place to cut down on all the hours we were spending on the train. Next semester I'm taking this intensive test prep strategy class and then Mom signed me up for a course at the Arts Students League.'

'That sounds like an awful lot to juggle, Chloe.'

'Well, colleges look at junior year most closely, Mrs. Jacobs. It's important to invest your time in worthwhile activities that show diverse interests and long-term goals.'

I choked down a mouthful of pancake instead of pointing out that we had faked her abduction so that she didn't have to worry about activities and SAT scores. My dad buttered an English muffin and said, 'Well, I thought you girls had the sheep for that.'

Chloe shook her head. 'We can't both apply with that piece. And it's really Finn's thing, anyway.' She smiled at me benevolently. 'You're really good with animals.' I had been working mostly alone in the stables anyway, even exercising

Caraway for her. 'My mom was an art history major. Everyone's always said that Cam got her artistic talent, but maybe . . .' Chloe shrugged and trailed off.

'I'm sure there's plenty to go around,' my mom said. 'And you've always had a great eye, Chloe.'

Chloe beamed up at my mom. 'Thanks.'

'So you won't be around on Saturdays?' I tried to ask casually.

'That's what's so great about the apartment. Mom and I can go in right after school and spend the night. We can get up in the morning and eat breakfast at a café in the East Village, and then I can go to my classes.' I wanted to poke her with my sticky fork, remind her that she hated her mom and that we made fun of girls who talked about the Village like it was some kind of kingdom of cool.

At some point, after Chloe went off to college, she'd talk about Colt River differently. It wouldn't be a place she grew up. She'd talk about being born and raised in New York City and moving out to the sticks for Cam's sake. She'll say, *I lived in the middle of nowhere for a while.* And maybe if she wanted to be intriguing, she'd add, *You might have read about my case in the news.* But Colt River would end up being just a weird interlude, something that made her a little exotic – she raised sheep when she was young. She had her own pony. She was kidnapped and beaten and crawled back home to safety. But she'd say, *Home didn't feel so secure afterwards.* She'd laugh bravely and ask, *Isn't it crazy that I had to come back to the city to feel safe?*

I could read it on Chloe's face the way you read the back

of a book to get the story. And it turned out that she didn't even wait until college. By the spring semester, Mrs. Caffrey officially informed the school board that Chloe would be home schooled. We read about it in the paper. Mr. Caffrey stayed at the farmhouse full-time with Cam, but Chloe and her mom spent most of the week in the city. My mom called it 'Brian and Sheila's arrangement'.

Chloe would float in some Thursday nights and her dad would drive her back to the train station on Saturday mornings. She didn't really come over for dinner or breakfast as much, but she'd gotten really into tea. She carried her own tea bags with her and we'd sit on the porch with a kettle of hot water between us. Mostly, Chloe would tell me about the city, about the people in her arts classes, the genius Cooper Union student she met at some sculpture show.

Sure, I was angry. Especially during the weeks, when I moved from home to school to the stables to more chores at the house, just shouldering through the kinds of days that Chloe and I used to laugh through together. It wasn't like I was spending time with anybody else. I sat through the same classes, ate my lunch at the same spot as always, and talked about the same usual nothing. So when Mr. Caffrey's jeep pulled in and Chloe hopped out before he'd even killed the engine, I had to stop myself from running out to meet her in the drive. I made myself wait until she rapped on the screen door and then finally I could run downstairs and see that she was okay. She was right there, listening and chattering and laughing like usual. I could relax a little and sit on the steps, lean back against the house, and exhale.

It was hard to be angry on those days that I just felt so grateful Chloe was home. But she came home less often, and then, when she did, we had less to talk about. We had all these silent understandings and eventually they outnumbered the conversations we had aloud. Once in a while, Chloe would show up at school on a Friday and everyone would fawn over her for a while. She'd sit through a couple of classes and sometimes she'd stop by to see Mrs. Holmes in the guidance office. Most people probably thought, *Poor Chloe – she's really struggling. She's never been quite the same.*

TWENTY-SIX

Of course we were never the same. Chloe took some tour of Italy the summer before my senior year in high school. Her mom traveled with her. She enrolled in some hotshot city prep school after that and quit coming back to Colt River so much. In December, when Mr. Caffrey told my dad that Chloe had gotten into Vassar, I remember thinking – she had a legacy there. She could have just filled in the application and sent it off with an essay about staying up nine straight hours for a lambing.

I sent her a text. She didn't write back. Maybe she knew I didn't have the same kind of news to offer. That would embarrass her.

It's not like my mom and dad didn't try. They lugged me up and down the East Coast. We sat through information sessions and roundtable discussions and informal presentations and whatever else colleges wanted to call them. I stayed overnight in a few dorm rooms and ate at the dining halls and collected a bunch of college experiences. And those kids existed on a different planet from me. Imagine me living surrounded by a thousand different Kenneth Rydens and Lizbette Markells. Or drinking at a party and then getting weepy about my best friend from high school. Imagine me rooming with another girl.

In the end, I made the choice that we all knew I would end up making. My parents sat me down for a few talks about it – about the importance of independence and how no one wanted to see me underestimate myself. But I also saw the worried corners of my dad's eyes relax a little. My mom canceled the ads she had placed to rent out my grandmother's place and they stopped planning for Grandma to move into the farmhouse. I'd go to Hawthorne University during the day and stay on in my bedroom across the hall from Mom and Dad. Grandma would give me her car to use, and in exchange, I'd run her on her errands and check in twice a week.

Everyone seemed relieved. It also meant keeping most of the animals. So life after high school ended up looking a lot like life during high school. I got to drive myself around everywhere and participated in fewer ruses involving the Amber Alert system. My mom would leave little notes around: *Ran into Molly Clairemont – Kara Mae would love to catch up! Give her a call!* Or she'd circle articles in the paper about Regina's upcoming dance performance – *We should head in and give her some hometown support!* She acted all casual about it, but the exclamation points gave her away.

I didn't feel like talking to anyone. And then when I did feel like it, I had no clue where to begin. Even if I could remember moving through the world before Chloe, none of us were ten years old anymore. My mom couldn't set up play dates or wrangle invitations to birthday parties. I took classes and kept my head down. I drove around and visited my grandmother. Once in a while, she would ask me to retrieve something – the fall wreath, then boxes of Christmas ornaments – from the cellar. I'd creak down the wooden steps and pretend I was visiting a room where someone had died. I felt the kind of chill there that people usually attributed to ghosts.

It wasn't until February that I followed Dean West. The holidays had passed and I guess I'd figured that Chloe would come home. Instead she sent a Christmas card addressed to our whole family. She and her mom spent Christmas in Paris. Mr. Caffrey didn't hang the lights again, but we saw him out and about with Cam more often. The rest of the town stopped asking about it. Cam still helped out with the horses and my dad went over there often enough. My mom would send him, armed with a casserole and a six-pack, but if they did talk, my dad would never share that with us.

People came home and Colt River felt like it filled up again. Kate had a party on New Year's and I went. A couple of us went sledding. As long as we were doing something I was fine – playing ping-pong in Kate's rec room, hurtling down the hill behind the high school. It was when things went quiet that I realized everyone else had more to say than me.

I didn't go out looking for him. My grandmother gave me a shopping list and the West place was on the way to the Stop and Shop. I looked over and saw Dean's truck in the drive. It hadn't moved by the time I drove back with the trunk stacked with paper sacks of groceries. I thought that maybe he'd stayed home like me and that it was a little crappy that my parents hadn't told me. Over the holidays, no one had mentioned Dean. People asked me how Chloe was, how she liked school, how she was getting along, and I'd always answered, 'Great.'

They usually went on to say something like, 'I still can't believe it.' Or 'God, wasn't that crazy?'

And I'd shrug, because what was I supposed to say? *We were crazy?* Or *You shouldn't have believed it?* But no one asked about Dean West. No one said his name.

At my grandma's, I tried not to rush through unloading the car. I waited patiently for her to tell me where to stack the cans of soup, the bags of rice. I even stalled a little, trying to prove to myself that it didn't matter whether or not Dean's truck was still parked on my next pass. But there it was, so I pulled up at the end of his street and waited for him to come out.

I almost just drove home. After a while, Dean still hadn't come out and I wasn't about to bound up to the porch and knock on the Wests' door. Seeing his truck felt like climbing down the steps to my grandmother's basement, though. It made me shiver and then ache.

He must have come out the side door, because next thing I saw him amble around the side of his truck and swing a huge duffel bag into the back. He looked around himself, in all directions, and I worried that he would see me. I reassured myself that Dean didn't have a reason to recognize my grand-mother's old Buick. He hopped up into the cab and I saw his eyes check his mirrors. Dean still acted like a suspect.

Part of me followed him out of curiosity, and then another part felt something closer to homesickness. It wasn't like I ever knew Dean well enough to miss him, but I missed the story we were both a part of. I remembered crouching in the school library with Chloe, waiting for him to pick up our latest message. And now I wished we hadn't aimed any higher than getting the cute shy kid to notice us. Or to notice Chloe, anyway.

I followed Dean all the way to the outskirts of Colt River. He turned on to Old Rutherford Road and drove toward North Dunham. The woods on the side of the road gave way to sparse fields and then to old factories, industrial complex-es. He made a series of quick turns, one after the other, and I needed to work hard to keep up. And then Dean pulled up at a little park, really just an island of concrete next to an underpass. It wasn't until he'd hopped out of the truck and came striding toward me that I realized that Dean hadn't been obliviously driving while I crept behind him. He led me to this spot.

'All right! What do you want from me?' Dean looked older. His face was angry and shadowed with a thin beard. 'C'mon! What do you w-w-want?' He bellowed it. And then: 'Finn?' He had charged up to the car, but now he stepped back. He raked his hand through his hair and looked around the small lot. His voice went quiet, but still glowered. 'W-What are you doing?'

'I don't know.' My voice shook, and for one agonizing second, I thought I was going to stutter. Dean kept scowling down at me. He wasn't going to let me get away with this. 'I was just driving by.' He snorted a little, crossed his arms over his chest. 'Really. And I saw you and just wondered what you were doing, what life was like for you.'

'Life is just fine.' His voice sounded frozen. 'You can tell Chloe that.' A slab of ice.

'I don't talk to Chloe.'

He looked up quickly. 'She okay?'

Sometimes I wished I could say *No.* 'She's fine. She's at Vassar.' I kept going. 'That's the college her mom went to. In upstate New York.'

'I know what Vassar is.' Dean sounded angry all over again. He looked back toward his truck. 'So what were you going to do?' I just stared at him, waiting for him to make sense. 'Follow me to my apartment? Make flyers with my address?'

'What?' I tried to imagine what Dean's life must have been like in those first few weeks after Chloe came home. Remembered the signs that Mrs. Caffrey and her friends waved outside the school's main entrance. The editorials in the township paper.

'No, I just saw your truck and thought – I live at home too – and so I thought—'

'You thought we could pal around?' Back in high school, when I imagined actually talking to someone like Dean, this was how he sounded in my nightmares. Cruel and revolted. He gestured toward his truck, the huge duffel. 'How do you know I'm not carting around some girl's body in the back there?'

I told myself how important it was to say the next thing clearly. And then looked him straight in the eye and said, 'I know you didn't hurt her.' My eyes almost watered, it was that hard to keep eye contact, but I didn't let myself look away like usual. Dean looked down first, and for a second I thought he would cry. His face crumpled and contorted. And then I realized he was fighting to pronounce something. It took whole minutes, but finally he got it out.

'Does Chloe know that?'

What would hurt worse? So I said, 'She never believed that you would do something like that.' True. 'But other people did, and she got swept up in that.' Also true. He pinched the bridge of his nose then and turned away. Dean squinted out toward the highway and I waited for him to stop himself from crying.

We stood there watching cars whiz by for a little while. An SUV slowed down on the road above us. I slid my eyes to Dean and saw he had tensed up all over. I tried to keep my voice steady. 'I really just wondered about you.' But that sounded like something you'd say when you were leaving someone notes and puzzles. I tried again. 'Maybe it's just me, but I haven't really talked to anyone since it all happened. And it was good, that time, to talk to you.'

I didn't have any right to lean on Dean West. But right then, he didn't know that. He said, 'There's a diner in North Dunham.'

And I said, 'I'll follow you.'

TWENTY-SEVEN

The Starlight sagged a little lower into the ground than Colt River's own Parkside Diner. Inside, someone had patched the blue leather seats with duct tape here and there, and they didn't have the little jukeboxes perched on the tables like at the Parkside. But the glass display case of cakes still had eight levels and the place smelled like scrambled eggs and coffee and pound cake. Dean relaxed a little there – he didn't look so hunted.

We sat down and the waitress came over, with Dean ordering coffee just for himself. I ordered a Coke and smiled up at the waitress until she asked, 'Nothing else?' in the nasty way that meant she considered a Coke and a coffee a waste of her time. Dean just stared up blankly at her and handed her the menu he hadn't opened. He didn't speak again until she blustered over with the pot of coffee and a sweaty glass of soda. 'That all?' she asked again and Dean didn't even glance sideways at her. His eyes stayed riveted on mine and he said, 'That's it' like it meant something, like I was supposed to gather some secret meaning – *I am it*. Or, *He has all he needs*.

But that wasn't real. Dean was just performing for the waitress; as soon as she turned away, his eyes dropped from mine and he busied himself pouring milk into his coffee.

'So I never knew what happened to you after you dropped out.' Even in the middle of saying it, I knew it was the wrong way to start.

'I d-d-d-didn't drop out.' Dean stirred his coffee and I could hear the spoon scrape the sides of the white mug. 'I probably had my diploma before your graduation ceremony.'

'That's great. That's terrific, Dean—'

But Dean looked up and shook his head at me. He did it quickly – almost tenderly – the way my dad would to try and correct me. 'Why is that terrific, Finn?' His quiet voice sounded disappointed in me. And then he tried: 'I heard you were at community c-c-college.'

'No. Hawthorne.' He made a face, like *Same thing*. 'It has some really good programs.' I had decided to focus on animal therapy. Not counseling animals. But treating people like Cam, helping introduce them to animals. I wouldn't even really be treating patients. I'd be helping the animal treat them.

But Dean didn't get it. He said, 'You're always selling yourself short, Finn.' I tried to argue, but he raised his hand up – he hushed me. 'No – you act like an animal would be better dealing with p-p-people.'

I wanted to tell him *Yes*. And *You have no idea*. But instead I asked, 'What are you doing now?' And even that came out bratty, like I was turning it back on him.

Dean just shrugged. He dragged a long gulp from his

coffee. 'I work at a gas station.' This time I dropped my eyes. I started focusing on his hands and then saw how red they were, the skin around his fingernails scraped raw and his knuckles chapped. It looked like Dean had been digging himself out of something. He held his hands up to the light. 'I must look like one of those OCD psychos. But you pump gas for while and then your skin soaks it up. You smell like gasoline all the time. It gets under your nails. Most guys I work with – their nails are black. It's sick. I just can't do that.'

'Because of cooking.' I said it while my brain was still putting the thought together.

But I was right and was rewarded with the bashful smile. 'Well, yeah,' Dean said. 'Nobody wants to eat food that smells like gasoline.' It got a little more comfortable between us. 'You don't live at the dorms?' I shook my head. 'That's a trek though, driving all the way out there.'

I shrugged and then made myself say something. Because I'd been waiting all this time to have a conversation with another actual human being. I came up with, 'I like to drive.' And then in an effort to sound a little less like a foreign exchange student, I added, 'It helps me think.'

'I get the feeling the last thing you need is more time to think, Finn,' Dean said. I didn't have anything to say to that. It was strange to hear Dean West talk like he knew me. We sat there and I let that wash over me – feeling noticed. Observed and understood.

'No one told me you were still at home.'

'I'm not,' he explained. 'Laundry. My mom does my shopping and laundry, but I try to stay clear of there for the most p-p-part. It's easier on them.' Over the past year, I'd imagined what it would be like if the whole town knew what Chloe and I had done. What it would feel like to have Colt River turn its back on you. Now I guessed it would feel like being Dean West.

'Can I ask you something?' I said. Dean tilted his head, waiting. 'And I'm not asking because I think you were the one who . . . hurt her.' I remembered the weight of the wood in my hand, Chloe's eyes – shut and bracing. 'I don't think that. But no one ever said afterwards and it made everyone else . . .' I forced myself to ask it: 'Why did you have her clothes?'

Dean's face went scarlet and I stumbled out apologies. 'No, that's fine – I'm sorry. She hadn't told me how involved . . .' Chloe and I used to talk about sex like it would happen to us in some next lifetime. I counted out the sliver of a second that my lips moved against hers. There were other reasons she wouldn't have told me.

But Dean shook his head. He opened his mouth to speak and then stopped. Then he started again, saying, 'It wasn't like that.' He bit his lip. 'She'd cut her leg on something. And she worried that it looked like . . . you know . . . girl trouble. A m-m-mishap.' By this time, Dean's face had deepened to full on crimson. I thought about Chloe insisting that we should leave her blood somewhere. On a branch near the woods. A hand print smeared on the horse. 'She had her gym clothes. She changed into those and wrapped the others in a plastic bag. And then forgot. It must have gotten shoved under the seat.'

'Chloe left a bag of bloody clothes in your truck?' I couldn't believe it.

Dean looked like he was searching the bottom of his coffee mug for answers.

He came up with, 'It's not like she could have known.' And that's what Dean told himself. When he woke up and the whole nightmare stretched out both behind him and before him, that's what he said to keep the days he spent with her preserved.

I knew because I did it too. Even knowing what Chloe was capable of, I heard myself repeating, 'She just forgot about it.' I thought of the lists we'd made and burned. How stupidly calm she'd stayed even when I told her the police had brought in Dean for questioning. I had worried that it was shock. Everybody underestimated Chloe. Even now when Dean talked about her, his whole face opened up in light. It must have been terrible to give up someone who thinks you're that extraordinary, hoping that then the whole world will turn your way, with that same look.

Dean threw his hands up, like he was asking me, *What are you going to do?* He paid for my soda, then sat back in the booth and told me he'd really like to come check out the horses. Maybe not back at the farm, but he could visit the stables down at college. I asked to see his new place and hoped it didn't sound like I wanted to lie back on his bed. We stumbled around moments like that and kept going. When Chloe first came home, she moved really slowly. At first, the doctors said the head injury had affected her fine motor skills. She had to go to physical therapy and everything –

that's how hard I hit her.

Right now, it felt like Dean and I were doing that – relearning basic skills. Keeping eye contact. Finding common interests. I thought to myself, *We could be each other's one friend for now. We could ease each other back in.*

But I already knew what I was going to do. And that afterwards Dean wouldn't be returning my calls. It helped, though, in that moment, to pretend otherwise. When we stood up, he helped me with my coat. Walked me out to the lot. My car was low on gas – I hadn't counted on driving all the way out to North Dunham. Dean said, 'I know the best little gas station.' He laughed, called it 'a local gem'. He led me there and then tapped on the horn to let me know he'd be driving on. That was it. That was our goodbye. The kid working the pumps waved at Dean's truck, then leaned into my passenger side window to get a look. He sent me inside to pay with a credit card and I could feel his eyes on me as I moved.

Inside, an elderly man behind the counter asked me how much I'd bought. I said 'Ten' and he rang me up. I wanted to say, 'You're going to be the last person to take me at my word.' But then I spotted the basket of muffins next to the register. They were wrapped in plastic, with familiar writing on the label.

He saw me looking and slapped the counter, grinning widely. 'One of my boys makes those – you believe that? Better than any kind of Girl Scout cookies.' His hand hovered over the register and I picked one out. 'That's right. That's a good one.' And so I carried Dean's muffin out to the car, set it on the seat beside me.

I don't let myself cry over baked goods. But I sat there for a second and pictured Dean as he pulls into the station in the mornings. He unloads a cardboard box from the truck and replenishes the basket before clocking in. I made myself imagine his shy smile when his boss tells him that he should get himself his own bakery.

It was dark by the time I got home. My mom and dad weren't home, but that was a relief, really. I'd probably just stand around, trying to memorize stupid, everyday moments: *Last conversation not punctuated by contempt. Last sincere laugh. Final family embrace.* I went outside to find that most of the animals had been fed – Dad had left the feed buckets turned over to let me know. I brought in Chauncey and stood on our porch for a second, glancing back at the Caffreys' place. I realized that it had been months since I'd caught myself checking for lights up in Chloe's window. Now I had different reflexes.

It took some time to dig up the card. And even when I found it, pinned up on my bulletin board, behind an article Chloe and I did for some safety campaign, I was still debating. For a few minutes, I reconsidered calling the police, but then saw Detective Stewart's stony face, the way they paraded Dean across the front lawn of his parents' home. I dialed the other number instead.

It was a woman who answered, but not the same one who used to be Andy Cogan's assistant. Maybe they fired her after our episode of *The L. A. Price Show* aired. This one didn't even sound annoyed, and I was calling on a Saturday night.

She just said, 'Explain to me who you are so I can make sure to communicate that to Mr. Cogan.' She said, 'It's okay – take your time.'

I had practiced saying it so much that I almost sounded professional. 'This is Finley Jacobs calling. Please tell Mr. Cogan I have an update on the Chloe Marie Caffrey case.' I paused, made myself breathe. And then, because she hadn't said anything, I added, 'You can tell him it's an exclusive.'

And that was it. She put me right through.

ACKNOWLEDGMENTS

My husband, Jeff Salzberger, is the original shy and misunderstood heartthrob of my life. I'm so grateful that he noticed me all those years ago.

Love and thanks to the Corrigan and Salzberger families, as well as Anne Glennon, Steve Loy and Pat Neary. Their kindness, care and belief in me have been invaluable and unwavering.

Jake Walters provided expertise on sheep that was essential to this novel.

Paula D'Introno, Bevin Donahue, Nandini Dutta, Lynn Hernandez, Eli Kaufman, Stacy McMillen, April Morecraft, Brian Pearl, Soma Plotnikov, Josh Powell, Morgan Powell, Sherry Riggi and Shawn Watts provided expertise on friendship that was essential to me.

Many thanks to Christine O'Brien and Imogen Cooper, who have stamped this novel's passport and ushered it overseas; I'm so thrilled to see a UK edition of *Accomplice*.

David Levithan has fostered me through four books and a full decade. I'm so thankful for the years I've worked alongside him, the chances he's taken on me and the calm he has carried into my nervous world.

Finally, I spend my days at Rutgers Preparatory School, surrounded by remarkable characters. I feel so fortunate to have the support and care of the faculty, staff, students and parents there. While no aspect of this book is based on actual people or events, our exceptional community inspires me every day.

OTHER CHICKEN HOUSE BOOKS YOU MIGHT ENJOY

STOLEN
Lucy Christopher

It happened like this.

I was stolen from an airport. Taken from everything I knew, everything I was used to. Taken to sand and heat, dirt and danger. And he expected me to love him. This is my story.

A letter from nowhere.

A vivid new voice for teens. MELVIN BURGESS

Tautly written and hard to put down . . .
INDEPENDENT ON SUNDAY

Paperback, ISBN: 978-1-906427-13-9, £6.99

 Find out more about Chicken House books and authors.
Visit our website: www.doublecluck.com

OTHER CHICKEN HOUSE BOOKS YOU MIGHT ENJOY

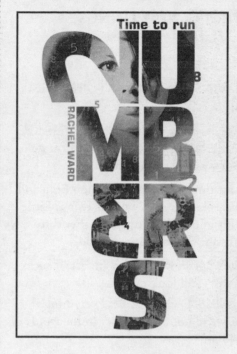

NUMBERS
Rachel Ward

Since the day her mother died, Jem has known about the numbers. When she looks in someone's eyes, she can see the date they will die.

Life is hard, until she meets a boy called Spider. Suddenly her world seems brighter.

But on a trip to London, Jem foresees a chain of events that will shatter their lives for ever ...

. . . intelligent and life-affirming.
PHILIP ARDAGH, GUARDIAN

. . . utterly compelling.
SUNDAY TELEGRAPH

Paperback, ISBN: 978-1-905294-93-0, £6.99

 Find out more about Chicken House books and authors.
Visit our website: www.doublecluck.com

OTHER CHICKEN HOUSE BOOKS YOU MIGHT ENJOY

PRETTY BAD THINGS
C. J. Skuse

TWINS IN CANDY-STORE CRIME SPREE ...

I know what you're thinking. Tearaway teens. Yadda yadda. Maybe you're right. But we're all out of choices.

Last time we made headlines, Beau and I were six-year-old 'wonder twins'. Little kids found alive in woods after three days missing, looking for our dad.

We've just hit sixteen and life's not so wonderful. In fact, it sucks out loud. Still no Dad. Still lost. Still looking.

But now we've got a clue to where Dad could be. Everything's changed. It's a long shot but we've nothing to lose. In the words of Homer Simpson, seize the donut.

It's so good, I'd even recommend it to people I don't like.
KEVIN BROOKS

. . . pretty damn good.
SUNDAY TELEGRAPH

Paperback, ISBN: 978-1-906427-25-2, £6.99

 Find out more about Chicken House books and authors.
Visit our website: www.doublecluck.com